"I never live to thirty?" Eryss gasped out as her heart fell.

Her thirtieth birthday was less than a week away. "Some man kills me? The same one? So many times?"

Midge nodded. "He must reincarnate, as well. And to find you in every lifetime? Has to be a curse. I am positive it was the same man in each reincarnation."

"Did you get a look at his face?"

"No. But you know we never reincarnate into the same physical manifestation. I didn't see your face, either. But that isn't what's important."

"Of course not. Who is he? What is he?"

The witch exhaled and leaned forward, pressing her palms to the table, and said carefully, "A witch hunter."

Michele Hauf has been writing romance, action-adventure and fantasy stories for more than twenty years. France, musketeers, vampires and faeries usually populate her stories. And if Michele followed the adage "write what you know," all her stories would have snow in them. Fortunately, she steps beyond her comfort zone and writes about countries and creatures she has never seen. Find her on Facebook, Twitter and at michelehauf.com.

Visit the Author Profile page at Harlequin.com for more titles.

TAMING THE HUNTER

———

MICHELE HAUF

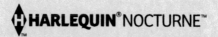
HARLEQUIN® NOCTURNE™

**Recycling programs
for this product may
not exist in your area.**

ISBN-13: 978-0-373-13986-6

Taming the Hunter

Copyright © 2017 by Michele Hauf

Printed in U.S.A.

Dear Reader,

The next few books I'll publish with Harlequin Nocturne feature a set of witches who live in Anoka, Minnesota. This real town is known as the Halloween Capital of the World. As far as I'm concerned, it couldn't be a more perfect setting for a witchy romance.

Most settings in my stories start with a real place and then I fictionalize it. The Decadent Dames brewery is located exactly where you'll find the real 10K Brewing in Anoka. The interior of the brewery in my story is the same, as well. You see, my kids own that brewery, and by the time this book comes out, they'll be celebrating a year and a half of it being open. It was fun for me to weave in little bits about the place because it was my way of giving a tip of the hat to my kids' successes. You'll also find a line of antiques stores across the street in the real town (although the people are completely fictional). So if you're ever in Minnesota and want to see where I set part of this story, stop into 10K and tell 'em Michele sent you.

Happy reading!

Michele

Taming the Hunter

Anacampserote (n.): something that can bring back
a lost love

Winter Solstice...

After padding through the soft emerald grass that car-
peted the floor of her sanctuary, Eryss Norling knelt before the altar she kept tucked between the pink-and-white
petals of bleeding hearts and the cool winter stars of
forget-me-nots. Behind those, crinkle-petaled hollyhocks
bloomed as if it were summer. A dragonfly flitted among
the leafy canopy that climbed to the top of the two-story
glass-walled conservatory.

Tucking her long, loose chestnut hair over an ear,
Eryss bowed to light the large yellow beeswax candle
on the simple wooden altar. Then she turned to light the
eight smaller blue candles she'd placed around the altar

to enclose her in a casting circle. Between each of the candles she'd placed rose quartz and garnet crystals to heighten the energy and fill the circle with love and happiness. And resolve.

Her silver-green velvet robe splayed around her knees and legs as she twisted within the circle, brandishing the lit match. Closed by three braided-ribbon frog hooks over her breasts, the robe was a favorite piece she wore often when casting a spell. Talismans of silver, crow's foot and bloodstone hung around her neck, sliding across the crepe-thin pink negligee she wore against her clove-scented skin. Blowing out the match dispelled sulfur into the humid air, and a waft of white smoke curled toward the morning glory vine climbing an iron trellis to the arched windows that formed a cathedral dome overhead.

Steeped in reverence, her movements were slow and thoughtful. She nestled a heavy, six-sided quartz wand with points at both ends in the sifting of black salt. After whispering a blessing for all that she had, all that she would know and all that changed with her footsteps through this realm, she bowed her head and touched her chest, where a tiny maroon line darkened her pale skin just below her breast. Her heartbeat thudded softly against her fingertips.

With her other hand she clasped the crystal-bladed athame and drew it across her forefinger, cutting a line through the whorls of her fingerprint. A few blood droplets splattered onto the black salt. Forget-me-nots bowing over the altar whispered delicious fragrance, entwining about the metallic tint from her blood, summoning earth elementals with the sweet perfume.

Setting aside the knife, she then beckoned forth the earth's energies with her hands, focusing it toward the quartz. Closing her eyes, she began to hum deeply and from the base of her throat, channeling the vibrations toward her heart and then releasing them throughout her body.

"I have loved only one so many times," she whispered. "In all my incarnations it has always been him. This I know."

And yet in each of those incarnations she had lost him for reasons she could not divine. Her portentous dreams had never explained that frustrating point. That wasn't the important question. What *was* important was that she *see* him, recognize him should he enter her life once again. For in her dreams, she had never seen his face. She knew no one reincarnated into the same visage.

There was only one way to recognize the one whom she had loved. And that was with a soul-deep knowing.

A cool cloud of red smoke diffused from around the quartz wand and billowed up over her hands. She kept her eyes closed, confident the elementals of earth and time participated in this sacred spell.

"When he returns to me in this life," she said, "allow my soul to recognize his soul. Bind us with a love of the ages so that only death will part us."

She blew out a breath through the red smoke. "So mote it be," she ended.

And a force walloped her chest, lifting her from the kneeling position. Arms lashing out for security, she was thrown out of the casting circle. She landed hard on the grass before the green velvet sofa.

"What the…?"

Opening her eyes, Eryss saw tendrils of smoke curl and form into intricate arabesques before darkening into soot and dropping onto the quartz. A startling image. What did it mean? And she'd been physically thrown out of the casting circle. That wasn't supposed to happen. What did such an expulsion portend?

Had she performed the anacampserote incorrectly?

"Yes," she reassured herself on an intake of breath. Crawling forward on the grass, she leaned over the salt line and touched the black salt and soot. Rubbing it between her fingers dispersed a scent much like an ocean surf. Weird. But she would remain positive the spell had achieved her intention. "All will be well with my soul."

Bowing to blow out the yellow candle, she then swept her hands to encompass the circle, taking out each flame of the smaller candles as she whisked air over them. An emerald-winged dragonfly swooped down and nestled in her hair as if it were a fancy barrette.

Now all she had to do was figure out what it would feel like when her soul recognized *the one*.

Chapter 1

Dane Winthur set aside yet another dusty accountant's box filled with cards that dated back to the early 1900s. While the Agency had been established only a decade ago, they had been operating unofficially for over a century. During that century, detailed cards had been written on each weapon or entity they had encountered and/or confiscated for secure storage. Dane had volunteered to go through the files and verify that each had been entered in the computer database.

His laptop sat on a stack of flat boxes to his right. So far, about 75 percent of the card files had been entered. But there was no rhyme nor reason why one card had been entered and another had not. It was a grueling, time-consuming task, but he was the newbie on the block in the Agency, having been with them for only two years, so he didn't mind some grunt work to prove his worth.

Besides, as a scientist by trade, he found the paperwork and attention to detail came naturally to him.

Now he fingered another yellowed piece of five-by-eight card stock that seemed newer than the other cards, most of which displayed frayed edges and coffee stains. Another weapon was listed on this one—a dagger that dated back to the thirteenth century. It had been marked as "To Note," not something the Agency had in hand, but wanted to keep an eye on. He scanned the rest of the notes.

"Belonged to a witch hunter, eh?"

He typed the weapon ID number into the database. It didn't bring up a matching record, so he was about to set the card aside on the "to be entered" stack when a name caught his eye from the description below the record ID information. "Edison Winthur?"

He read the description carefully and muttered the last line out loud. "Last known owner: Edison Winthur, California."

Blowing out a breath, Dane sat back against the stack of boxes behind him in the depths of the storage facility the Agency had leased for the old records. A strange smile curled his lips, and he flicked the card between his fingers.

"My father?"

Two weeks later...

"I've tracked down a location for the dagger, Winthur," Jason said over the phone.

Phone clasped to his ear, Dane tossed aside his surfboard and wandered across the sand to sit on a smooth boulder edging his property. A thermal wet suit allowed him to surf in the fifty-degree waters. January was always the best month to catch some killer waves. He'd noticed his cell phone glowing when he'd landed on the sand and had returned the call immediately.

"The witch hunter's blade?" he asked Jason Meadows, who worked in Research out of his apartment in New York. All Agency positions were "in situ," since there was no home office or official headquarters. Jason was a cyber guru who could tease out the most hidden of information from a jumble of bits and bytes.

"Yes, that one. Let me text you the address. It's currently owned by an antiques store called Stuart's Stuff. Hang on."

Dane smiled at the flock of seabirds swooping over the beach. But his levity was more for the discovery he'd made weeks earlier while going through some of the Agency's old files.

Dane was head of Weapons. Well, he was the only one in the department. It was newly created because there had been a need. Their crew was small and distributed across the United States and Europe. Tor Rindle was the head of the Agency and had been visiting the States when he and Dane had met—over the disintegrating fur, flesh and bones of a werewolf.

Yeah, that had taken a lot of philosophy-changing faith on Dane's part. He was a geologist who had never met a conspiracy theory he didn't want to debunk. But the werewolf? Dane had no choice but to believe. And he had been strangely thankful when Tor had told him about the Agency and offered him the job. Such work aligned with a weird memory he'd had from when he was eight. The Agency was secretive, which was cool. James Bond gadgets were not in abundance, though. They used science to debunk myth and the paranormal—to keep humanity safe from the real monsters.

Whether or not the dagger listed on the file card possessed any sort of paranormal powers hadn't been recorded. Dane's job was to rule out that sort of stuff. Or if not, to put a spin on it. Not that this was an official job. He was simply curious. Or rather, compelled after he'd seen his father's name listed on the card. A man he had known only for the first few years of his life, and "known" simply meant that he'd been his son and had existed in the man's life.

And to think the word *compelled* set his heart racing. The first time he'd learned the meaning of that word he had been eight. And the few times since then that a compulsion had come upon him, he'd always been whisked back to that time when his mother had found him standing in the basement, sword in hand. She'd been so angry. Outraged. He hadn't understood.

But he was compelled to understand now, because it might fill in some integral knowledge he required to become completely whole. To simply *know*.

"Sent it," Jason said over the line. "Do you know this one has a legend attached to it of belonging to a witch hunter? Not sure if the blade itself is supposed to possess magical capabilities. But you know, witches."

"Yeah. Witches." Dane chuckled. "It's always something."

Though he'd not encountered witches in his service to the Agency, he was always up for an adventure, both physically and mentally. And learning about new creatures? Fascinating stuff. Because really? The world was a better place thanks to the Agency's ability to think fast and to explain away the unexplainable with complicated scientific terms and theories.

"So why this blade," said Jason, "if I can ask? I mean, this isn't an assigned job. What's so remarkable about this item?"

Dane twisted at the waist and turned, which flexed his abs. His muscles were rapidly cooling, even with the warm suit to protect him from the chilly temperature. He wasn't much of a sharer. Then again, Jason was an okay guy, and it wasn't as though he was going to call up the boss and tell him Dane was using Agency time to pursue personal issues.

"The last known owner was my father."

"Oh man, cool. So, was he the witch hunter?"

Dane chuckled. "I doubt that very much."

On the other hand, what did he know about his father? Edison Winthur had died during a cave spelunking expedition. He'd fallen five hundred yards down a narrow chute, and his body had never been recovered. It had occurred a year after Dane's mother had divorced him. Dane had been three when Edison died.

And still his mother's words resounded loudly in his thoughts. *Don't be like your father. He was such a dreamer.*

"Should I schedule you for a weeklong vacation so we don't overbook you?" Jason asked.

Dane had to shake himself back from the haunting warning his mother had issued so many times. "Uh, sure. Give me a few days, at the very least."

"Fine. I have a contact name for the shop owner. I'm texting that to you, too."

"Where is this place?"

"In a northern suburb of Minneapolis."

"Seriously?" Dane winced as a sea breeze skinned his face with a cold kiss. "Isn't it, like, thirty degrees in Minnesota right now?"

"Do I sense an inordinate fear of the weather from the guy who surfs in January?"

"Never. But you know, anything below fifty is crazy cold."

"Ha! You'll have to bring along a sweater. Give me a

call when you have the dagger in hand. Unless…you're doing this one under the radar?"

"Not at all. The dagger wasn't an assigned job, but I have no intention of keeping it a secret. Whatever I find will be documented, and I'll address any issues regarding spin or how it should be stored when I've had a look at it."

"Cool. I've got you scheduled through the week. I can arrange a flight for you, as well. Will text the details."

"Thanks, Jason."

Dane hung up and tugged at the zipper on his wet suit.

The key goal in finding this dagger would, with any luck, answer the questions he'd asked himself since he was eight. Was this the same dagger?

The secondary goal was more emotionally rooted in the limited knowledge he'd been given about his father. He'd always wanted to learn as much as he could about a man his mother had described as "having his head in the clouds." And he'd lost track of how many times she'd admonished Dane not to be like his father.

Having one's head in the clouds didn't sound dangerous to Dane. Only if one also lacked logic and rationality, which he subscribed to. Always.

What an opportunity that would be, to hold something his father had actually owned. Or rather, to hold it once again.

But had the old man been a witch hunter?

"Doubt it," he muttered, and grabbed his board.

Dane had joked with Jason about Minnesota being thirty degrees on this January day. Actually, it was two. *Degrees*. He'd left the beach for two degrees. And he felt both those single digits breeze through his lightweight wool jacket and permeate his tweed vest and the dress shirt beneath as the chill fixed itself into his skin and sent out wicked feelers for the network of his once-warm veins.

He rushed down a sidewalk edged with dirty snow heaps the city plow had pushed up as his cab had parked in the nearby lot. The concrete was white from the chemicals added to the sodium chloride used in abundance on the roads. The first time he'd ever heard the term "salting the roads" Dane had imagined a large kitchen saltshaker suspended from the back of a truck. His childhood imagination had been so vivid (when his mother wasn't aware).

He had that very imagination to thank for being here right now. And he wasn't sure whether or not it was something he should be thankful for. Fantasy was best served in small doses, and even then, only on the silver screen or the pages of a novel. Very well; his mother had been right.

Dane whispered his thanks when the antiques shop door opened to whoosh a welcoming warmth across his frozen cheeks. He huffed and clapped his gloved hands together, stomping his feet, even though there was no snow on his leather loafers. The weird stomping-clapping performance managed to get the warmth flowing through his system.

A kind-looking woman, who looked to be in her eighties, appeared from behind a glass case and sailed over to the counter, which was littered with an assortment of Halloween ornaments and wooden black cats, bright orange Halloween Festival buttons and a plethora of orange-and-black garland.

"I'm Dane Winthur," he announced, with a chill invading his tone. "A colleague of mine should have called about a dagger two days ago?" Jason had said he'd handle alerting the shop that Dane was on his way.

"A dagger?" The woman shook her head and adjusted the frothy white hair piled loosely atop her head.

"Yes, uh… I was told Mr. Stuart is the owner? Is he in?"

"Mr. Winther, I'm so sorry, my brother and his wife are out of town for a family funeral. Just left this morning, actually. Oh, wait now. I do recall him mentioning something as he was going through the list of things for me to do in his absence. You're the scientist, yes?"

Dane bristled but tried his best not to show it. The owner of this antiques shop had known he was coming to pick up the dagger. Traveling halfway across the United States and—he wasn't here? That took some kind of nerve, to up and leave without calling to let him know.

"Yes," he answered, calming his rising ire. "I've traveled from California to your lovely yet icy state for the dagger." He patted his vest pocket, where he'd tucked the dossier and a printed photo of the dagger, and pulled it out. Unfolding it, he showed it to the woman. "Did Mr. Stuart leave it in your care?"

"Not exactly." She squinted as she studied the photo. "Harold did mention you were coming as he headed off to the airport. He was in a hurry because they managed to snag a pair of last-minute standby seats for the flight to Hawaii. I'm so sorry, Mr. Winthur. You know how funerals are. Can't plan for them."

"Of course. Well. Does *not exactly* mean no, not at all, or maybe, I might know where the dagger is?"

"It means maybe, I don't know where it is. I mean, I do know where it is, but I don't have access to it. We were going to close the shop, because I'm not much for handling inventory and the finer items my brother stocks, but I do like to hand out my cookies to the locals. Help yourself." The woman gestured to a plate of chocolate chip cookies on the counter that Dane hadn't noticed before.

Now that he did, his frozen senses thawed and the scent of sugar and chocolate teased sweetly. He picked up a cookie. It was warm, bless the cookie gods. Had he been annoyed about something? Who could remain angry when biting into chewy, warm chocolate and sugar?

A funeral. He couldn't possibly be rude and insist on anything, but he would nudge as best he could. "How long will your brother be away?"

"Four or five days. The flight takes almost a whole day, so that's two days of travel time right there."

"The funeral is in Hawaii?" A much better place—for a vacation or a funeral—than this Arctic tundra. "Lucky fellow."

"Ah? Hmm…" She tugged the plate back to her side of the counter.

"Sorry. I mean, *really* sorry. For the, er, bereaved." So he wasn't a master at compassion. Feelings were so… complicated. "Did Mr. Stuart leave the blade in a safe or some such?"

"Oh, he did, but it's a newfangled fancy-doodle kind of thing that requires him putting his eye up to it to open."

"Oh. Biometric, eh? Quite a fancy-doodle thing, indeed."

Especially for a run-down little shop that currently offered a sale on 1970s disco balls, as displayed in the front window. After New Years Discount! Get Them Before They're Gone! Had he stepped into the seventies?

"I really do need to get my hands on that dagger," Dane said. "The information I've collected about it states it once belonged to Edison Winthur. He was my father."

"Oh, my. That's mighty interesting. He's passed?"

"Yes, when I was very young."

"I'm so sorry." The cookie plate was pushed closer. "Harold should have left the dagger out for me to sell to you, but he's always been so careful about the weapons he sells. High security, and all that fiddle-faddle."

"Fiddle-faddle can be a bother." Dane crossed his arms high on his chest and fought to keep from asking if he could take a look at the safe. But it would be impossible to crack if it required the owner's retinal scan.

"The agency I work for has a penchant for tracking down weapons with a fantastical legend attached to them." He never explained the Agency beyond that. What people didn't know regarding the Agency, they didn't need to learn. "I'm also a geologist. The metals used in ancient swords and blades fascinate me."

"I thought geology was rocks?" the old woman asked.

"It is, but the cold iron used in the—" Dane winced and nodded. "Yes, just rocks. Uh, so your brother will be back…when?"

"Friday."

And today was Monday. Must he stay here an entire week? In what closely resembled a storm-ravaged tundra? And the old man had insisted someone pick up the dagger in person. He hadn't wanted to send it by post. A wise decision when it came to weapons that could possess a volatile nature. Of course, Mr. Stuart couldn't know about that. Or could he?

Hmm…

Dane smiled at the woman through a tight jaw.

"Will it be a problem for you to stay in our fine little town for a bit? There are hotels along Highway 10, not far from here. Oh! And there's the Winter Fantasy Ball this evening over at the Bleekwood mansion. You might stop in. I suspect the local girls would love to marvel over such a fine, er, studious fellow as yourself."

Dane nodded appreciatively even as he felt the back of his neck heat. A geriatric flirting with him? It was sweet. But a week in this icebox? He wasn't sure his sand-and-surf blood could manage that long without freezing.

A biometric safe. Just his luck.

On the other hand, he did favor a rousing adventure. Learning to survive in the icy tundra? Sign him up!

He shoved a hand in his pocket, where he touched the comforting curve of a plastic Bic lighter. He always carried one with him. He wasn't a smoker, but when he became agitated, he calmed himself by flicking it over and over.

Hey, to each his own.

He palmed another cookie and bit into it. "Tell me the best place to stay around here?"

Chapter 2

"Oh, Eryss! You look gorgeous!"

Eryss Norling turned to spy her coworker Mireio Malory flouncing toward her in an eighteenth century ball gown, replete with a pink powdered wig and décolletage cut low enough to make promises without a single spoken word. Eryss hugged her and smiled at Mireio's signature sugar-candy scent, then tucked a stray bright red curl up under her friend's wig.

"You must be Marie Antoinette?" Eryss guessed.

"Natch," Mireio said, with a flutter of her lush false lashes. "She's my spirit animal, you know."

"I thought that was a mermaid."

"That, too! And in a poufy dress! But look at you, all silver and blue and looking like the Snow Queen herself. Love the wig."

Eryss adjusted the too-tight tinsel wig with a tug above her ear. She'd found it at the local costume shop just down the street from the brewery. "I wanted to get into the snow fantasy. Winter *is* my season."

"And you never feel cold. Always so warm." She clasped Eryss's hand and squeezed. "See? You're warm as toast. And my tits are in desperate need of a nice warm sweater. Or I'll take a handsome male head lying on them if I can manage that. The eligible bachelor pickings tonight are slim. Have you seen Valor?"

"I think she headed to the kitchen to check the keg. We should have enough Iced Kiss for tonight, but there's a lot of people here."

The ice beer they brewed had a high alcohol content— and a touch of wintergreen mixed with quartz gem elixir— and they served it in shot glasses shaped like icicles.

The town's annual Winter Fantasy Ball, held in the Bleekwood mansion every January, had been featuring The Decadent Dames's microbrews for four years, as long as they had been in business in Anoka. Eryss was proud of their beers, but despite the rumors, she'd never confess that the four witches who owned the place also stirred in a bit of magic with each batch.

"I'm heading home," Eryss said. "Your eligible bachelor count is correct. Unfortunately. And I'm restless. I need to ground myself in the conservatory."

"Still having those dreams about the man? I thought you were going to cast the anacampserote?"

"I did perform it on solstice eve. Haven't had another dream until last night. I dreamed again of the great love I once lost. I can never see his face. It's a portent, I know. But with the spell cast, I should be able to recognize his soul should he come into my life. Though, you know, it might not be today or tomorrow. For all I know, it could be thirty *years* from now."

"I don't think so. You will find your great love when you are still young. Maybe you'll get him for your birthday?"

Eryss turned thirty in a week.

"Sure, maybe. But I am in no mood to wander these bleak halls in search of some steamy man flesh. It isn't going to happen tonight. I'm restless because I—aggh, I just need some hot and heavy sex, you know?"

"Darling, I know." Mireio fanned her bosom and cast a glance about the ballroom, where the band had just ripped into a bouncing jitterbug. "There aren't many men left in this town we haven't served at the bar."

"And after getting to know them from across the bar," Eryss added, "I want to clock half of them over the head."

"You're telling me. We should drive downtown to Minneapolis one night. On a man hunt. Or try Tinder!"

"Ugh. Dating apps are for hookups."

"Yeah, but sometimes a hookup is all a girl wants. You know? But wait, maybe you don't know. You're the one looking for the happily-ever-after. Oh, sweetie, you'll find him."

"I know I will." Eryss chuckled at her friend's hopeful dramatics. Friends would never admonish one another for wanting some mind-blowing, no-strings-attached sex once in a while. She hugged Mireio. "Oh, you *are* freezing."

"It's the décolletage, don't you know." She ran her fingertips over her corseted bosom. "I can never stay warm in winter. Remind me why I live in Minnesota?"

"You were born here, and you love the changing seasons." Eryss took Mireio's hands and held them together between her palms. "Warmth," she whispered with intention.

"Thank you," Mireio said. "I felt that magic all the way to my toes. But just so you know, if your plan to open another brewery out of state comes to fruition, I vote for California."

"Me, too. And it is on my list. I'll see you tomorrow at the brewery." She kissed Mireio's cheek, being careful to avoid the little black heart patch. "I'll make sure Valor has the new keg in place."

"See you tomorrow!"

Valor had indeed already replaced the spent Iced Kiss keg with a new one. That, along with the half keg of the Uff Da IPA Lot, should last for the remainder of the evening. That beer name had been all Mireio's doing.

On the way out, Eryss said her goodbyes to everyone. She knew many and many knew her because they frequented the brewery. A few knew her because they'd had occasion to *believe* and had been desperate. A love spell here. A breakup spell there. The repulsion spells against violent lovers were always difficult but necessary. Those who received the benefits of her craft kept their mouths shut, guarding Eryss's secret.

It wasn't easy being a witch, even if the town she lived in was the official Halloween Capital of the World.

At the top of the stairs that fronted the mansion, she stepped out onto the patio where a bonfire toasted partyers regaled in myriad costumes. The air was warm and tainted with ice and burned oak. Dozens of people stood around the fire with plastic champagne goblets and beer mugs in hand. Among the elves and witches and faery princesses were snowcat racers (the easiest way to bundle up and dress in a sort-of costume without looking out of place), loggers (lots of flannel and thick, warm boots)—oh, those lumbersexuals—and one daring caveman who wore a fur Fred Flintstone number that strapped over one shoulder. Poor guy, he might develop frostbite in places he'd never imagined possible.

Chocolate and marshmallow oozed out between graham crackers as s'mores were handed around. A game of ice bowling was set up along the side of the patio. The balls and pins had been chipped out of ice harvested from the nearby Mississippi River. Laughter sprinkled the air as if it were crystal snowflakes. The evening could be magical—if a girl had a man on her arm with whom to share those sweetly tempting s'mores.

Yet Eryss was an introvert and didn't feel at all guilty about leaving the party early. She'd come to make nice with the locals because area businesses and the city council always invited the brewery to Anoka events, and—okay, she'd had the gown. Why not use it?

Though she wouldn't have minded dancing, if any man had asked. Of course, she might have had to hang out near the dance floor for that to happen, and well, introverts didn't tend to do such things.

With a nagging hankering for gooey marshmallow and chocolate teasing her, Eryss turned and was roughly bumped into from the side. "Oof!"

Though a deflection spell teased the tip of her tongue, she wisely held off from speaking the words. She and her fellow witches did their best not to flaunt their craft at public events.

"I am so sorry." The man's cold hands gripped her forearms to steady her. "I wasn't looking. That was entirely my fault. I slipped on the ice."

There was no ice on the fire-warmed concrete steps, but Eryss wasn't about to point that out once her gaze landed on the man's face. Deep brown eyes were shadowed by thick black brows. She had never seen such a rich iris color and thought perhaps there were also glints of gold winking back at her. A five o'clock shadow brushing his jaw emphasized an exquisitely masculine bone structure. Thick coal hair, swept messily back from his face, screamed for her to touch the loose curls that tickled those red ears.

And suddenly, her heart performed a skip and every part of her being stood up in recognition. Was he...?

"I've been looking for you," she murmured in awe.

"Uh...you have?"

Giddy warmth flooded her heart. Her veins. Her skin flushed and she—well, she felt it in her very soul. This was the man. The one.

He had to be.

"Oh, what?" Eryss shook her head out of the deliciously muddling awe and back to reality. "Sorry. Did I say I was looking for you? I mean, uh..." What to say? She couldn't come right out with the revelation that she suspected he was her long-lost soul mate. Just because the man gave off smolder vibes did not make him receptive to her beliefs of reincarnation. "You need a hat," she decided quickly. "Looks like your ears are burning."

He gave a funny wince. Obviously, he'd picked up on her comment, but wasn't going to press. "They are. The blood vessels in my ears have started to constrict and blood is being shunted away from my extremities—ah. Ha-ha!" His smile revealed bright white teeth and squinting eyes that captured Eryss as if a love spell had been cast. "Sorry about that. I have a tendency to expound on silly things. Suffice it to say, I'm from the West. Didn't expect it to be quite so cold." He touched an ear and winced again.

"We call it frostbite here in Minnesota." She marveled over the lingering laughter in his smile. Wonderful. And he was hers. Maybe? Yes, he had to be. But how to know for sure? "We should step over by the fire."

"Yes, but you seem to be on your way out?"

Her gaze wandered to his broad shoulders, down the white shirt, rolled to his elbows to reveal a manly dusting of dark hairs on his—oddly, tan—forearms, and to the thick veins that corded the back of his hands. Leave now when she'd just stumbled into the man she'd been waiting for?

"Leaving? Heck, no! Will you join me for a hot chocolate?"

"I should be honored to share libations with such a lovely queen," he replied.

Libations? The man most definitely was not the standard bar slug or even a hipster (the brewery's standard customer). And Eryss remembered that she had been feeling horny not too long ago. How lucky could a girl get to find her soul mate and have him be übersexy, as well?

When he offered it, she took his arm and allowed him to lure her over to the bonfire. They found a spot close enough to warm their hands but far enough away so as not to ignite Eryss's sparkly skirt. The man with the sudden and seductive laughter got them hot chocolates from the bar posted outside the front of the mansion. It served eggnog, hot chocolate, hot brandy and some kind of drink called a Dirty Snowman. Despite her trade, Eryss didn't like beer all that much, so she was thankful to sip something sweet with just a touch of alcohol.

"I'm Dane Winther, by the way." He handed her a paper mug. "I was on my way inside to find my coat, but I suddenly find the need for warmth has dissipated. And I've yet to take a sip of this thick brew." He winked at her. "Must be the company."

A charmer? She could work with that. "Eryss Norling." She offered her hand, which he shook. "Stand closer to the fire. You really need to warm those hands."

He moved closer and wrapped both hands around the

mug. After blowing over the hot chocolate, he took a sip. "Norling? I believe that means something like 'they who come from the north'?"

"Got it in one guess. But I've always lived here in the north. I own The Decadent Dames brewery in town."

"Ah, yes, I noticed that place. Across from the antiques store? I had wondered how decadent a beer could be, but you were closed when I passed by."

"We had to finish kegging the Iced Kiss for tonight. We'll be open tomorrow. And I promise a very decadent experience if you try the oatmeal cream stout."

"I do like a nice dark beer. And chocolate." He held up his mug, tapped it against hers in a paper-thud toast, then tilted back a swallow. "Mmm…you Minnesotans do know how to do hot chocolate. I think there's booze in this."

Eryss smirked. "It's got crème de menthe in it. We call it a Chocolate Kiss."

A bemused smile danced in his eyes, and once again captivated by his utter and easy merriment, Eryss swayed, but stopped herself as soon as she felt her body lean toward him, toward his interesting ocean-surf scent. It was a scent she'd recently smelled. But…where and when? Wow, she was really leaning close now. She did not want to scare the man away because he thought she was weird. Or excited over finding someone she had known for ages.

"Mmm, yes, it's got a touch of mint in it. A kiss, indeed." He grinned and took another sip.

His eyes actually smiled. And with all that thick, carelessly swept hair that virtually demanded a woman run her fingers through it, could the man be any cuter?

Eryss stepped closer until they stood shoulder to shoulder before the bonfire. The blaze toasted her cheeks. Or was that Dane? She loved the name. Very Nordic.

Did he feel the same way about her? As if he knew her? She jittered on her toes, knowing she stood next to *him*. The one!

Maybe. She shouldn't get ahead of herself. She could simply be feeling giddy over bumping into one heck of a hot man.

"I'll have to stop in to your brewery," he said. "I find I'm on a forced vacation in your chilly little town. I was supposed to pick up a rare dagger from Stuart's Stuff, but the proprietor is out of town."

"Hawaii for a funeral. Isn't that lucky?"

"I said the same thing, but I don't think the owner's sister found the humor in my wishing for warmer weather. Though she did allow me to take a second cookie."

"Ha! Gladiola Stuart is discerning about whom she allows to have a cookie. Apparently, you passed the test. And I can see why."

Eryss cautioned herself from drawing her gaze up and down his body in an indiscreet droolfest. She wasn't that kind of girl. Mostly. She was much more stealthy, and had already checked out his ass when he'd gone to get the hot chocolates. Nice and tight. And no, he hadn't given any indication that he recognized her in any way.

Chill, she cautioned inwardly. *Do not freak the man out.*

"Where *did* you come from?" she asked over her steaming mug. "I'm guessing someplace warmer by your thin shirt and vest? And the tan?"

He palmed his chest. The tweed vest granted him an astute, teacherly vibe, which, when added to the smoldering dark looks, Eryss found intriguing.

"I'm from Santa Cruz, about an hour from San Francisco. I'm afraid the tan is a permanent condition. And I had to buy a warm coat in the Minneapolis airport after

I'd arrived. Can you believe I've never experienced snow before? And I'm a geologist."

"You'll be baptized by fire, or rather ice, here in Minnesota. What branch of geology?"

"Geochemistry. Which means I really like rocks. But I also dabble in botany and anthropological genetics. I like to have options."

"I guess you do. I like rocks and plants. Genetics is beyond my grasp."

"It's my weakest field of study. But the little I know tells me that you had at least one blue-eyed parent to be sporting the color yourself. Gorgeous."

Eryss parted her lips to speak, but then couldn't think of a thing to say. He smiled a little when she caught him staring into her eyes. It was a flirtatious moment that made her giggle.

"So what are you dressed as tonight?" she asked.

"I didn't have time for a costume. Gladiola Stuart told me about the party earlier. I guess you could say I'm a scientist."

Eryss purred over the steamy chocolate. "I suddenly find myself quite fond of science."

His brow lifted and a smile glittered in the man's deep brown eyes. And like that, Eryss's ovaries did the dance of joy.

"To science." He offered his mug in another toast.

Eryss tapped her mug gently against his and shivered one of those good, warm-all-over shivers. First handsome man she'd met since the anacampserote, and here she was thinking he was the one.

Or was she overreacting because he was also the sexiest thing on two legs that managed to touch her with his dancing eyes and laughter?

"So you said you're in town for a while?"

"Seems Mr. Stuart won't be back for a week. Can you recommend some good restaurants and places to visit?"

"I probably can. But you'll have to drive into Minneapolis for culture and fine dining."

"I may do that. If I can find a car rental place. I took a cab here. Though I'm not so sure how I would fare driving on these snow-encrusted streets."

"It does require some talent to navigate the black ice. But you'll have a few good days before we get walloped again."

"Walloped?"

"There's snow headed our way. It's going to warm up to the twenties, which provides great conditions for snow."

"Warm up to the twenties," he muttered, shaking his head. "I suppose you think that's downright balmy?"

"Oh, it is." It was always fun to tease the out-of-towners. In reality, Eryss wasn't much for the below-zero weather, but she took it all in stride. Living in Minnesota afforded her all the seasons. Too bad winter generally lasted almost six months. "So what kind of dagger would a scientist be looking for?"

"There's some fantastical lore attached to it, but I'm mostly interested in it because it's supposed to be thirteenth century. The lore says it was forged with cold iron, and don't get me started on the fascinating aspects of ancient forged metals. I'll nerd out on you."

"I like a nerd." Especially one smelling like chocolate and mint, mixed with a hint of tweed. "I'm a bit of a brew nerd myself."

"So you actually brew beer in your little place?"

"Yes, we're a microbrewery. Me and three other women are all part owners. We've been friends for ages."

"The Decadent Dames. *Decadence* is such a delicious

word, don't you think? It speaks of glamour and ritual, embellishment and desire."

"And velvets and silk, and sweet spices and honey," Eryss chimed in.

"I love that. What about warm summer grass threading between your toes and constellations of fireflies buzzing about the midnight sky?"

"Wow. You really miss summer, don't you?"

"I do." He sipped the cocoa. "But I'm learning winter does have its sweetness in the form of a lovely snow goddess."

"It's the tinsel hair. You just want to run your fingers through it, don't you?"

"It's the whole look. If you were carrying a wand that shot out snow sparkles from the tip, I'd totally buy into it."

"You've seen *Frozen*."

"How to avoid it when even the cereal I buy features the characters on the box? But I confess, I did see it. It was for a date."

"You took a woman out to a Disney movie?"

"I wasn't my first choice, but I didn't complain. I got to pick the restaurant, so it was fun all around."

The man was racking up some seriously sexy, dateable points. And Eryss wouldn't even begin to calculate how many points he'd earn if he truly did turn out to be her soul mate.

"What kind of food do you like?" she asked.

"Seafood and good wine."

"I can recommend an excellent Scandinavian restaurant for you to check out while you're here. It would be a shame for you not to try lutefisk and lefse before leaving."

"I've heard of lefse. A Norwegian staple made with flour and…"

"Potatoes. It's like a very soft flatbread, and you butter it and sprinkle sugar on top. Roll it up, and have at it!"

"Sounds like a treat. Do I want to know what lutefisk is?"

"It's seafood. Sort of. Whitefish soaked in lye. But if you cook it right, it's awesome." She noticed his distasteful swallow and laughed. "I haven't eaten it since I was a kid. I know better now." She winked at him.

Behind them, strains of music echoed out from the mansion. Dane took her hand, the one clasping the empty mug, and she startled. "Would you like to dance?"

Suddenly feeling more ungrounded than she ever had in her life, Eryss delighted in the airy lift to her being. "Yes, please."

The winter queen bewigged with tinsel knew how to dance a waltz. And so did Dane, thanks to his mother's insistence that a well-rounded man could make his way through life with ease and grace. Of course, she didn't have to know he'd also taken martial arts classes and was a damn good hand at knife-throwing, courtesy of his own desires to round out his life. But as they glided about the dance floor and the song came to an end, he was thankful for the next, slower song so he could hold his partner closer and look into her eyes. Those mysterious blue eyes.

There was something about Eryss that he couldn't quite put a finger on. She was pretty, but not in a conventional, overdone way where men's jaws dropped and they stared long after she'd passed. She had flawless skin and bright eyes. A soft pink mouth and no visible blush on her cheeks. And yet Dane felt as if he had scored a dance with the most gorgeous woman in the world, for her attention warmed him to the bone and he was quite sure he hadn't stopped smiling since they'd taken the dance floor.

He leaned in close, brushing her cheek with his. He should have shaved. But she didn't flinch or seem to mind his stubble. In fact, she nestled in closer, pressing her breasts against his chest and bringing their hands down so they swayed together in the middle of the dance floor, barely moving.

Yet his heart raced. He felt like the awkward geek he'd once been at high school dances. Nervous. Unsure. Most definitely not as suave as he liked to think he was. Was everyone staring at the fumbling nerd? And yet he'd scored the cheerleader this time, and hell, yeah, he wanted everyone to look at him.

Eryss tilted her head and whispered, "I feel airy when I'm with you, Dane. Not at all grounded."

"Is that a good or bad thing?"

"I haven't decided."

Hmm…well, he didn't want her to decide it was the latter, so he clasped one hand across her back and held her securely. Grounding her? He wasn't sure how that worked, but the feeling took him and all he wanted to do was hold this beautiful queen and forget the unfortunate luck he'd had at the antiques store.

Something about this embrace felt…familiar? It was an odd thing to notice. He'd never met this woman. Surely he would remember those blue eyes. And he'd never once set foot in Minnesota before today.

He'd take the feeling for whatever it was, and count his luck as having turned toward the good side.

When the slow music segued into a bouncy beat, they paused and her eyes sought his. She asked, "Want to come to my place?"

Dane's reaction went from surprised, to curious, to

aroused in a matter of seconds. That had been an abrupt invite.

She didn't blush so much as glow, even under the silly tinsel wig. "Uh, I think I can show you a little taste of summer. I promise I won't molest you."

He intentionally dropped the smirk. "Now I'm disappointed."

She laughed. "Unless you want me to? Come on. I know where summer lives."

He clasped her hand, and sucked in a breath at the sudden electric zing that coursed from that connection. It felt as if he'd been jolted by static electricity directly on the heart.

"Is something wrong?" she asked innocently.

Eryss peered into his eyes once again. He'd never seen this woman before. And yet...*had* he?

"You do recognize me," she said with an effusive smile. And with that weird announcement, she tugged him off the dance floor. "Come with me."

As they grabbed Dane's coat and glided down the mansion stairs, Dane felt as though he was following a familiar path to something he had wondered about for so long.

Chapter 3

Bemused was one way to describe Dane's mood. He'd only just arrived in Minnesota this morning. Had nearly slid into the ditch at the mercy of an angry cab driver while being transported from airport to northern suburbs. Plowed his way to the antiques shop. Learned he'd have to stay a miserable week in the tundra. Decided to check out a costume party on a night that featured single-digit temperatures. And now he was about to hook up with a pretty woman smelling like chocolate, mint and sage.

Maybe. This might not be a hookup. She could be taking him to her house to—hell yes, it was a hookup! With a woman wearing a silver wig and a blue gown glittering with spangled snowflakes. But he could see beyond the costume and knew she was more interesting than a meteor dug up from a farmer's field. And he wanted to get to know her better. He had a week in this town. Why not start it off with a bang?

"Do you do this often?" he asked as she navigated her Prius down a dark road that was *just out of the main city*, as she'd stated. *Her own little bit of sanity that edged the suburbs.*

"What? Navigate icy roads wearing a snow queen costume?"

Dane chuckled. "No. Pick up stray scientists you've found bumbling about fire pits on frozen winter nights."

"Ah. All the time! Though I'd never assign the word *bumbling* to you." She laughed, and a slip of dark hair fell out from under her wig. "No, this is a new one for me." She clicked on the turn signal and slowed for a right. "But how could I resist a scientist looking so out of his element and in need of a little tender-loving summer?"

"Out of my element? Yes. I prefer carbon."

"Ha! A science joke. My element is earth, in case you're wondering."

"Earth isn't exactly an element. I'll assign you silica, since that is abundant in sand, which is earth. Of course, you could also be nitrogen, because when that freezes— well, it's icy and fun to play with."

"I'm not an ice queen, I just play one at the annual winter festival. And if you're not nice to me, I'll turn around and you'll never see summer."

"Sorry. But I will reserve judgment on your summer-invoking abilities until I can feel the grass beneath my feet."

"It will happen. Promise. Just ahead. So where are you staying?"

"I found a hotel next to an Applebee's. Classy place, the hotel. They even offer all-you-can-eat pastries glopped with thick pink frosting in the mornings. I could not contain my enthusiasm when I learned that."

"Really?" She flashed him a genuinely doubtful look.

"I'm kidding. I have a tendency to find sarcasm in all the wrong places. Sorry."

"Don't apologize. You're a breath of fresh air, Dane. I don't run into men like you around town all that often."

"So you've snatched me up and now you're going to do *what* with me, exactly?"

She waggled her eyebrows and pulled the car into a garage set beside a Victorian-style house. "Just wait and find out. Come in, if you dare." She turned off the car and opened the door.

And Dane followed with the eagerness of a scientist discovering a new element. This could be interesting. Or at the very least, a distraction from the local television reruns and stale sheets he had been headed for back at the hotel.

Inside the house, the lights were low and the kitchen vast, four times the size of a normal kitchen. Dane was drawn to the center, where a butcher-block table stretched ten feet and was paralleled by random unmatched bar stools in a range of heights. Above the table hung various dried herbs and flowers among copper pans and light-bulbs caged by chicken wire.

He drew in a breath, infusing his senses with lavender and rose, sage and thyme, and he detected cinnamon, as well. Summer, indeed. But it wasn't grass, as she'd promised. Still. He took in the rest of the kitchen, the pale gray clapboard walls harmonized with the stainless steel appliances. Country chic with a dash of bohemian, from the bright red and violet dish towels to the deep garnet glass dishes stacked neatly in the doorless cupboards.

"This is like something from a movie set," he said. "You live here alone?"

She nodded and then tugged off the tinsel wig to reveal a spill of chestnut hair that tumbled down her shoulders. Straight as a ruler and thick. She blew a few strands from her bright blue eyes. And how those lush lashes fluttered as she waited for him to speak. He could not ignore or dismiss what those enchanting eyes did to his heartbeats—thudding toward some cliff was how it felt.

"Dane?" She nudged forward, inspecting his gaze. "Is something wrong?"

"Uh, no." Had his mouth been open in wonder over her simple yet utterly gorgeous appearance? He needed to check himself. This was a little unsettling, standing here with a woman he'd met an hour earlier. Sure, he'd romanced her a bit at the party. But then he'd been the prince swishing around the dance floor with a queen. Now he felt slightly unsure. Playing the science nerd was his game. And he hadn't much of a game to claim in the first place.

"So where's summer?" he asked.

"Let me pour you a lemonade first, and then we'll head into summer. You like mint?"

"Yes, please."

He sat on a stool and shrugged off his wool jacket. He'd need to buy something warmer if he intended to go out and about for a week in this frigid weather. And he could hardly imagine sitting in a hotel room that whole time. He had some weapons reports to work on for the Agency, but he always got antsy if he sat before the laptop too long. Best way to counterattack a work slump? Hit a few waves or punch the bag for a while. He wondered if there might be a gym in the hotel. He'd ask at reception when he returned later…but how would he get to the hotel? He had no vehicle.

Eryss pulled a glass pitcher from the fridge and then crushed a few fresh mint leaves she picked off a plant near a window over the sink.

"I want to change out of this silly dress," she said as she handed him a glass of cloudy yellow brew sprinkled with emerald leaves. "I'm going to send you into summer on your own, and then take a few minutes to myself. Deal?"

He sipped the lemonade. Tart! And followed by a tendril of sweetness laced with a minty gush that tickled his nose.

"Oh yeah. That hit the spot. Uh, and yes, go do whatever you wish. I can sit here until you return."

"No. You are in desperate need of a summer infusion. Follow me."

He didn't need to be told twice. Dane followed Eryss's swaying blue skirt into the living room, which was as large as the kitchen and decorated with velvet and silk furniture coverings and plants. Bohemian yet fresh, he thought. A far cry from the white walls and steel and leather furniture that filled his small Santa Cruz apartment. Down a hallway they neared a glass-block wall, and then he saw the doors and realized a two-story conservatory was attached to the house.

Eryss opened the door and gestured for him to enter as one low inner light flickered on. He strolled inside and the humidity hit him softly. He swallowed the heavy air and smiled. The warmth was incredible and the green smell of plants transported him to...

"Summer," he said in a hushed voice.

"Told you. Here." She handed him a lighter, then turned and flicked a switch. A stirring of gears began to lower what he saw was a massive crystal chandelier in the center of the glass hothouse, and it stopped just beside a curvy emerald velvet sofa. "Light the candles and I'll be back quick as I can."

"Uh, sure," he said, as he absently flicked the lighter

on and off. He couldn't get over the incredible place in which he stood.

Eryss disappeared out the door and into the house. And Dane stood there, a lemonade wafting mint in one hand and a lighter in the other as he noticed the emerald-crystal candelabra was fitted with real beeswax candles. And was that—did a *dragonfly* flit about the massive chandelier?

What kind of Wonderland had he stumbled into? And was Eryss more Alice than Snow Queen?

"Does it matter?" A grin teased at him and he relaxed into the intriguing madness of it all. "Here's to Wonderland."

Confident she'd left the man in a wondrous state, Eryss tugged off the satin gown and tossed it across the bed as she beelined into her closet. It was a walk-in, but was only half filled with clothes and shoes. The other half was stacked with boxes of crystals, herbs, tinctures and other magical accoutrements she didn't have room for in her spell room—which was the conservatory.

Geneva, one of her brewery partners, had scoffed at this tiny closet. That woman owned an entire store of clothing, and a high-end one at that. She hadn't been at the party tonight because she was still in Greece, ending a two-month-long affair with a millionaire. Or maybe he was a billionaire. Eryss couldn't keep track of Geneva's conquests.

Tugging on the long, gray, crushed-velvet sweater that was more a dress because it went to just above her knees, she decided against the wool leggings she usually wore with it. She wiggled her bare toes, which glinted with bright green toenail polish. Checking her appearance in the mirror, she turned before it as she buttoned up the sweater dress. When was the last time she had preened for a man?

"He's so cute. And smart. And hot."

Now the question was: to hook up or not? She had no moral qualms about taking to bed a man she had just met and felt confident wasn't a serial killer or nose picker. Some magnetic vibes had formed between them while dancing.

Had her soul really recognized his soul? It was a feeling she'd never known before, and she wanted to place it as a result of the anacampserote spell. But she mustn't rush into believing such things. Finding her soul mate was monumental. And she had known Dane all of an hour.

"Oh, Eryss, you have to chill and relax. He's just a handsome man. End of story."

Or, with hope, the beginning of a story.

But she could not deny something about him seemed familiar.

"Maybe we've dated in a previous life," she said. That was always entirely possible because she had reincarnated many times. "Or were we married?"

Who knew? The possibilities were endless. What mattered was that she felt Dane had bumped into her tonight for a reason. And she never ignored intuition. So she'd follow his lead, and see where they both landed. She was willing to follow.

Browsing over her jewelry tray on the vanity, she selected the rose quartz pendant and pulled it on over her head. "For the heart."

She skipped down the stairs and picked up her lemonade from the newel post at the base of the steps, and then sailed into the humid warmth of the conservatory, which she kept verdant and healthy with the help of earth elementals. Hopefully, they would remain out of sight tonight. They didn't normally show themselves around anyone but her and her witch friends, but she would cross her fingers for an uneventful evening in the summery haven nonetheless.

Dane had settled onto the emerald sofa, head tilted back and eyes closed. He seemed to be taking it all in. With dark curls spilling over his forehead and his powerful hands clasped loosely across his lap, he looked like a dozing faun king amid the wilds. Powerful, virile and of the earth. Eryss felt compelled to lean over and kiss him. Taste the sweet lemonade on his lips and breathe in his solid, masculine presence.

But he hadn't kissed her at the dance, so she didn't want to leap too quickly. Not until he gave her some sign he was interested in more than chatting.

"So, is it summery enough for you?" she asked as she sat next to him. The lush grass floor was the product of a spell that she didn't have to tell him about. She loved feeling it tickling her toes.

"It is. How do you do this? In the middle of winter? I get the thick glass and the heating system, though I couldn't find a source for the heater. And some plants are very hardy in cooler climes, but the grass? Are there heat coils *beneath* the sod? It's frozen out there. There must be some means to heat the ground. Otherwise, it's not scientifically—"

"Science has nothing to do with it, Dane. It's magic. And if I told you how it worked it wouldn't be magic anymore. So don't question it. Deal?"

"I don't believe in magic."

"I'm sorry for you. So much in life is a direct result of magic and unexplainable phenomena."

"It's my job to explain such phenomena. Everything

has a reason and a source. Down to the very atom. I should probably tell you what I really do."

"What? You're *not* a scientist?"

"Oh, I'm a scientist. But for the past few years I've been, well, you might call me a debunker. I disprove paranormal phenomena and other items associated with myth and legend."

"Seriously? Like a myth buster?"

"Yes, exactly."

"How does a guy happen on to a job like that?" Now a little uncomfortable knowing she sat next to not only a scientist, but one who went out of his way to prove people of her sort a myth, she turned to face him, tucking up her legs and propping an elbow on the back of the sofa. "Was there an ad in the paper?"

He chuckled. Oh man, the guy's laughter. It hit Eryss in all the feels.

"No," he said. "I was recruited. It's important that the public gets the right information about the things that tend to grow fantastical roots with remarkable speed via popular culture and social media. Human brains have a hive mentality, and if someone says a vampire exists it doesn't take long for the rest to agree. Thus." He splayed a hand before his chest. "The calm in the storm."

"You?"

"Me. I'm doing what I love. Using science every day. And really, I can't let the world sit back and actually believe in vampires, can I?"

"Fantasy *is* good for the soul," she suggested.

Though she did agree with his purpose, if not his actual work. Vampires and witches? The fewer people who believed in them, the safer and easier it was for them to exist among the humans. "So you've debunked vampires?"

"On more than one occasion. I live in Santa Cruz, but my work frequently lures me to San Francisco. That city is oddly rife with murders staged to look as if a vampire did it. You would be surprised the lengths some go to get the teeth impressions just right. But they always drain too much blood from the body. If a vampire did exist, he could not exsanguinate an entire body in such a short time. I'm sorry. This is a morbid subject."

"No, I'm interested in what you do. Does your being here in Minnesota have to do with your job? Should I be keeping one eye over my shoulder in fear of vampires?"

"You should not. And I'm here on a personal project, actually. Although it is also related to my work. I work in the Weapons division and am charged with debunking weapons of historical interest that have a legend of magic attached to them."

"So, like Excalibur?"

"Yes, but I believe that legendary weapon was last seen tossed in a lake."

"Not so. I'm pretty sure the lady living in the lake handed it to King Arthur."

"Right. Because it's entirely possible for a woman to exist in a lake. Mermaids are theoretically implausible. She may have been called the Lady of the Lake, but not because she actually lived in one. Of course, it doesn't matter. The Arthurian Chronicles *are* fiction."

"Wow. You haven't a fantastical bone in your body. Did your mother never read you faery tales when you were little?"

"No, she read me the table of elements and notes from her psychology papers."

Eryss gaped at Dane. He didn't catch her shock as he sipped the lemonade. Poor guy. But she didn't want to get into a deep conversation about childhood traumas and lack of fantasy play. The night outside the windows was gray, illuminated by the snowy ground and nearby forest. The air inside was fresh as summer, and all she wanted to do was touch his hair and…kiss him.

"It's a good thing our pasts do not define us," she said, even as she inwardly kicked herself for saying it. She, the woman who was obsessed with finding the lost lover from her previous lives.

"Indeed. But my past is what brings me to Minnesota. I'm after a weapon once owned by my father. It's got some paranormal legend attached to it, which could make it an item of interest to the company I work for, but that's not the important thing."

"It was your father's," she stated.

"Indeed. He died when I was three." Dane shook his head and ran his fingers through his hair. And Eryss sighed inwardly as the glossy black strands swept over his ear. "Enough talk about what I do and why I'm here. I want to enjoy summer!"

Now he turned an absolutely delicious smile on her. He set the glass down in the grass and turned his body toward her. He set his shoulders back and spread his arms across the sofa back and arm. He was open to her, beckoning without words.

And if that wasn't an invitation, Eryss was losing her wiles. She moved in for a kiss. His stubble brushed her cheek and the heat of him surrounded her, sending a shiver of delight across her skin. The tang of lemons sweetened her lips, and she inhaled mint as if it were his pheromones.

He'd rolled his sleeves up to his elbows and she glided her fingers up his arm, rough with dark hair and the map lines of thick veins. So masculine. She turned into him and he paused the kiss. His eyes held her, bewitched. "Is this all right?"

"Yes. Why wouldn't it be?"

"I'm feeling a little out of my element. As if I'm stumbling here."

"Really?" And here she'd thought the invitation overwhelming. "You're doing fine."

"Not with the kiss. I mean, this feels too good to be true, Eryss. We just met an hour ago and now here I am, kissing you beneath real candlelight on a sofa set amid an enchanted garden. It's sort of blowing my mind."

"I bet it takes a lot to blow your mind."

"It does, actually. Your success is duly noted."

"You like to think a lot."

"I do."

"Then that will be your challenge." She swished away a curl from his brow. Yes, so soft. "You can't think around me, you just have to be in the moment."

"This *is* a good moment."

"I agree. Now, stop thinking and kiss me."

Her smile lured him to her like a night flower draws one to inhale its perfume. Dane kissed her and pushed his fingers up through her hair. His mouth fit hers in a way that was confident and yet so sweet. She knew him, and perhaps he knew her but didn't realize it. It was a fantastical way of thinking, but there you go. She was a witch. It helped to have an active imagination.

"Come here," he muttered, and pulled her onto his lap as he leaned back on the couch and looked up into her eyes. "Candlelight becomes you. It dances in your hair." He stroked her hair and pulled it to his nose. "You smell like ice and sage."

"I must still be working some of my ice queen mojo. You taste like mint and lemons." She straddled his legs with hers and leaned in to kiss his jaw, licking the short stubble. A fern tendril had crept over the back of the couch and tickled her forehead. She giggled against his mouth. "The plants approve of this moment, as well."

"If I didn't know better, I'd think they were sentient beings intent on seducing the two of us together."

"Plants are sentient. And we are together. Haven't you ever been seduced, Dane?"

"I, uh, well, sure. Not in such a manner, though. It's so…"

"Interesting?"

His eyes dropped to the rose quartz crystal dangling above her breasts. "Quick."

He was having trouble with their sudden embrace? Yes, well, she had not followed his lead, as she'd told herself to do. *Bad witch.* Eryss sat back on Dane's thighs and smoothed her palms over his tweed vest buttoned neatly over a crisp white shirt. "Do I intimidate you?"

"Honestly? A little." He ran a hand back through his hair. "I can't believe I confessed that. Normally I'm the one questioning if I'm the intimidating one. You're a fascinating woman, Eryss, and I think it's either that I can't believe my luck or that maybe you really are some kind of snow queen and you've bespelled me."

If he only knew.

"I think I should step back and slow down," she said. "I'm sorry."

She started to rise, but Dane took her hand and pulled her back to sit on his legs. "No, I'm sorry. This is what I want. You. Kissing me. Hugging me with those long legs and making my heart beat faster than a neutrino spray."

"I don't know what that means, but I can work with it."

This time he kissed her deeply. And while Eryss was still wondering if she had done the right thing with the anacampserote, she had to remain true to her intuition.

And her soul felt she was in the right place with the right person at this moment in her life. That's all that mattered.

Dane's hand glided up her hip and along the gray sweater. She wanted him to touch her everywhere, to learn her. To know her.

When his hand stopped just beside her breast, but not quite touching it, he broke their kiss. "I should leave before I don't want to leave."

He certainly did vacillate from one extreme to the other. "And you do want to leave?"

"I do. I don't. Eryss."

"I know." She did know. They were moving quickly. Racing, even. Not that she minded, but she wanted the guy to be all in, too. No sense in forcing a man to be something he wasn't ready to accept. How could he? He surely had no clue she suspected they were soul mates. "You can take my car back to your hotel."

"Really?"

She nodded. "If you can be back here tomorrow around eleven to pick me up, I'll show you around the brewery. Then I have some work to do for the afternoon."

"I can do that. I have some reports to fill out that will keep me busy."

"You really debunk vampires?" she asked, as he stood and stretched. "What about witches?"

Dane came out of the stretch with a chuckle. "Bunch of silly women who play with crystals and herbs and think their cats can talk to them."

"Ah. Wow."

The man had no idea how many points she would take off for that comment. On the other hand, the less he knew, the better. He'd be shocked to meet a cat-shifting familiar that could talk to humans. She bet he'd never debunked a creature like that before.

"You're sure?" he asked. "About me taking your car? Do you trust me driving on these roads?"

"They're clear of ice and snow. Mostly. I trust you."

She kissed him again. All of him smelled so good, like a place she could cuddle up in to get away from the rain. Or like a long-lost sanctuary that she'd found again.

She patted his chest. "I know your soul." He gave her a wonky look of disbelief, so she flounced toward the doors. "I'll get the key!"

Telling him she knew his soul had probably been rushing things more than if they'd almost had sex. And she wasn't positive she recognized his soul. The whole night had been a heated surrender to passion and lust. It was time to start thinking rationally.

"Like a scientist," she murmured, as she picked up the car keys from a copper bowl on the kitchen counter.

A scientist who debunked paranormal beings and who thought witches were silly? If they were going to get to know one another any better, Eryss sensed Dane's every belief would be duly challenged.

Challenge was necessary to a great life. So she'd bring it on, ready or not. The man had just stoked a silly witch's passions.

Chapter 4

Eryss strolled into the brewery, leaving Dane outside on the sidewalk. With a shovel. The heavens had dropped a light dusting of snow overnight, which left the sidewalk coated, and Dane had commented that it could be dangerous. So she'd gotten out a shovel from the basement storage and handed it to him. He'd grinned at her and accepted the challenge.

Hey, if the guy wanted to comment on their upkeep, then he needed to put up or shut up. Trial by fire, baby. Or rather, by snow.

After shedding her coat and mittens at the end of the bar, she shook out her hair and glanced over the hardwood floor. It was in need of a mopping, which she'd get to soon enough. A clinking sound came from the dishwasher, which was being fed pint glasses by Mireio. Mireio was an early riser and was always first into the brewery. But then, she rarely closed. Such a schedule worked well for all of them and their half-dozen other employees (none of them witches, and none of them aware of their employers' otherworldly abilities).

"So?"

Eryss met Mireio's hopeful gaze and knew exactly what she was thinking. And she wasn't even psychic. Eryss aligned a few pint glasses on the stainless steel counter and then tossed a dishcloth in the sink. "So what?"

"That looks like a fine specimen of man shoveling our sidewalk. Where did you find him? Dial-A-Manhunk?"

"At the party last night."

Mireio's eyes widened and she clutched her hands together hopefully before her chest. "And he's still with you this morning! Ooh! Did you have sex last night?"

"Really? Of all the things you want to know about that amazing hunk of man with the biceps of steel and hair that glistens like black gold, all you can think to ask is did we have sex?"

Mireio nodded eagerly. "What else is there to know? You must have taken him home with you, since you two are together today."

"I did take him home with me. We made out. But sex would have been pushing it a bit quickly."

"Good call." Mireio's gaze was pinned to Dane. "Maybe? Oh, how could you have *not*? Look at him!"

Eryss had. And knew exactly what wild and delicious scenarios involving naked flesh and moans and sighs were running through her friend's imagination. "He's a scientist."

"Ooh. A nerd. I love a sexy nerd." Mireio toyed with her springy red curls. "Don't find them wandering around Anoka very often. So when *will* you have sex? Because if you let that one slip out of your hands without tapping—"

"I'll give it my best shot. The man's kisses do not lend themselves to patience."

"Did you tell him you're a witch?"

"Mireio, he's a *scientist*."

"I got that. Oh, you don't think he'd believe you?"

"It's not that I need him to believe anything about me. Since when do we just toss it out there that we're witches?"

"True. But can you imagine the conversations you'd have trying to convince him you can control the earth and its elements with nothing more than your little finger?"

"I blew his mind with the conservatory. I liked seeing his surprise. But here's the kicker—he's a scientist who debunks paranormal phenomena."

Sudden worry fluttered Mireio's lashes. "What do you mean?"

"Like he proves vampires don't exist and thinks witches are crazy old ladies."

"Oh." Mireio shuddered. "Not cool. But he saw your conservatory. Who could actually believe something like that can exist *without* magic?"

"He's convinced I have heat coils running under the soil."

Mireio accepted that with a nod and a shrug. "Could happen."

"Doesn't matter. I don't want to get into it with him until I'm sure."

"Sure you want to have sex with him?" she asked eagerly.

"That. But also, sure that he's…the one."

"The one?"

"The one my soul pines for. I had a weird moment of recognition last night with him, Mireio. What if the anacampserote called him here? What if he is *the* man I fall in love with every time I'm reincarnated?"

"But he doesn't even believe in witches. I don't see that working too swell in the romance department."

"Right. But this man from my former lives might not have always been in my life for very long. He could have been a one-night stand or brief affair on many occasions. How often do we really reveal ourselves to our lovers?"

"If they are quickies, never. Too risky for witches. But if you think he's your soul mate, don't you think you'll have to tell him sooner or later?"

"I would love to have him know me as I know him. But that's the kicker. I don't know him. It was just a moment of knowing last night. So I could be wrong."

"But you want to be right."

"Goddess, yes. He's so sexy." They both turned to watch Dane push snow off the sidewalk outside.

Had she made a mistake by not encouraging him to have his way with her last night? "What am I going to do? He's only in town for a week."

"You can make him love you, then spill the beans about being a witch. Or you can tell him now and challenge his beliefs."

"Sounds like a game. I don't play games."

"Oh yeah? What about the one where you think he's your lost love and you want to keep him close to you without saying anything?"

"That's not fair."

"All is fair in love. War just sucks."

They both laughed, and Eryss couldn't find an argument against Mireio's suggestion to challenge his beliefs. She'd invite Dane to dinner. Tonight she'd prepare a feast to seduce. And she would pay attention to every sign she saw or felt toward him. If her soul really did recognize him, she wanted to be sure. And do what she could to help him recognize hers.

* * *

She had prepared a meal to seduce, Dane thought as he rolled the rhubarb wine across his tongue and inhaled the savory scent of tomatoes, garlic and pine nuts from the plate before him. But he didn't need to be seduced by food. The dress Eryss wore was more than amply urging his desires to the surface. She had on a soft, pink velvet dress that stopped at her thighs and was fringed with delicate lace about her décolletage, which kept drawing his eyes *right there*. And when she laughed her breasts jiggled, and then he couldn't remember what he was doing.

Oh, right, eating. With a fork. That he'd almost dropped onto the plate.

Making the save, Dane cleared his throat and offered, "I liked shoveling this morning."

"I noticed. You shoveled the whole block. The pet store next door appreciated that."

He shrugged. "I think I could handle Minnesota once in a while."

Eryss lifted a questioning brow.

"Mostly. Probably. In the summer, for sure."

"Does surfer guy miss the waves? Do you surf this time of year?"

"Oh, yeah. Some of the best swells roll in during January. Put me in a heavy wet suit and I'm good to go."

"But even with a wet suit, the water must be cold."

"In the fifties. So you see?" He pounded his chest with a fist. "I'm hardy."

"Then I challenge you to do the polar plunge. I think that's happening sometime next week over in Saint Paul."

"Is that what it sounds like?"

She nodded. "Jumping into the lake through a hole cut in the ice. But don't worry, there are towels and hot beverages waiting to warm you up after."

"I think I'll stick with fifty degrees and epic surf."

Eryss's giggle lifted her breasts in a jiggly don't-look-away come-on. The water glass Dane held tilted, and cool liquid splashed his wrist.

"Whoa!" She grabbed the glass and pressed a towel to the spill on the table. "Got it."

"Sorry." He reclaimed the glass and set it carefully before his plate. Even a child could manage such a skill as lifting a glass to drink. Of course, children's distractions were far different from a grown man's. He smirked at Eryss's darting look. So he confessed. "You distract me. Your cooking distracts me. The warmth from the hearth fire is distracting in a good way. And everything about you and this house is distracting. I'm normally much more pulled together."

She stroked a finger along his wrist. "And here I thought I was the only one having a hard time concentrating on the pasta. You know you have a few silver hairs in your beard stubble and above your ears that are devastating to a woman's better judgment."

Dane rubbed his stubble, which was trying to become a beard. He wasn't that old, but indeed, he did have a few silver strands. Had he inherited them from a father he'd never known? The only photo his mother had ever saved of Edison had been taken from the side, and was blurry. He had dark hair in it, but it was hard to tell if gray had yet invaded. "They say a few gray hairs give a man a distinguished air."

"I'd call it downright sexy. But I assumed you were about my age."

"Which is?" He managed to fork in a bite of pesto without spilling. Points for the distracted scientist.

"I celebrate my thirtieth in a week. What about you?"

"I'm a January baby, as well. My day is the twenty-eighth. We're both looking at thirty."

"That's interesting! I'd love to read your cards."

"My cards? You mean like tarot? Wait. Don't tell me." He cast his gaze about the kitchen, seeing what he'd seen once before, but this time really taking it in. "You've got all the plants, the minerals and crystals sitting everywhere, and you told me you believe in magic. Of course you do tarot."

"Tarot is not done. It's read. And yeah, I've got skills." She licked her fork clean, and the sight of her tongue dragging along the silver tines disturbed Dane's sense of propriety. "I just find it interesting that two people born one day apart have found one another. Our souls are clinging to each other."

"Souls, eh? Tell me you don't believe in the afterlife and reincarnation and all that blather." A necessary rebuttal. He had made the comment to her yesterday about witches being silly. It was a standard reply in his line of work. Couldn't let anyone actually know he believed in real witches.

"I innately know that I have lived many lives. And your lack of belief in an afterlife, or that souls exist in many forms for many lifetimes, doesn't bother me. You are a scientist, after all. You're designed not to see the greater picture."

"Is that so?" Dane pushed his plate forward to lean an elbow on the table. "All scientists do is seek the greater picture."

"Unless you're a microbiologist."

She had him there. They tended to study the small stuff. But still, there was a vast and greater world within their study.

And Dane's sudden rising indignation settled. He

didn't want to start a fight debating science and fantasy with this beautiful woman who had successfully plied her seduction skills on him. Not when his eyes again strayed to her cleavage and he suddenly wondered what dessert she would offer.

"You mentioned you're also a geologist," she stated. "Besides the debunking stuff, you study rocks, right?"

"That's a vague and expansive way to summarize what I do. But sure, I study rocks."

"So if I tell you I use crystals to gain insight and heal myself, then where do you stand on that?"

He chuckled, then saw her nodding as if she'd expected him to react that way. "Well, seriously. Rocks don't heal." And that wasn't a line; he simply knew it to be fact. "And people who claim to read stones or get some kind of voodoo vibrations out of them are…"

"Are?"

He was not going to answer that one, even if she threatened to have him stomped on by a thousand elephants. He might stand on the side of logic, but when a man was trying to impress a woman it was far better to plead the fifth at times.

"Everything is energy, right?" Eryss said.

"Of course. We are all atoms bouncing up against one another."

"Including this table, the chairs we are sitting on, the rocks on my kitchen windowsill, the ones in the copper bowl down the table there, and those outside hidden under the snow. Yes?"

Whatever point she was trying to make, he sensed he would not agree. But again… "Yes."

"Energy vibrates those atoms and makes all things living entities. Why is it so hard to believe that two en-

ergies can combine to work with each other? The rock
and the healer?"

Dane blew out through his nose. She had an infini-
tesimal point there. But if given time, he'd refute it with
ease. More often than not his job did not result in protecting the masses, but rather a mentally unbalanced in-
dividual. Eryss was not one of those.

He hoped.

"Will you let me show you something?" She leaned
forward, an eager look sparkling in her eyes.

"Always and ever," he replied without thinking.

She stretched to the side to grab a stone from the copper bowl she had just mentioned. It was an egg-sized
piece of rose quartz, roughly cut and unpolished, yet it
gleamed in shades of pink and white under the subtle
candlelight.

She held it between them. "This crystal is one of my
favorites. I use it often on my heart chakra. The energy
it puts out is tangible."

Uh. Huh. Okay, so perhaps she was a kitchen witch of
sorts? That was the only explanation Dane had for those
women who were involved in such things as chakras and
souls and crystals with energies. A ridiculous enterprise.
But a harmless hobby, all the same.

Still, it annoyed him.

"Take it." She held out the crystal.

He decided to amuse her and took the rock. It had a
good weight and he couldn't deny it was a lovely specimen. But it was simply a rock mined from the earth. His
studies tended to ignore the beauty and instead read the
history within the striations and deposits that the mil-
lennia had formed.

"Now." She straightened and dipped a finger to her décolletage, pulling down the dress a bit to reveal the inner swells of her breasts. "Place it here, on my heart chakra."

"You want me to…" Dane held the stone before her. His eyes danced over her breasts. He hadn't touched them last night. Had he been out of his mind? They were firm and full, and perfectly sized, and… "You're not wearing a bra."

He caught her lift of brow, and chuckled. "Right. I just sounded like a fourteen-year-old boy, didn't I? I'd apologize, but it's inevitable a man's mind goes certain places when a woman slips down her dress like you just did."

"No need to apologize. I'm not completely without my wiles." She fluttered her lashes. "But let's do the energy experiment first. Place the quartz here." She tapped her chest between her breasts.

So, with as much fortitude as he could muster—but really, it didn't require anything more than that lash-fluttering invite—Dane pressed the stone against Eryss's chest. His fingers brushed her warm, supple breast, and he sucked in a breath to imagine stroking his tongue along the skin. Tasting her. He met her gaze and, while she wasn't smiling, he felt the acceptance and smile in her eyes. He relaxed—and the sudden shock of an electrical charge forced his fingers from the stone.

Eryss caught the rose quartz in a palm.

"What the—" Dane touched his fingertips together. Grabbing the stone from Eryss, he turned it over, checking for compromise. "Felt like I'd touched an electric fence. A weak one, but…"

"That was the energy of the crystal aligning with my chakra. It felt great, you holding it against my skin." She took the stone from him and replaced it in the copper bowl. "But I suspect, given the proper amount of time, you'll find a way to refute what you've just experienced."

He wouldn't refute the experience. Because he had felt the energy. But...how? Okay, sure, if he went deep he knew there were scientific claims that stones and trees and even flowers carried measurable energy. A particle detector could pick up radiation from stone. He'd verified as such many times in the lab. But never by merely placing a rock to a woman's chest.

"Dane?"

"Good trick. We should change the subject," he suggested. Because while he welcomed a good debate, he wasn't stupid. Arguing semantics about make-believe magical stuff would never get him the girl.

"Yes, we should," she agreed. "A new topic. How about we discuss your distraction."

"My distraction?"

"You and that fourteen-year-old boy haven't stopped staring at my boobs since you sat down to eat."

"Ahem." He rubbed his jaw. "I confess, the view is distracting. Man, do I sound like a creep."

"I don't mind your distraction." She tickled the lace framing her décolletage. "I did put on a low-cut dress for a reason."

"It's working. From the pine nuts in the pesto to the soft music and candles, I am feeling the seduction."

"Excellent. I have more candles lit in the conservatory. Let's move out to summer, shall we?"

"What about the dishes?" Dane gathered up the plates and silverware. "I'll rinse them quickly for you, and I see you have a dishwasher."

"A man who insists on doing dishes? Now you're seducing me. I'll meet you out among the wild!" she called, and her pink skirt swept the air with her exit.

Dane made quick work of the dishes, a skill his mother had taught him. He could never leave a table now without cleaning up. He wiped off the butcher-block table, grabbed his glass of water, considered it, then checked the fridge. There was a bottle of corked wine, three quarters full. He pulled it out, selected two goblets sitting next to a blue calcite crystal from a shelf, and…he walked over to the table and picked up the rose quartz from the bowl.

Turning it over and inspecting it carefully revealed the many beautiful striations and cracks. It was cold to the touch but warmed in his palm. He knew nothing about chakras, but was aware the woo-woo folks had assigned seven chakra points to the body and each were color-coded and meant various things regarding health and welfare. A bunch of hoodoo nonsense.

And yet, he had been physically repulsed from holding the quartz.

"Interesting," he muttered, and set the rock down on the table.

While Dane was putting away the dishes, Eryss lit the emerald candelabra and turned off the main light. The conservatory glowed softly and smelled like the newly bloomed freesia, her favorite flower when it came to fragrance. It flooded the room with a heady perfume.

When he wandered in, barefoot, she smiled. She'd like to see him in a wet suit peeled down to his hips, revealing abs and, she suspected, a hairy chest, for tufts of dark hair peeked out the top of his white shirt.

He poured two goblets of wine—good man for taking the initiative of bringing in the wine—and handed her one. He sat on the couch and stretched his feet over the grass.

"You know, I'm a bit of a scientist myself," Eryss confessed. She sat beside him and sipped the wine. "Formulating the beer recipes takes math skills, knowledge of yeasts and bacteria, and boiling points and the gravity of sugar. One miscalculation of time and temperature during the boil and I've got something so bitter even the triple IPA aficionados will spit it out."

"Sounds complicated. I'll stick with drinking the finished product."

"And you," she said. "You are more connected to nature than you want to believe."

"Oh, I do believe in that connection. Electric rocks aside. Surfing is more about knowing the water and myself than any logical reasoning. Though math is involved when calculating a point break or peak. Okay, we connect in the middle ground. And I'll give you the rose quartz adventure. I do know some scientific research has been done on crystals and their energy. But I'm still going to pass on the tarot reading."

"Fair enough."

"I think we should focus on the intentions we both presumably have for this night."

"Intentions?"

Dane took her glass and set it in the grass and then leaned in to kiss her. He tasted like wine and pesto. He slipped his fingers through her hair, then kissed her cheek and down to the base of her earlobe, where she could feel his pulse against hers.

"Life. Energy. Atoms," he whispered.

"Don't think like a scientist, Dane. Respond with your body, not your brain."

"I thought that's what I was doing."

He slipped the sleeve from her shoulder and kissed her there with a soft moan that mined a deep and animal part of her. Eryss tilted back her head and wrapped her legs about his hips, pulling him down onto her. His hot mouth landed on the upper curve of her breast, and his fingers carefully pulled back the velvet to expose more and more of her breast without quite going to the nipple. He lingered on her skin, tracing it with his tongue as if designing runes. She felt it all the way to her toes and back up to her pussy, which was already warm and wet for him.

After unbuttoning his tweed vest, she slid her hands up under the crisp white shirt beneath, her fingers gliding through the dark hairs and around his rib cage, which was strapped with tight muscle.

"For a science nerd," she said against his mouth, "you're ripped."

"It's the surfing. I can't spend all my time formulating and postulating, can I?"

"You most certainly cannot."

He nudged down her dress strap, which exposed her breast. The first lash of his tongue to her nipple teased a moan from her. She squirmed beneath him, pulling him closer.

"It's very warm in here," he said.

"It is. We won't feel the winter chill if we shed our clothes."

"Your postulation is correct." He gave her breast a quick kiss, then glanced back up to her eyes. "There's something about you, Eryss. It makes me want to dive in. Like I'm so comfortable with you that I forget this is only our first official date."

She tilted her head against his shoulder. "Curse you, rational thinking."

His laughter echoed in the room and the leaves shuddered, reacting to his energy. And Eryss couldn't prevent herself from reacting, too. She straddled him and pulled down her dress straps further. "This is my body telling me to take what I want. I am a goddess of earth and winter, and I desire that you worship me. Kiss me right here, Dane. On my heart chakra." She tapped between her breasts. "And don't stop until you know I'm satisfied."

His smile was so infectious, she felt joy in her core. He leaned in to kiss her and the sweet, firm touch branded her softly. Stubble brushed her breasts with a tease. And he dashed his tongue over her curves, avoiding her nipple, which frustrated her in a good way. When he explored the underside of her breast, he paused and traced her skin with a fingertip.

"This dark mark here. It's not a scar?"

"No, a birthmark." It was about an inch long. A dark line right under her breast and between two ribs. She'd studied it often, wondering over it. "They say birthmarks are scars from a previous lifetime."

"I assume those who say that believe in reincarnation?"

Oops. She wasn't about to let him start thinking now.

Diving in, Eryss kissed him hard and deeply, rubbing her breasts against his shirt and vest. His fingers found her nipples and he pinched them gently, then not so gently. She moaned deep in her throat and rocked her hips upon his lap.

Moving too fast? Could one ever move fast enough toward destiny?

"Dane, let's do this. Share energies."

He kissed her jaw and nuzzled his nose against her cheek as he whispered, "Does that mean what I think it means?"

"Yes."

Suddenly Eryss was airborne, and she landed on her back on the couch. Dane crawled over her, unbuttoning his shirt as he did, and she helped him pull the clothes down his arms and fling them to the floor. She pressed both palms to his chest, reveling in the solid muscle and warm, tickly hairs.

"You're beautiful," she said. "Surfer guy."

He laughed that wondrous and soul-touching laugh, and she laughed because it was infectious and she wanted to take on the energy he put out.

"You are the beautiful one," he said as he bowed to kiss her between the breasts. "You and your energetic heart chakra."

He slid his tongue along the curve of her breast and glided up to suckle at her nipple. Raking her fingers through his hair, Eryss held him there, gasping as his expert touch moved the energy from her breast out through her body and to all parts that now tingled and curled. Her toes dug into the velvet couch.

She reached down and unbuttoned and unzipped his pants, and he chuckled from his throat as he moved to her other breast. A confirmation that she was on the right path. Shoving down his pants to his hips, she then danced her fingers around to land on the head of his penis, which had escaped his boxers. Hot and hard, it filled her palm. He gasped when she clasped her fingers over the top of his erection, and his movement pulled him down through her grasp. She quickly caught him again and this time controlled the pistoning action herself.

"Your energy is definitely very focused," he said as he glanced up at her and winked. He closed his eyes, and she controlled his silence with a firm grip of his cock. He was able only to moan then, and that pleased her immensely.

"You don't want to go up to the bed, do you?"

"No, I like it here in the jungle." He shook back a loose strand of his hair from his eye. "Uh, do you have birth control? I don't have a condom."

"I'm good. Birth control," she replied. It was her standard way to explain that she conjured a birth control spell once a quarter under the harvest moon. But the guy never needed to know the method, or anything beyond that she was safe.

She wiggled her hips as he slid her dress down to her thighs and then her knees, until she eventually kicked it aside. And all without letting go of his cock. So talented.

"You've got the hold of someone who must prefer driving," he commented as he looked down at her firm clasp.

"It's just so fun to hold. You don't mind?"

"Not at all. As long as you don't mind me kissing you here." He slid up alongside her so she didn't have to let go of him, but also bowed forward to place a kiss at the apex of her thighs. And he didn't stop there. His tongue dashed out to explore and taste and devour. "You smell like coconut here."

"I always use coconut oil in my body lotions."

"I like it. I think that stuff comes in handy as a lube, too, if I'm not mistaken."

"Oh, lover, we are not going to need it," she cooed, and met Dane's winking smile.

Had she seen that smile so many times in her various reincarnations? Possibly.

"Come inside me, Dane," she whispered.

He moved up to kiss her mouth, and his fingers stroked her folds still, tendering her most sensitive spots with ease and devotion. When she guided his erection between her legs, he propped up on an elbow and met her gaze. In the soft candlelight his eyes twinkled, and as he entered her, the intensity in his irises held her mesmerized. He owned her with his eyes, with the smile that grew as his rhythm began and the thickness of him filled her.

Eryss clutched at his hip, beckoning him faster, and never losing eye contact. The expressions on his face moved from a tense, lip-biting agony to a cool, smirking confidence. And then his eyes closed and his body trembled. His thrusts grew deeper, harder. She dug her fingernails in at his hip, begging, pleading for the mastery.

And the tug and tease of his erection at her clitoris summoned an orgasm that shook her very bones at the same time that he gasped and clutched the couch near her head. They came together.

As they had through the centuries.

Dane was startled awake by Eryss's cry. They lay entwined on the emerald sofa amid a wild and weird winter jungle. Still in the clinging throes of sleep, he watched as she sat up and touched her ribs just beneath her breast. Right where that weird birthmark darkened her skin.

"You okay?" he muttered, fighting the urge to come fully awake.

She nodded sleepily. She was fighting wakefulness as well. It was still dark outside. "Just a weird dream."

She settled beside him and he pulled her close. As her skin melded against his, his erection took note and he smiled against her shoulder.

"Really?" she murmured.

"It'll settle," he said. "Unless...?"

"Come inside me, Dane," she said in a beautiful sleepy tone.

And so he did, slipping into her hot wetness and not even feeling the need to thrust. It just felt great being inside her. And together they drifted to sleep again.

Chapter 5

Dane strode out of the bathroom and down into the kitchen, veering toward the fridge only because it was a natural inclination to seek snacks after sex. But instead he grabbed a glass from the shelf and poured some tap water. He retrieved his cell phone from his coat pocket and propped a hip against the butcher-block table.

Scratching his bare abs, he checked his emails. None. Not that he'd expected any. He was on an unofficial vacation. But he always strived to stay in touch with the Agency. There was a possibility someone might want to get ahold of him. He'd emailed Tor that the dagger pickup would be delayed, but it wasn't a problem. The Agency was pretty sure the dagger was neither cursed nor contained active magic.

Because sometimes weird stuff did happen around the weapons he debunked. It all had to do with the energies. Blades and weapons made from metal could pick up magnetic properties, and if you stood in the right place at the wrong time, the thing could be propelled toward you due to paramagnetism.

He loved stuff like that. Made the job more interesting than it already was.

"Energies," he whispered now, and his thoughts returned to last evening when Eryss had asked him to place the rose quartz over her heart chakra. "Who'da thought?"

So he'd give the idea of stones possessing energy credence. Because he had witnessed it, and was pretty sure she hadn't tricked him with a low-voltage device such as the type magicians palmed for unsuspecting suckers. That didn't make her a real witch, just a woman connected to nature.

And there was absolutely nothing wrong with that.

He almost tucked the phone back in a coat pocket when cool morning light glinted over the window above the sink—and he noticed a symbol that frost crystals had formed on the glass.

He padded over and studied the window. Sunlight fractured through the ice crystals in blue, red and violet. It was almost a mandala, though not symmetrical. A fractal of sorts, but again, more homemade than precise. Impossible to have been formed by frost. The only way was if someone had traced a finger on the window first, which was likely the case.

He raised the phone and snapped a picture of the symbol. He always recorded stuff that fascinated him. And his job made him extra perceptive for out-of-the-ordinary happenings. Eryss's house was full of fascinations. She thought stones could heal? And now this symbol. And the full garden out in the conservatory. And reincarnation and souls. Talk about open-minded.

Perhaps a bit too open, he thought with a grimace.

Could she really believe she was a natural-born witch? No, she hadn't said as much. She was simply someone who was fascinated by crystals and plants, which might naturally lend to the more woo-woo sorts of artwork like the one on the window.

She seemed too smart for that, a woman who would never blindly accept the unknown without the facts. Yet if she were a real witch…that was another scenario entirely. But he had no reason to consider it.

Setting his phone on the table, he glanced to his coat, which hung by the door. He didn't wish to spend the next few days sitting alone in a hotel room. He could, but that wouldn't be fun. So a fling with a sexy woman who could seduce him with her cooking and a conservatory overflowing with summer?

"Bring on the magic."

Eryss woke on the couch alone. Had her lover left in the early morning hours? But had he *walked* back to town? No, Dane must have gone looking for the bathroom or—what was that incredible smell?

She shot upright and the chenille blanket fell away from her bare breasts. She wrapped the blanket about her shoulders and waist, forming a snuggie sort of cape, and then padded into the house, following the scent of cinnamon and…

"Bananas?" she said as she wandered into the kitchen.

Dane stood before the stove, spatula in hand. He wore nothing but the black pants he'd worn last night, no shoes or socks. The back view of him gave no clues that he was a nerdy scientist. Those delts and lats. Mercy, she was glad she knew her anatomy. On the other hand, who cared what those hard stretches of muscle were called? Oh, but what was that?

She touched his hip, above the three red scratches.

"Wild woman," he said over a shoulder.

"I'm sorry. Does it hurt?"

"A deliciously painful reminder of a night well spent." He turned and kissed her forehead. "I'm a bit of an early riser. And since I have no way of getting back to town without absconding with your car once again, I am at your mercy. So I thought I'd butter you up with banana pancakes. Gluten free, thanks to your almond flour in the pantry. And a nice lemon and blueberry syrup."

"Wow. If this is the bonus round, I'm in."

"The bonus round?"

She hugged him from behind. "Last night was incredible. Now you're upping the stakes by making me breakfast. It's not very often a girl brings home a man and scores so highly."

"You don't know me well yet. I have a terrible habit of leaving my beard clippings in the sink, and you don't even want to ask about how often I do laundry."

"Then I won't. Can I help?"

"No, you sit down. These will be ready in a few minutes. I like the morning attire."

She wiggled her butt, which was half revealed by the short blanket as she walked to the table, where he'd already set two plates and silverware. She picked up the creamer and sniffed at the blueberry syrup, which was still warm. He must have crushed the fresh berries from the fridge for that. Were hidden culinary skills present in every scientist? Or was the man just too good to be real? Her intuition told her no, he was real and quite the catch.

And her witchy senses said the same. He was hers. Had been for a very long time. Now, what to do with him?

"My mother used to make these all the time," he said as he delivered the steaming pancakes to her plate with a flip of the spatula, and then sat down beside her. "I added some chia seeds. The omega-3s are good for the brain, you know."

"I do know that. Did your mother teach you to cook?"

"Yes. It was just the two of us when I was growing up."

"I'm sorry."

"It's okay. Well, not okay. I miss someone I never knew. But I did grow up as the man of the house, while also developing an inordinate ability to pick out the most decorative drapes, and I can iron linen like a pro."

"A well-rounded man. I like it. I've always been on my own."

"Really? But you must have parents?"

"Yes, but they used to go off adventuring all the time. Sometimes they'd tote me along, but most of the time I stayed at home so I wouldn't miss school. Mrs. Mc-Alister, our neighbor across the alley when we lived in town, was sort of my surrogate granny. She taught me... so much." So much that she could never tell Dane about. Mrs. McAlister had recognized the witch in Eryss and been her mentor in witchcraft, despite her parents never telling her for fear she'd be ostracized. "By the time I was fourteen, I was taking care of myself. Being a book-worm, purveyor of garden-tending and nature appreciator, I never really fit into my parents' adventurous lifestyle. It was too rush-rush for me."

"I get that. You are the free-spirited bohemian who likes dancing skyclad beneath the moonlight."

"How did you know?"

He laughed. "Really? You do that? Maybe you are a witch."

"I could be. What makes you think—oh, mercy. This pancake is amazing. So fluffy and moist. I think I'll have to keep you around. You *are* a virtual prisoner here, unless you want to forge through the snow to get back to town. A couple more inches fell last night."

"You forget I am now a master snow shoveler."

"That'll get you a narrow aisle up to the mailbox. You'll need the snowblower to clear out the whole driveway."

"I considered buying some snow boots, but then rethought it since I'm only here for a week. Now I can see the error of my ways. Weather isn't so much my forte, as is what the snow and ice can do to three-million-year-old granite and limestone. If you don't want to shoo me out, I have no problem sticking around and checking out the aforementioned snowblower. Though I suspect you've work to get to?"

"I have to stop in to the brewery today. In a few hours. We're good for now. Although I may take you up on blowing the driveway." She licked the blueberry syrup from the fork. It was just sweet enough, with a tang of lemon. The man was a chef.

Dane ate a few pieces, then brushed his dark curls over an ear. A devastating move to Eryss's wanting heart. Much like his laughter.

"So tell me about that dream that woke you early this morning?" he asked. "Do you often have nightmares?"

"Oh, uh…"

She'd forgotten about the dream that had woken her from a dead sleep. It had been a doozy, but she couldn't tell him the details. She didn't even believe the details. But all dreams had meaning, and she really wanted to know what that one had meant.

With an absent rub at the birthmark beneath her breast, she said, "It was nothing."

"Nothing? It woke you up like a lightning bolt. You cried out."

"I did? No, you must have been dreaming, too."

"I heard you. It was a horrified cry. Was the sex that bad?"

"Ha! No way. It was probably the best sex I've had. And I have had some blissful sex."

"I'll take that as a compliment. And I'll have to accept it as truth when you say the dream was not related. That plant over the sink is mint, yes? I hope it isn't catnip. I added a little to the syrup."

"You're good. No cats in this house."

He was on to a new topic, which was fine with her. Because to tell him that in her dream she had felt a blade pierce her heart as some faceless man had shoved it into her chest? So not cool.

She certainly hoped the soul seer could fit her in today. Because a dream like that was not something a witch should ignore.

"I plan to rent a car today," he said. "Perhaps you could drive me to the rental place on your way to work? I want to drive around, maybe go into the city. I might check out the Minneapolis Institute of Arts."

"They're featuring an exhibition on ancient Greek weapons right now. Sounds right up your alley. But watch the traffic on the way home. You'll want to head out of the city by three with the storm coming in."

"More snow? Does it ever stop snowing in this wretched state?"

"You don't like all the snow? It's a good reason to cuddle and share body heat."

He raised his eyebrows. "Duly noted. I'll return early and cook for you tonight, if you're up for that? Having me around yet another night?"

"You really have to wonder? Dane, if you like, you can stay here for the rest of the week."

"Really? Hmm. I hate to impose—" She kissed him with lips that were sticky with blueberry. "Mmm." He lashed his tongue out to trace her lips. "Do that again."

She got up and leaned against his thigh, moving in for a better kiss that he tasted as eagerly as he'd eaten the pancakes. He coaxed her onto his lap and his hand slid down between her thighs, the blanket slipping from her shoulders to her elbows.

"I'll pack my things and bring them over later, along with something for supper," he said against her mouth. "You good with that?"

She murmured a positive sound but didn't make the effort to speak as she crushed her mouth against his and danced her tongue with his. And when his fingers found the moistness between her legs, she spread them a little wider and invited him in.

Eryss dropped her purse, coat and mittens at the end of the bar.

Mireio popped up from the stainless steel mash tun wielding a plastic shovel full of steaming spent grains. She dumped the earthy-smelling oats, barley and rye into the twenty-gallon Rubbermaid tub sitting on the floor and blew a stray strand of bright red hair from her lashes.

"I was in at seven this morning," she declared. "No rest for the witchy."

"I guess that means you didn't hook up last night?" Eryss slid onto a bar stool and pulled the brewery's iPad before her. She opened up Excel to check the numbers for last weekend and ensure the inventory was up to date.

"Seriously? I haven't been out since the festival and that night was a bust. Yet you're in rather late. What's up with that? Usually you're the one to scoop out the grains and clean the tanks for me."

"Sorry. I was occupied this morning," she said, not hiding the lilt of happiness that brightened her voice.

"What?" Mireio hastened down from the two-step ladder she'd been standing on and swung around the side of the bar to sit on the stool beside Eryss. She leaned her elbow onto the bar and rested her chin in her hand. "Spill. Did the scientist come over again? Did you finally have sex with him?"

"Finally? It's only been two days, Mireio."

"I know, I know. So tell!"

"He did come over. I made pasta last night with pine nuts—"

"I don't care about the food. Although you do score aphrodisiac points for the pine nuts."

"Exactly."

"You know what I want to know, woman!"

Sitting up straighter and drawing in a breath, Eryss announced, "We did."

"Yes!" Mireio pumped a fist. "I knew there was a reason for that peachy flush to your cheeks, and your hair is extra glossy this morning. Tell me all about it! This is the man who believes science proves everything and nothing magical or supernatural can ever occur?"

"Exactly."

"I'm sorry for you."

Eryss laughed. "You shouldn't be. He was a breath of fresh air, trust me on that one."

"Did you tell him you're a witch?"

"I did not, but we did have a heated discussion over the efficacy of crystals as instruments of energy. I never come right out and say 'Hey, I'm a witch, what's your problem?' And can you imagine trying to convince a man like Dane of that? He debunks the paranormal for a living."

"Yeah, that's a tricky call. So was he, you know... good?"

Eryss nodded. They'd shared sex details before. It was a girlfriend's right to either spill or not spill, and she loved spilling to Mireio. "Devastatingly so."

Mireio let out a hoot and pumped the air with both fists. "That means he rocked your bones. And the moon was new last night. Let's see, that means creativity and fertility—oh."

"Don't *oh* me, Mireio. I've cast a birth control charm on myself. Do it every quarter. Nothing to worry about."

"Sure, but you know. It was a new moon."

A new moon meant one of the most powerful times for fertility and creation. And creation could mean, very possibly, a new life. But she'd had sex plenty of times during the new moon and had never...well, she couldn't be positive she'd ever had sex specifically on the night of the new moon.

No. Eryss was confident in her birth control charm. And she would not give it another moment's thought. "I'm good," she reiterated. "Trust me."

"Oh, sure! Are you seeing him again today?"

"I gave him the key to my place and told him to give up on the hotel. He's only here for a week. And if I can have that hunk of science in my bed for a few more days, I'm going to make it as easy as possible for him. He's having trouble with our snow."

"He did a fine job of shoveling yesterday."

"He did, and he confessed he liked it. But I don't think he's seen snow. Ever."

"That's weird, but good for him. I'd totally give up all the snow for the ocean." Mireio leaned an elbow on the bar and caught her chin in hand again. "Too bad I could never give up my friends. This poor mermaid will suffer the indignities of the dry air and cold for friendship."

"Your sacrifice is much appreciated. You do have that fabulous bathtub, though."

Mireio cooed and fluttered her lashes. "A mermaid's dream."

The woman wasn't actually a mermaid, but her focus was water magic, and her bathtub was a monstrous, round, freestanding bowl in the center of her ornate bathroom. It was the size of a hot tub; she took baths more often than showers. Eryss often thought Mireio should have been born mermaid.

"If I ever get around to opening another brewery it'll probably be in California or Florida," Eryss offered.

Mireio raised her hand. "Dibs on management!"

"You got it."

Mrs. McAlister had often told Eryss there would come a day when she'd need to uproot and replant herself to expand her knowledge and open her skills to the universe. So why not California, specifically Santa Cruz? Hmm…

"So what other details are you willing to spill about your fabulous sexfest last night?"

"Oh. Well."

"What? What!"

Eryss rubbed her brow. "I…woke up in a dream this morning."

"I'll bet."

"No, I mean the dream woke me up. It was actually a nightmare."

"Not the one where you dream of a long-lost love?"

"Not that one. That one really is a dream. But I don't think I need that dream anymore. I think the anacampserote worked."

"You mean… *Dane* is the guy you always dream about? Does your soul recognize him?"

"I think so. I mean, I'm not sure what that feeling should be like, but I feel something when I'm near him. Something very familiar. I'm instantly at ease with him. And I felt a tremendous summoning toward him at the winter festival. But the nightmare I had this morning was different. I think I woke Dane when I called out."

Mireio sighed.

Eryss set the iPad down and turned to her witchy sister. "I dreamed that a man stabbed me through the heart with a knife. And I was wearing medieval clothes. And he had blood coming out of his chest, too."

"Yikes. Did he look like Dane?"

"I never see faces in any of my dreams. It's so frustrating. But I don't think it had anything to do with Dane. It couldn't have. We had a great night. But the dream troubles me."

"Dreams are portents."

"I know. That's why I called Midge."

"You going to have the soul seer peer into your dreams?"

"Yes, she said she can see me in an hour. I can't let this go without looking into it."

"A wise woman never ignores her dreams. And you are the wisest chick I know. I'm so sorry." Mireio squeezed Eryss's arm. "But I'm not sorry for the hunk of manflesh you got last night. Just one tiny detail?" She squeezed her fingers together before her wide blue eyes. "Weird quirks or even, you know…size?"

"Where's Valor?" Eryss asked, smirking as Mireio's shoulders deflated.

"I think she's with Sunday. They're working on a motorcycle or something. She said she'd be in this afternoon to keg the stout."

"Sounds good." Sunday was a cat-shifting familiar. Her husband, a werewolf, headed a local pack. "I'm going to run to the appointment. Talk later."

"Did you ward yourself when you were with Dane last night?"

Eryss paused before pushing open the brewery door. What a simple question. The answer was obvious—and yet she *hadn't* warded herself. Normally, a witch put up a gentle ward against psychic invasion whenever she was out with a man. It was just the smart thing to do. She hadn't felt the compulsive need or worry to do so when talking with Dane, however.

That was the first time she'd been careless with a man. Truly, she felt some kind of comfort when she was in his presence, and that must have been why she'd forgotten.

"Sure," she muttered, and left before Mireio could sense the lie.

Chapter 6

Dane tried on the leather gloves and curled his fingers. They were lined with fleece and were not at all bulky, as he would expect from gloves designed to protect your fingers in below-zero weather, as the tag advertised. The store clerk said they were must-haves for the Minnesota winter, "don't ya know."

Dane did take particular glee in listening to the Scandinavian accent. Eryss had a touch of it.

So he was buying winter wear because he was stuck in Minnesota, but also because he liked the girl. And if she asked him to shovel or blow the snow from her driveway again, he'd do it. Because it was fun, and because he wanted to help her. Maybe impress her, as well. It was a biological trait to want to show the opposite sex that he was capable of protecting, supporting and nurturing.

He chuckled at his rambling thoughts. Hell, he just liked having sex with her. And eating with her. And talking to her. Okay—so he liked her. A lot. And he felt compelled to be near her.

And that strange feeling of compulsion gave him a shudder that was not a result of the cold. He'd never forget what he'd said to his mother when he was eight years old and she had found him going through one of his father's old chests. Dane had sneaked into the basement and pulled the old wooden chest out from under a blanket that he suspected his mother thought would keep it a secret. But secrets fester in a little boy's head, and before long, he thought about that chest all the time. He had to look inside it.

Inside had been shirts, and books on things like geology and rock climbing. A few of the images in the rock climbing book had interested Dane. He'd tried to rappel off the deck a week later, only to realize he was not a knot-tying expert. He'd fallen into the sandbox, onto his back, but had hurt only his pride.

Beneath a red shirt, at the very bottom of the chest, had lain a sword. Actually, when Dane thought about it as an adult educated in weaponry, he realized it had been a dagger. But to an eight-year-old? It had been a mighty sword!

Knowing he'd get in trouble for touching a sharp blade—his mom always admonished him for going into the silverware drawer—he had leaned over the chest and stared at it. And a weird feeling had overcome him. He couldn't *not* touch the sword. In fact, at the time, Dane had felt as if the thing had whispered to him, "Pick me up."

He hadn't heard his mother's clickety high heels come down the wooden steps, but he had heard her scream. "Dane! Put that down!"

And, sword in hand, he'd said, as if in a trance, "The witch must die."

His mother had freaked. Pulled the blade from him and tossed it in the chest. She'd swatted his butt and sent him to bed without supper. It was three days before Dane could find his way back downstairs while his mother had been out in the garden. The sword was gone.

Ever since, Dane had always felt disturbed whenever a feeling of compulsion came upon him. It instantly took him back to that afternoon in the basement when his mother had swatted his behind and told him he was a bad boy.

And yet, he'd never forgotten that sword.

Could it really be the very same dagger? Obviously his mother had not tossed it out. She must have realized it had value and sold it. How else had it ended up in an antiques store in Minnesota?

Well, he was here to find out. And to see if that weird compulsion still existed. But killing witches? He wasn't sure where his child self had conjured those words to say. Probably from a movie he'd seen one late night while his mother had dozed on the sofa after a long day at the office.

Standing outside the store, he pulled off the leather glove and took his phone out of his pocket. Damn, it was cold! He stepped back inside the shop, but just as he scrolled to his contacts, he realized he didn't have Eryss's phone number.

Of course, she would be at the brewery. And he now had his own rental vehicle, so he could drive over there. He hadn't asked if she wanted to go along with him to the museum this afternoon. Even though he'd heard her say she needed to work, he wouldn't forgive himself if he did not at least extend the invitation. And much as he enjoyed navigating new cities on his own, having Eryss alongside him would be what the surf kids called milfy. Extraordinary.

Ten minutes later he raced across the street and into the brewery to avoid the brisk wind that seemed to cut at his epidermis with razors. What had made him think a quick trip to Minnesota was a good idea? Oh, right, it was supposed to be a *quick* trip. Not a week.

The consolation prize? He'd hooked up with the prettiest, most sensual woman in the whole town.

"We're not open!" someone called from the far end of the bar.

Dane scanned the room, done in brick and hardwood. Eryss had mentioned it had been stripped to the original flooring and brick walls from the late 1800s when they'd rehabbed the place four years ago. The ceiling was open to expose the pipes and air ducts. It smelled like oat and roasted barley. The earthy scent made his mouth water.

Three large brew tanks stood before the far wall, their stainless steel exteriors gleaming like chrome on a Maserati. Bent over one of the tanks was a pair of legs beneath a very short skirt.

Dane called back, "Uh… I stopped by to see Eryss?"

"She's not—" The woman half immersed in the big steel tank pivoted on her center of balance, dropping her feet onto the step stool before the tank, and popped up a head of bright red hair. She eyed him and dropped a small plastic shovel onto the floor with a clatter. "Well, well, you must be him. I wasn't introduced after you shoveled for us."

"I am Dane Winthur. Sorry to have caught you at such an, uh…inopportune moment."

After stepping down quickly from the stool, she swung around the bar, tugging at her short floral skirt. "That's all right. You couldn't have seen anything in particular. I like to keep my particulars covered." She fluttered her dark lashes and giggled. "You want a brew?"

"I thought you were closed?"

"We are, but you're *him*. And that's all that matters."

"Indeed, I am him." Dane wondered what that meant exactly, and then realized Eryss must have spoken about him to this lovely bit of spunk and cherry red. And wow, that hair—she had dipped it in paint, surely. "Is Eryss around? She said she would be working here today."

"You just missed her." Behind the bar, the woman grabbed a goblet and poured a dark beer from the tap. "She's heading over to, uh, hmm…get something, from… someone."

A bald lie if ever he'd heard one. But he wouldn't press. He wasn't lord and master over Eryss. She could do whatever she wanted. And he had told her he had plans, so surely she wouldn't spend all day waiting around for him to drop by. Unfortunately for him.

He pulled out the ever-present lighter from his pocket and flicked it a few times. The redhead gave him a curious look so he stuffed it back in his pocket. "Sorry. Habit."

The woman set the goblet before him. A bold head of creamy foam capped the dark brew. Dane inhaled the caramel and cream scents.

"It's our vanilla oatmeal stout," she offered. "Sweet, dark and bold. Great for a cold winter day. If you want a shot of nitro coffee in it, it'll stay with you all afternoon and keep you flying into evening."

"I think I'll pass on the caffeine. Cheers." He lifted the glass. "With whom do I have the pleasure of speaking?"

"I'm Mireio Malory. Master brewer and Eryss's friend for ages. I mean, like centuries, seriously. Because you know, reincarnation. Oh! That's stuff you don't believe in, right? Eryss says you're a scientist?"

"That I am. And reincarnation is one of those fantastical things that some like to grasp on to as a means of explaining life after death. I err on the side of life *and* death. One time around, thank you very much."

"Poor guy. You'll learn differently. Sooner or later." A wink dusted her lush lashes over one of her bright blue eyes. "Drink up."

Dane did so, and glanced to the coaster that bore their logo, The Decadent Dames, which gave him pause. The dame featured in the oval retro frame wore what looked like a pointed witch's hat and dangled a pentacle-shaped pendant in between two sharply pointed fingernails. Interesting. And…disturbing.

"Witches, eh?" he muttered in question.

He'd been told the town was the Halloween capital. Of the world. Certainly the local shops liked to capitalize on the paranormal to go with the city's theme. Stuart's Stuff had enough Halloween ephemera to fill an industrial-sized pumpkin patch. But it was a little strange considering the things he'd noticed about Eryss so far.

"Sure." She hooked a hand on her curvy hip. "We put spells on our brews."

He set the goblet down. A glance to the front window revealed there were no suspicious mandalas or symbols designed in frost. He'd forgotten to look that up at the hotel. But two women spouting the same witchy lore to him? They *were* friends. And they did work together. Hmm…

"Perhaps a man should not drink anything a witch has brewed." Offering a cautious smile, he teasingly pushed the glass forward on the bar. "I don't wish to be transformed into a toad."

"You believe in witches?"

"Not at all." *Yes, but—* "My job is to debunk them, actually."

"Eryss told me. But don't worry. We're just normal chicks." She picked up his goblet and sipped from it. "See? No poison."

To show good faith, Dane took a hearty swallow. It was a nice, dark stout that warmed his belly. "Nope, no poison."

"I was joking with you. It's our thing, you know. If you have a business in the Halloween Capital of the World, it certainly helps to play up the spook factor. Know what I mean?"

He nodded and relaxed his shoulders. "I guess so. I should have come in October."

"It's crazy around here then. It's much quieter in the winter."

"With temps barely reaching ten degrees today, I can see why. Though there are people everywhere—out shopping, talking on their phones, walking their dogs."

"We don't let the deep freeze bring us down. Or keep us from spending money on things we don't need. Whew! Eryss really found herself a hot one."

He was almost beginning to feel as if he'd forgotten to wear a shirt, based on the way she looked at him. Wasn't such blatant ogling supposed to flatter a man? Instead, he felt disturbed by her playful mention of witchcraft.

"Will Eryss be back soon? I didn't get her number and wanted to ask if she was interested in going to the museum with me this afternoon."

"She's booked through the evening. After she's done with—er, then she's returning to help me finish the pale ale we've got brewing in the tanks."

"I see." The woman was definitely keeping a secret

about where Eryss was. "I promised I'd make her supper. And she did give me an extra key to her house. Can you suggest a grocer in the area to pick things up for a romantic dinner?"

"Oh, you are so perfect." She tapped her cheek with a bright red nail that matched her hair. "There's the co-op just down the block from us. But if you're headed into Minneapolis you can stop at The Wedge. They have wine, too. Eryss prefers wine over beer. Go figure."

"Thank you, Mireio. This stout is excellent."

"It's the henbane," she offered with a wink. "It'll give you hallucinations."

Sure she was teasing, but not completely. Dane winced, but did manage another sip, because a man never refused a deep, dark stout on a cold winter day. "Will I be able to drive?"

"Sure. You need to drink a few pints to start seeing chickens," she said with another ineffable wink. "See you later, surfer guy!"

He waved as he left the bar, and shook his head, wondering what the real effects of henbane were. As the wind kissed his face, he decided to wait until he got in the car before pulling off a glove to search the internet for that information.

Ensconced in the front parlor of Midge Olson's Victorian house in Saint Paul, Eryss slowly came out of the hypnotic state the witch had invited her to enter. Her goal was to catch a glimpse of the lost lover about whom she wanted to learn more. Scents of thyme, sage, beeswax and cherry cola filled her nostrils. She shook her head, rising into the present.

"What did you see?" Eryss asked eagerly.

Midge sat on the other side of the small TV tray, covered over with black velvet. Her crystal ball sat in the center of the table, surrounded by crystals to amplify her visions. Midge herself was a real number. Her long hair was dyed black, and she sported Bettie bangs and a ponytail that was tipped in fluorescent green. Matching green eye shadow distracted from her deep brown eyes. A T-shirt stating I Want to Believe and a Hello Kitty ring on her littlest finger finished the look.

"You said you cast an anacampserote?" Midge asked.

"Yes. I've always dreamed about a lost love. I wanted to bring that love to me and to recognize it when it arrived. I think he's arrived."

"I wasn't able to confirm that. I'm sorry. I didn't see a man's face or even romance for you. But that doesn't mean anything. You could be unconsciously keeping that one to yourself."

"I doubt that. I mean, I want to know who it is. Is it Dane?"

"I love that name." Midge swallowed a sip of cola. The drink was one of many bad habits she wasn't afraid to cop to. "So Nordic. Like a Viking warrior."

"He's a scientist."

"A nerd?" One of her coal-black brows arched. "Interesting."

"Yes, but not the sort you would expect. He's sexy. And his stubble…" Eryss caught her chin in her hand and sighed.

But if Midge couldn't see her soul mate, then what did that mean? The woman was a soul seer. She viewed another witch's soul as if it were a TV show. At least, that's how she had once explained it to Eryss. Of course, she hadn't done a soul gaze, so the hypnosis had provided a mere peek into Eryss's psyche.

"You mentioned having a nightmare," Midge prompted. "Was that related?"

"I don't think so. I was stabbed by a faceless man."

"*Another* faceless man? And you *don't* think that's related?"

Eryss shrugged. When she put it that way...

"Will you let me read your soul?"

Eryss pulled her hand from the table, clasping it against her gut in a protective manner. If they held gazes for a long time, witches could read one another's souls. It was terribly revealing, and no witch would ever allow another into such an intimate part of him- or herself. It was like handing over the keys to your life in a few quick movements.

"I know, it's intense," Midge said. "But that dream you had about getting stabbed was a portent. And with a new man in your life, one whom you very possibly called here by the anacampserote, things just got interesting."

"I didn't summon him. I just asked for the ability to recognize him when he arrived."

Midge tilted her head with a fierce stare that said what Eryss knew she never would with words: *Really? You're buying that?*

"Fine. I do want to know what's up with the nightmare. But how will doing a soul gaze get that answer? It's not as if I have the information. And if you couldn't see my soul mate, how will this help?"

"You know you have the information somewhere in there." Midge tapped her own temple. "We both know you've reincarnated many times."

"Dozens, for sure."

"Could be hundreds." Midge held out her palm. "I've seen your life line. It's insane."

Eryss rubbed her palm up and down her arm. Yeah,

she'd studied it, too. Long and dashed through with many lines, as if each were an indicator of a past life. Once she'd counted twenty-one dashes. If she had reincarnated twenty-one times, she could be a soul originated from medieval times. Which would be cool. Then again, time was not linear. So she could never prove that she'd moved through the ages. Perhaps instead, she'd leaped and bounced and circled all around.

Her dreams of the lost lover were obviously from past lives. Which meant the nightmare could be from one, too.

"So maybe somebody killed me in a past life," she offered. "It might not be a portent."

"It may not be." Midge clutched the pop can and rapped her fingernails against the thin aluminum. "What do you believe?"

Her immediate reaction to the dream had been that, indeed, it was a portent. But Eryss didn't say that. They both knew it was.

"If you don't want me to look further—"

"No, let's do this." Decided, Eryss sat forward on the chair and placed both palms on the black velvet cloth. "Look into my soul. I would never ignore a portent. I need to know whatever you can find."

"Excellent." Midge inhaled deeply, let out her breath and closed her eyes a moment to center herself. Then she took Eryss's hands. "I'm going to block my soul because this doesn't need to be reciprocal."

Eryss nodded. "Yes. Good. Do that. I don't care to ever look into another person's soul."

"You have any personal wards up? I didn't feel any when you entered."

Wards were like personal guard walls against evil, danger or magic. "No, I'm clean. I always come to you trusting and open."

"Great! Here goes the whole pot of lutefisk."

The witch leaned forward and peered into Eryss's eyes. This was nothing like Dane staring into her eyes. Touching her. Knowing her in ways perhaps even he had not comprehended. This was almost technical. Eryss wanted to blink, to look away and close off her deepest secrets from the woman. But she did trust her. Whatever she saw would stay between them. And if anyone could do a soul gaze, it was Midge Olson.

Midge's fingers curled over the tips of Eryss's. The two were silent, intent with one another. Sharing energy, feeling the subtle vibrations of breath, blood and bone. Between their hands sat the crystal ball, dark but sparkling with an inner vitality. The rosemary and thyme scents faded and Eryss shivered.

Midge sucked in her lower lip, but didn't speak or make a sound. She looked…pained.

Was what she saw so terrible?

"Clear your mind," Midge whispered urgently. "I'm in." She maintained her gaze, unnerving Eryss, but fortifying her to continue the staredown. "Flashes of…different times. Nineteenth century. Painting. You were an artist once. Oh, look at that huge skirt! Wait. So much crimson. Ah…" She shuddered.

Eryss felt Midge's fingertips curl into her palms. The nails hurt and she pulled away from her touch.

"Whoa!" Midge blinked and shook her head. She swiftly downed a long swallow of pop. "Uff da, that was interesting. Over and over…so much…you're only…not even…and it happens every time. Thirty?"

Suddenly the witch smacked her palms together loudly, breaking any connection they may still have had.

Eryss sucked in a gasp. She hadn't breathed for several moments. It felt as though the world was coming back into focus. Lemon thyme filled her senses and the beat of her heart thudded with resounding intensity.

She grasped Midge's wrist. "What did you see?"

"You have lived many lives," she said quickly. "But again, we knew that. I saw bits of a few. You tend to be very stylish over the centuries, you know that?"

"Sure, whatever. What else?"

"The murders." Midge cringed and shook her head. Drawing her pinched fingers over her head to her shoulders and then down her body, she appeared to be pulling on a white light, but Eryss sensed she might also be cleansing any bad energies.

"Murders?" Made sense if she had dreamed about being stabbed. But— "Plural? As in more than one?"

Midge nodded. She swallowed, looking nauseous. "He—always the same one—stabs you in the heart. And yet you—you stab him, as well. The two of you always die together. Over and over. And the number. What does it mean? Ah! You...never live to your thirtieth birthday. Ever. Whew!"

Midge got up, the chair clattering across the floor as she did so. She paced before the TV tray and ran her fingers through her ponytail, meeting Eryss's gaze only briefly.

"I never live to thirty?" Eryss gasped out as her heart fell. Her thirtieth birthday was less than a week away. "Some man kills me? The same one? So many times?"

Midge nodded. "He must reincarnate, as well. And to find you in every lifetime? Has to be a curse. I am positive it was the same man in each reincarnation."

"Did you get a look at his face?"

"No. But you know we never reincarnate into the same physical manifestation. I didn't see your face, either. But that isn't what's important."

"Of course not. Who is he? *What* is he?"

The witch exhaled and leaned forward, pressing her palms to the table, and said carefully, "A witch hunter."

Chapter 7

"Eryss, breathe."

Responding to Mireio's calm instructions, Eryss drew in a breath and exhaled repeatedly, allowing her lungs to expand and deflate as she silently urged herself to relax. She'd driven straight to the brewery to report to her friend what Midge had seen during the soul gaze. And she hadn't even told Mireio everything before it had all overwhelmed her, and she'd started to gasp for air.

What was wrong with her? She was the calm, cool, collected one. Nothing could ruffle her feathers.

"Finding out a witch hunter is after your ass is a hell of a way to end the day," Mireio said. She poured a half pint of hefeweizen and handed it to Eryss. "Drink. It's the one with the chill spell on it."

"Thanks." She downed the beer in two swallows. Rare were the beers they served *without* a spell. But none were too strong, basically just homeopathic approaches to keep their customers happy, cool and eager for more. "Pome-granates and chamomile. That is tasty. You only serve that to the rowdy ones, right?"

"Mellows them up fast. And prevents broken dishware and possible fist punches through the bathroom walls. I am so over patching up the men's bathroom. You feeling more relaxed now, sweetie?"

"I am. Sorry. I just—right. One more second." She exhaled and dropped her shoulders. Finding her center, she inhaled deeply and then, envisioning her anxiety exiting out of her as if it were a dark cloud drifting off into the atmosphere, she mentally gave it a flip of the bird. "I'm good now. It was a lot to find out. That every time I've reincarnated I always wind up being murdered by a witch hunter."

"The same one *every* lifetime?"

"That's what Midge saw. Weird, right? She suspects the witch hunter is under a curse. Or both of us. I just wish I knew *why*. Because if I did, that might give me a method to stop it from happening again. Mireio, she said I die *before* my thirtieth birthday."

"That's only…" Her friend did not say what they both knew.

"Oh, my goddess." Eryss pressed a palm over her heart, tendering her pulse and trying to relax.

"Oh, witch's warts, now I need a drink."

Eryss pushed her glass toward the taps. "Fill me up while you're at it."

"So how will you know who this witch hunter is?" Mireio asked as she handed over a full glass.

"No clue. Midge couldn't see his face. Nor could I see a face when I had the nightmare. But I assume any man who comes charging toward me with intent to kill is a good guess."

"You think it's Dane?"

"What?" She hadn't considered such a thing. "No. That man is not a hunter, he's a scientist. A geologist, for Herne's sake—he studies rocks."

"Yes, but the nightmare did arise when he came into your life. And there's not much time before— You can't ignore that and brush it off as coincidence."

"Seriously? You think Dane is a dangerous witch killer who is softening me up for the slaughter by cooking for me and making insanely fabulous love to me? No. That's…no. It doesn't feel right. He's my lost love. He's got to be," she said in a whisper that was trying to encourage her frightened heart more than anything.

"Of course he is. A sexy guy like that? He doesn't have a dangerous bone in his body. So who else could it be? I didn't think there were that many witch hunters around. I know they have to register.

"That's it!" Mireio set down her pint. "We can check the registry and see if we can find locations for witch hunters currently in the United States."

"I don't think witches have access to that registry, for a very good reason."

"Oh. Right. Sorry. Well, you're going to arm yourself, aren't you? Both psychically and with real weapons?"

"Of course. Midge said I always kill him, too."

"You go, girl!"

Somehow being congratulated for ending a man's life—as he did the same to her—didn't sound like an occasion for confetti and streamers to Eryss. She wanted to live. And the only way to do that was to actually kill another? She was not a murderess. And apparently causing another man's death *didn't* grant her life.

"I can't harm another soul. What if I didn't kill him?" she posited.

"Then you'd still be dead."

"Right. According to Midge I always die. Oh, Mireio, I have to think about this one."

Mireio handed her a coaster with an ink scribble on it. "Your sexy scientist stopped in right after you left. He wanted to bring you along with him to the museum but didn't have your phone number, so he left his. Explain to me how the man can have a key to your place, has thoroughly put the sex mojo on you, and yet…no phone number?"

Eryss blushed as she took a sip of beer.

"Right. No need to answer the obvious. He's sexy. And smells so freakin' good."

"He smells like ocean surf."

"Ocean surf with murderous intentions?"

Eryss flinched as Mireio smacked her fist into her palm. "You're not helping my nerves."

"No, you're right. He's not a hunter. The man is gentle. But strong—I saw those biceps when he was shoveling. Yet I don't see the predator in him. But it's still not a bad idea to put on a white light when you're around him."

A white light was a gentle ward that protected her from negative energies.

"Good call. Oh, goddess. I invited him to stay at my place for the rest of the week. I don't know if I should have done that after what I've learned today."

"Sure you can. Neither of us believes he could be the witch hunter. You said he debunks the paranormal? The last thing such a person would actually do was hunt for witches—oh. Hmm…"

Eryss swallowed roughly as she picked up on the same thing Mireio obviously had. Who *better* to hunt for a witch than a man whose job it was to debunk them?

But no. A man couldn't hunt for something he didn't believe in. Right?

"Don't worry about it, sweetie." Mireio tucked a couple red curls behind her ear. "And with Dane around for a few days it'll take your mind off the dire stuff. Are you going to shelter yourself away and hide, waiting for the big bad man to come after you?"

"No. That's stupid. I would never run from my life, or the challenges it has in store for me. And talk about challenges. Whew! I had only wanted to bring the soul of my lost lover into my life, and now look what entered. I need to find that crystal blade my grandmother gave me. It's so sharp. And it fits in my purse."

"You should wear a thigh strap like Valor does."

Eryss and Mireio both chuckled. Valor was a balls-to-the-wall tomboy with a twist of velvet and sage.

"He said he was going to make supper for me tonight," Eryss said, tugging out her phone to call Dane.

"I know. He asked for a good place to find groceries. I told him to check down the street."

"Good girl. I trust him. I do. I mean, he's the one, right?"

"I sure hope so, sweetie."

Eryss couldn't quite smile at Mireio's weak encouragement. She certainly hoped he was her soul mate. And not the man who would sink a knife into her chest before her thirtieth birthday.

Dane had just found the symbol in the online directory that matched the one he'd photographed from Eryss's kitchen window and begun to read, when she'd pinged him that she was on her way home. He hadn't had a chance to finish reading about what the symbol meant, but it troubled him that he'd found it on a "witch" site.

Since working for the Agency, he'd had no choice but to step over to belief. He believed in witchcraft. Yes, him, a scientist. But real witches were born, not made. His opinion of people who believed themselves capable of magical powers was that they were lacking something in their emotional lives that required them to latch on to some sort of religion or ritual that spoke to them and provided solace. Or even the illusion of power. It was a waste of time, as far as he was concerned.

Did Eryss really consider herself a witch? A real witch, in possession of authentic magical skills? She owned a brewery that served beers with witchy names. Even the woman he'd spoken to this afternoon, Mireio, had joked about witchcraft.

Was it merely a way to speak to a city that marked its fame as the Halloween Capital of the World? Perhaps. But still. He'd ask her about it tonight. He'd just come out with it, and make it clear to her that he was getting some confusing signals from her about the witch stuff. Maybe she was teasing him because she knew he debunked the paranormal?

Yet it didn't feel right. Eryss was true to the bone. He innately sensed that about her.

"I'll ask," he muttered. "And then I'll have nothing to wonder about."

He went into the kitchen, set the laptop on the butcher-block table, then pulled the vegetables he'd purchased from the co-op grocery store from the fridge. Time to start chopping. He had a bean and lentil soup to prepare.

Twenty minutes later the soup simmered on the stove, imbuing the air with sweet tomatoes, savory thyme and rosemary. Dane hummed "Hotel California" while he worked, which he'd heard on the way home from the museum. He smirked when he realized the lyrics resonated with him; he could check out of Minnesota anytime he liked, but…he could never leave. Ha!

The side door opened to emit a woman bundled up against the cold. Dane tilted his half glass of red wine toward her. "Good evening." He felt only a little strange greeting a woman he had known for three days as if they had been dating for years. And the fact that she'd given him free reign in her home was also not as odd as it should feel.

They had grown instantly comfortable with one another. In fact, he had felt a weird sort of familiarity with her the evening he'd met her at the ball. And while the scientist in him demanded he question such an instant and easy attraction, he did not. He liked this ease. Bypassing all the usual dating worries, misinterpretations and hang-ups? He would take it.

Eryss unwrapped a scarf from around her neck, releasing a spring of chestnut hair over the fake fur rimming her coat hood. She managed to shed her boots, mittens and coat all at once and parked them on the hooks and sisal mat beside the door.

Beneath the winter armor, she blossomed in a summery green dress dotted with red flowers. Her red tights matched the flowers. She met him at the table with a cold kiss.

Dane flinched at the first touch of her lips to his and her nose was so cold! But when she giggled, he dived in for the chilly reward of warming her up. Her mouth opened against his and their tongues touched, igniting an instant and provocative spark. Her cool fingertips curled into the chest hairs at the base of his neck.

"It smells great," she said. "I'm going to run upstairs and freshen up a bit. Pour me some wine!"

She glided down the hallway, leaving him with a smile on his face. Domestic bliss so quickly? He was doing something wrong. Or was it oh so right?

Maybe she *had* bewitched him? Had she used her powers to enthrall him in a blind devotion so that he would cook for her and greet her with supper after a long day at work? What had been in that beer?

"The only witches in this town are kitchen witches," he muttered as he poured her a goblet of red. After setting it at the place beside his, he checked the soup. "And the only thing bewitching around here is Eryss's beauty and personality. She just has an…aura about her."

Yes, that was it. She exuded a bohemian, otherworldly charm so different from the usual women he dated—the scholarly associates he met and knew from work, those with whom he could hold a conversation about the acceleration rate of gravity and learn a few things in the process. Or the cryptozoologist on the Agency staff who was an expert in fantastical beasts of myth and legend. She was hardcore science, using her knowledge to make mush of those who would predicate the existence of anything not human.

And they were all blondes. Sexy, shapely and smart. He did have a type.

So why was he suddenly compelled to a woman of light and airy-faery? *Well, she is beautiful.* Dane ladled the soup into bowls. *She is an amazing lover.* He sprinkled a bit of asiago cheese over the surface of each serving. *And she's different.*

That was it. She was something he had yet to discover and label and attempt to debunk. Eryss was a puzzle, from which no scientist could look away. He would like to learn her intricacies. Not to prove them wrong or convince others she was just plain old normal, but to infuse his knowledge with the essence of her. Her very being attracted him like a dragonfly in a conservatory seeking the sunlight.

"Compelled," he muttered, feeling an unease shadow his eagerness.

No, he wouldn't let that incident cloud what was going on with Eryss. She didn't need to know about his weird childhood find and how it haunted him to this day.

As he turned to bring the bowls to the table, he was stopped by Eryss putting her arms around his waist from behind to hug him. "Hot soup!" he warned.

"Can I help?"

"No, you sit down. It's a simple meal, but you have to allow me to do the whole serving thing so I can stretch it out and make it feel a bit grander."

Twirling around in her green-and-red dress, she settled onto a stool before the table. "Anytime a man cooks for me it's grand."

"Does it happen often?" He set a bowl before her and sat beside her. He'd found linen napkins in a drawer and quaint mason jars for the lemon water.

She sipped the wine and smiled at him. "This is a first."

"I'm sorry for that. Perhaps if we men pampered women more often the world would be a kinder, gentler place."

"You're going straight to seduction tonight. You keep talking like that and I'll be naked before dessert."

"Sorry, there's no dessert."

She slid a palm along his thigh. "I beg to differ."

He grinned at her salacious suggestion. "Well then, let's eat before dessert gets cold, shall we?"

"Did you make it to the museum?" she asked, blowing on a spoonful of soup. "Mireio said you'd stopped by the brewery."

"I did. I wanted to see if you were interested in accompanying me. The Greek weapons exhibit was interesting, but I've seen much the same a few years ago. Still, it was fun to navigate Hennepin and Washington Avenues and drive by the Vikings stadium. And I got out of town before three, as you warned."

"I wouldn't even go out tomorrow," she said. "There's a storm heading in tonight, just after midnight. I can feel it."

"More than the snow that already fell?"

"The weatherman predicts at least six inches."

Dane felt his heart clench. "I may never get out of this town alive."

"Oh, come on, surfer guy, you can handle it."

"I do like the snow." At her questioning lift of the eyebrows, he said, "I do. It's…fun. Not as thrilling as surfing, though. January offers some of the best waves out there. Pull on a nice thermal wet suit and I'm good. It's the Viking in me."

"Wow. Descended from Vikings. I'm Scandinavian, too. Which is why I always seem to end up stuck in Minnesota."

"Always?"

She sipped the wine and smirked from over the goblet rim. "Reincarnation."

"Oh, right."

"Have you debunked that?"

"Not…yet."

But if she kept talking about it, he'd have to ask, if souls were simply refurbished over and over, how to explain the population overgrowth. Past lives? Merely memories from television shows or the intense desire to believe in something greater that offered the promise of finally "getting it right"?

"It's not something that science will ever accept," Eryss said. "Some things are simply innate. You accept them on faith. But I suppose you're not a religious man, either?"

"Not terribly. Which doesn't mean religion cannot serve a purpose. Faith can be comforting in times of suffering and need. I would never make a statement against it."

"So you do have a soul in there beneath the armor of particles and atoms and scientific theory."

"Of course I do. And when I die, my soul will cease to exist."

He winked at her and quickly spooned in more soup. If he didn't ask now, then he might lose the opportunity. He might be ruling out some delicious sex for dessert, but—damn him, the scientist had to ask.

"I noticed interesting symbols on the windows and traced inside some of the cupboard doors in your pantry."

"You were snooping?"

"I had to look around to find a few ingredients for supper."

"Your science background doesn't have an explanation for the mandala over my kitchen sink?"

"Well, sure. And I looked it up. I couldn't *not* look it up. It's my job to be curious about these sorts of things."

"I understand that. So what did you learn?"

"Well, the symbol on the window above the sink traces to pagan lore. It could be construed as a sort of alchemical symbol nowadays. But it doesn't impart magic or summon—"

"I'm a witch, Dane."

He set down his spoon and wiped his hands on the linen. "I see." That was not what he'd wanted to hear from her. She was misdirected, that was all. And now he really had to lay the disbelief stuff on thick, or risk exposing his work to her. "Well, we all have our religious endeavors. Not me, of course. Raised nondenominational."

"It's not a religion, it's a lifestyle. I was born this way. Witchcraft is what I practice. A witch is what I am. Does that freak you out? Do you think I'm mentally unbalanced?"

"Well, I, uh…no." But the lie was difficult for him. She had been so perfect. Why had he asked? He should have never asked!

And yet she'd said she was born that way. His inner alarm bells clanged loudly. Real witches were new to him. And he hadn't come prepared to deal with such entities.

Eryss leaned forward and asked softly, "Do you now regret having sex with me?"

"I could never regret a moment spent with you," he said truthfully. He lifted his glass in a toast. "And much as my knowledge—my very job—would have me argue against your *practice*, I won't. To each his own. And let's leave it at that, shall we?"

They clinked glasses and Dane took a moment to ignore his raging need to explain to Eryss how a woman couldn't possibly possess magical skills simply by worshipping some goddess or calling down the moon or combining herbs into an ineffectual potion. Whatever it was that she thought she was he'd have to overlook. He was in town for only a week. And he did enjoy her company, both in and out of bed.

If born a *real* witch, she could possess magic—which he had yet to witness. And every fiber of his being did not want to witness such things. He'd been told witches could be nastier than a tribe of vampires. The thought made him shudder.

"I'll have you know I admire science," Eryss offered. "It is an exquisite way to explain how most things exist."

"All things."

"Most." Her grin told him she was ready for the challenge of an argument if he pressed.

"Tell me about the brewery," he said. Best to change topics. "How did that come about? You said you are the owner?"

"A diversion? Not what I expect from a man of science but…okay. Fine." She pushed her soup bowl aside and leaned an elbow on the table, crossing her legs and leaning suggestively toward him. "I am the owner of The Decadent Dames, along with three other women. I've always been a home brewer. Of all kinds of brews."

Her smile was both wicked and teasing. Dane wouldn't take the bait. He. Must. Not.

"I've been friends with the women who work with me for years," she continued, "so it was a natural progression to open the place and share our passion with the public. Mireio is the master brewer, although I formulate a lot of the beers for her. Valor is the muscle who likes to haul bags of grain and mill it, and she's also our promotion guru. And Geneva is our good luck goddess. She's out of the country at the moment. On holiday with her latest billionaire."

"Her latest?"

"She doesn't like to settle in with anyone. Just hang out long enough to have some fun. We're all very young. Relationships should be fun and easy and not too serious, don't you agree?"

"I do. But what if you meet the one? You do believe there is one out there for you?"

"Of course, I dream about him all the time. Oh." She pressed her lips together. "That wasn't for sharing."

"Does this dream lover have a name?"

"No. Not even a face."

Dane gaped at her.

"Not like that. He has a face. I just never see it in the dream. Okay, fine. I've confessed I'm a witch, so I might as well roll out all my strange secrets and really chase you away."

He touched her hand and she curled her fingers into her palm, but he wouldn't let go. He didn't want to. "It will take a lot to send me fleeing from you. I promise. I do have an open mind, much as you might believe otherwise. I always listen to both sides, research, check stats and perform tests, before coming to conclusions."

"That's so not sexy."

He smirked. "I realized that the moment it came out of my mouth. But it is my truth."

"I get that."

"So what, beyond being a witch, is your strange secret?"

She huffed out a sigh. "I dream about a great love I once had and lost. You know, in my past lives. I feel as though someday I'll see him again. Recognize him. Like…"

"Like?" He bowed his head to catch her straying gaze. She was telling him something she didn't ordinarily share with others; he sensed that. So he didn't want her to clam up. And if he were to form an opinion about this woman, he must get all the details. It wouldn't be fair to her to make a judgment based on a few pagan symbols he'd found in her home. "How will you recognize this man if you've never seen his face?"

"My soul will know his," she said. She suddenly clasped his hand and stared hard at him. "Dane?"

"Yes?"

"Do you…" She tilted her head. Her eyes were ever so blue. An ice queen's prize. "Well, I know you don't. As you've already said, you believe we all come to this earth for just the one lifetime. Death takes us. Nothing more."

"Exactly. Why would there be anything else?"

"For the very reason that we have much to learn—or rather remember—and it takes more than one mortal lifetime to do so. Have you ever wondered, though? I mean, just for a moment?"

"About life after death? Never." Dane sat back, baffled over her sudden intensity. He'd asked her how she would recognize the man in her dreams and she'd looked at him as though—no. She couldn't possibly believe that. He was no woman's dream man. And he did not believe in reincarnation, so that ended any possibility that her lost love could be him. It was simply a wish for a man who could sweep her off her feet and into happily-ever-after.

But he couldn't help but wish they did have a deeper connection.

"I believe," Eryss said with quiet confidence, "and that's all that matters to me."

"So these visions you have…is this to do with the nightmare that woke you this morning?"

"No. I'm not sure. I certainly hope not. That man— you couldn't possibly be him."

He really didn't want to know.

Maybe a little.

All right, fine, he *needed* to know. "Him?"

"I suspect you haven't a mean bone in your body," Eryss said with a strange note of hope in her voice.

"Mean? I think I've fallen off this conversational track, Eryss. Weren't you talking about soul mates?"

"Sorry. Yes, in the one dream, it's my soul mate. But

in the nightmare I had this morning…oh, I'm rambling. And you don't need to hear this. I'll figure it out."

A sudden gust of wind rattled the window in its frame.

Eryss shrugged when Dane looked to her with raised brows. "Storm is coming. I forgot to close the garage door. Do you want to park your rental inside? There's another space. You probably should. It's going to get cold tonight."

Colder than the icebox this state already was?

"Uh, sure." She'd abandoned the conversation thread too quickly. Had he been cruel to dispute her beliefs? He didn't think so.

"Give me the keys," she said. "I'll run out quick and do it."

"I can do it."

"I want to shovel the walk from the garage to the house while I'm at it. Keep ahead of the storm. And I need to check the gas in the snowblower. I suspect I'll be blowing snow in the morning."

"Uh." Dane raised a finger. "Man in the house here. I could do that for you. Besides, I rather enjoy playing with the snowblower."

"Okay." Then with a wince she asked, "Are you in or out for the night?"

"Which do you prefer?" he countered.

"In. But I don't want you to feel obligated to stay with a person you can't understand."

"Religion, or lack of it, should never be the wedge that separates two interested parties."

"It's a lifestyle, not a religion. Witch." She pointed at her chest as she stood, then carried the dishes to the sink. "If you're in, you're in. If not, I won't feel bad if you drive away."

"Really? I was hoping you would feel something if I decided to leave."

"Oh, I would. I mean—screw this talking around the subject. I want you to stay the night, Dane."

"Then it's settled." He grabbed the garage keys from the copper bowl. "I'll drive the rental car into the garage, then check the gas in the snowblower. Afterward, I challenge you to a snowball fight."

"Is that so?"

"Yeah. And I'd say your odds of winning are quite good, matched against this surfer guy."

Chapter 8

By the time Dane pulled the rental car into the garage, the sky had begun to toss down light, fluffy flakes. Eryss had walked around the side of the garage, disappearing from view. She wore only a coat and boots, thin gloves and a light scarf. Minnesota woman. He did respect her resilience.

As he got out of the car in the garage, he pulled up the wool coat collar to his chin and shivered, then clapped his gloved hands together. He knew he'd never experienced this kind of bone-deep cold while surfing the fifty-degree waters.

A quick check to the snowblower's gas gauge confirmed the shiny red machine was ready for further adventure in the morning. Did he really like the girl that much that he'd suffer the frigid cold so he could get a little snuggle time?

"Yes," he confirmed out loud.

But what about the witch thing? He really needed to address that. Was she completely delusional, or had she actually been born a witch?

Either way, he wasn't going to like the answer. How to deal with a real witch? But did he have to *deal* with her? This was not a job. And besides, Agency workers didn't approach paranormals in a confrontational manner. They simply made sure none were out to cause innocents harm, and judged the situation as either safe or possibly volatile. From there, decisions were made. Sometimes the Order of the Stake was called in to handle violent vampires. But Dane had no clue what the protocol was for witches.

On the other hand, no proof had been put forth.

"Kitchen witch," he muttered, and left it at that.

He walked outside and spied Eryss with her arms spread out and head tilted back. Big, fluffy flakes landed in her hair and on her face. And he forgot any worries he'd just been considering.

She motioned for him to join her. "Like this." She leaned back and stuck out her tongue.

Dane closed his eyes and tilted his head, mimicking her.

"You have to look," she said with a giggle. "It's a trick, knowing when to close your eyes and when to keep them open."

It took a few seconds for him to catch a snowflake. It melted instantly across his tongue. "Ah! Got one!" He pumped a fist, then swung around and swept her into his arms. "I know when to close my eyes." He held eye contact until their noses touched, then he closed them and his cool lips met hers.

And winter was swept away as her body warmed his shivering bones. While snowflakes melted on their hair and cheeks, Eryss's kiss melted Dane's reticence about engaging with a possible witch. She pulled him closer and hugged him. His deep growl, without breaking the kiss, urged her to seek more. Their tongues dancing, she hiked up a leg and he caught it with his hand. And…they toppled, and landed in a thick coating of fresh snow.

"Sorry," he said against her cheek. "I didn't calculate the angle of two bodies swaying in bliss to the instability of the snow cover."

"Stop being a scientist and start making a snow angel." She rolled away from him and swept the snowy ground with her arms and legs.

"I can do that," he said decisively. After rolling a few feet in the other direction, with his head pointed toward hers, he began to do the same. "These are the only kinds of angels that exist, you know!"

"Dane!"

Right. He was not trying to debunk angels.

"Sorry! Not being a scientist right now. Just being a guy. A guy who is freezing his ass off lying in the snow trying to impress a girl."

Her face appeared above his head and she smiled upside down. "You're not doing a very good job. Your angel's left wing is crooked."

"Don't judge the disabled." He cracked a smirk and she swatted loose snow onto his face. The ice crystals stung and then immediately melted. He reached for her head upside down, and bracketed her cheeks. "Answer me this one."

"What?"

"Tell me why you live in a place where the air hurts your face." And on a whim, he raised his left arm and blasted her in the face with a fluffy ball of snow.

Eryss gasped and then backed away. "Oh yeah? Guess

it's time to teach surfer guy how to lose in the battle of the Snowmageddon."

Dane stood up from the angel as Eryss bent to scoop up some snow. He thought he'd made a reasonably good one. And since angels did not exist, it could look however he made it. Opening his mouth to correct her assessment of his creativity, he got a mouthful of snow.

"Yes!" Eryss pumped her fist and scampered off into the yard beside the conservatory, bending to scoop up more fresh-fallen snow.

The next snowball just missed his head. He saw that one coming and managed to dodge it. He flung his own ball toward Eryss, but without aiming. She laughed as it landed five feet in front of her, a dysfunctional missile. He shrugged and grinned.

"Listen," she said suddenly. The snow queen closed her eyes and tilted her head again, lustrous chestnut hair falling over the scarf and down her back.

Dane studied her as she listened—he didn't hear anything—and observed snowflakes falling softly in her dark hair. Melting in tears down her cheeks and kissing her mouth more reverently than he could imagine doing himself.

Please let her be normal. Not delusional.

He cast his gaze around her yard, but didn't spy squirrels or anything that could make a noise. "I don't hear anything."

"Exactly." She opened her eyes with a wide smile. "The exquisite quiet of a snowfall. Isn't it the greatest thing ever?"

Now Dane closed his eyes, focused on the fall of cool flakes hitting his face and realized there was no sound. Scientifically, he knew the snowflakes were getting in the way of the sound waves, scattering them so that less sound reached their ears. Also, the snow absorbed sound. And yet he felt as if he stood in his own world. With Eryss.

When he turned his head to agree how great it was, she stood next to him. He saw the kiss coming half a second before it landed on his mouth.

She wrapped both legs about his hips and he carried her up the side steps without breaking the hot, heady connection between them. He crushed her against the door and moved the kiss to the edge of her mouth. He licked away a melted snowflake with a dash of his tongue. "You taste like winter and wine."

He playfully nipped the edge of her jaw, then tugged aside her scarf to kiss her neck. "We could make out here in the storm," he said, "but I sense we'd melt a hole right through to the grass for the heat we're generating."

"Take me inside, lover."

He opened the door and strode through, stomping his shoes clean of snow without setting her down. Eryss kicked off her boots and let them drop, and he followed suit. Then he angled them both through the kitchen and toward the stairway. "Conservatory or the bedroom?"

"Upstairs!" she said with a giggling laugh, and he took the steps in a bound, clutching her to him for the bouncing ascent. "You're so strong."

"You weigh very little. And we've asserted that I work out. Any more obvious facts you want to point out?"

"Only that that was a sarcastic way of calling me an idiot."

"No. Ah." He paused before her closed bedroom door, setting her down. Eryss let her shoulders relax against the wall. "I'm sorry. The guys I work with are so…it's a work thing. Scientists battling for king of the lab."

"I bet you're king a lot."

"Not so often as I care to be, but on occasion, yes. Would you forgive my cruel words if I did this?" After tugging off her scarf and dropping it to the floor, he opened her coat and kissed his way to her breasts.

"Forgiveness is yours," she cooed as he kissed her through her dress and gently bit her nipple. "But I'll be even more forgiving when we get all these clothes off."

She backed away from him, drawing her dress down her shoulders and slipping it off. The red tights followed just as quickly. The woman was not into bras or panties, and he was just fine with that. Shedding his shirt and unbuttoning his pants, he quickly disrobed to his skivvies and swept the naked seductress into his arms once more and walked her into the bedroom.

"Whew! You're still cold." He bent to lick her rock-hard nipple. "Do I make you hard?"

"You do. And soft. And hot. And—" she lashed her tongue along his jaw "—wet. Strip off your boxers and let me warm up that hard-on, yes?"

He shoved down his boxers as he set her on the bed. Eryss quickly grabbed him by the cock, and while astonished she was in such a hurry, he was also eager to sink himself deep inside her heat. So when she directed him there, they both groaned in pleasure, and he bowed his head to her shoulder.

"I am at your mercy, Ice Queen."

Chapter 9

Dane rolled over, his arm sliding off the side of the bed. He smiled at Eryss, a dreamy, sex-satisfied grin that twinkled in his eyes thanks to the candlelight.

"What?" she asked.

"Everything," he said. And then he turned his head away from her, as if that was all he was willing to offer.

Not "nothing" but "everything." She wanted to ask him more. But it didn't matter. She felt the same. Everything about the man was awesome. He was sexy, handsome, kind, generous, smart, even accepting of her being a witch. (Though he didn't believe it for a second; she knew that.)

What was wrong with Dane Winthur?

Not a thing. And even when a little voice in her head that sounded a lot like Mireio suggested that he could be a witch hunter, Eryss shoved it away in disbelief. Not this too-perfect man. If anything, he was her long-lost love. She had found him. They had a future to explore together.

And then the dreaded thought that he was leaving in a few days shot her down from the high. She rolled to her back, trailing her fingers along his arm and to his buttocks, where she tapped lightly. How to keep him here longer? Did she want to do that?

What kind of vindictive luck had delivered her the first man she'd really connected with in a long time and…he was just passing through?

And yet her soul did recognize him. She hadn't wanted to explain that one to him over supper. But she knew, with her very soul, that he was that long-lost love. She'd never felt this way with a man before. As if they'd simply fallen back into one another's arms after being away for a short absence.

Just because Dane didn't believe in reincarnation didn't mean it hadn't occurred for him, as well. How had they lost one another in previous lives? Was there a way for him to tap into his soul and experience the same recognition she did? If she could recognize him, he could surely do the same.

Of course, she believed. That was Dane's main obstacle.

He leaned over the side of the bed and picked up something from the floor. "What's this? Is it a decorative thing? It's so delicate."

He rolled over to show her the crystal blade she'd left sitting out after cleansing the bedroom during the new moon. Normally she tucked it away in the nightstand. How it had gotten on the floor was beyond her. Well, she hadn't been using the most logical side of her brain since she'd met Dane, that was for sure.

"It's not decorative." She took it from him. The leather-bound hilt warmed instantly in her grip. "It's a real weapon. I like to…keep some means of protection close. I am a single woman living alone."

"Sure, but…the blade is crystal. That hardly seems a useful weapon to me."

"Surely in your line of work you must have come across crystal weapons?"

"I have. Once even a three-foot-long blade. But it was decorative. What sort of weapon would that serve as? Is it even sharp?" He shook his head. "The things they make these days to appeal to female consumers."

"I didn't buy it as a decoration, Dane." Eryss turned the blade to point upward. "It was given to me by Mrs. McAlister, the neighbor I told you about who was virtually a second mother to me. She used it as an athame."

"Ah."

There was so much in that simple utterance. Disbelief. Condemnation. And a professional debunker wondering if he should laugh out loud at her.

"A witchy sort of thing?" His smirk told her she should steer clear of further discussion that might lead to more disdainful comments about her species. "You know, it's been said that a woman is better off unarmed, because in most cases the attacker will be stronger and more powerful, capable of wrenching the weapon from her hands and, thus, arming himself."

"Oh yeah? You want to try me, surfer guy?" She held the knife at the ready, very much capable of defending herself with the blade. Valor had given her a few pointers.

"I would never harm you, Eryss. And I suspect that you are skilled with that thing."

"Damn right." She made a fake stab toward him, stopping the blade a good ten inches from his chest, when out of nowhere a vision flashed in her mind.

* * *

The man beneath her screamed and clasped at the blade stuck in his chest. Blood pooled out in a rich crimson flood over his thick wolf's fur coat. His face was spattered with blood and he growled, cursing her as a witch. "My soul will not rest until yours has burned," he hissed out, along with some spittle.

She clutched her chest, which burned with pain. Blood coated her fingers and the edge of the blade cut her skin. But not from the crystal blade. She, too, wore a blade in her heart. And she, too, cursed the hunter in turn. "My soul will live forever with your love."

"Eryss? Watch it with that thing. Eryss!"

"Huh?" Startled out of the vision, she dropped her hand, then realized she was still holding the blade, and at the last second managed to snatch it away before the tip slid across Dane's chest.

"Whoa. Woman, what is up?" He shuffled to lean on his elbows, his gaze fiercely tracking the crystal blade.

"I'm sorry, I had a moment of…distraction. I'll put this away." She leaned over him, opened the nightstand drawer and tucked it in. "There. All gone."

"All gone? You almost stabbed me with that thing."

"No. I was just going to show you that I have the skills."

"By sinking the blade into my chest?"

"Never! Would you stop freaking out?"

"Sure, but for a moment there you had such a look in your eyes. Is everything all right?" He stroked the tips of her hair, hanging near her elbows. "Did I do something wrong?"

"Wrong?" She forced herself to snuggle up beside him, putting the horrible vision away for a moment when she could be alone and think it through. "Are you crazy? You just rocked my world."

"Right. Uh…" He glanced to the nightstand where she'd tucked away the crystal blade.

"Can we drop this, Dane?"

"I…yes. I'm just…"

"Not tired?"

"After what we just did? Not at all." He kissed her forehead and slid a hand down her arm. She sensed he was still thinking about the blade, because his body tensed against hers.

She had seen herself and a man, a fearsome man, stab one another. He'd said he wouldn't stop until she burned. Only a witch hunter would say such a thing.

"Since I'm now well and thoroughly awake, want to do it again?" Dane asked. The night was lightening, but snow still battered the glass in sleety ticks. "The weather deems to keep me here, snug with you."

He kissed her stomach and Eryss forgot all about being stabbed in the heart by a witch hunter.

Eryss breezed into the brewery and tossed her purse behind the bar. A leather jacket with The Decadent Dames logo stitched on the back in red and white threads was lying across the bar. Valor must be in the basement, filling the kegs with the stout Mireio had brewed a month earlier. Eryss decided to review the brew schedule for the month, so she parked a stool at the end of the bar and opened her laptop.

She'd had no problem leaving Dane back at her house. They hadn't gotten the promised six inches of snow, probably just two or three, but even so, Dane had offered to plow the drive. She'd left him to it. And it was a good idea because the weatherman had promised the real storm would hit tonight.

But now she caught her forehead in her palms and squeezed her temples. That vision she'd had of holding the bloody knife returned to her. She had grasped for a blade stuck in her chest. In that moment she had felt the painful cut of the steel through her heart. It had struck right where she pressed her fingers now—through the birthmark below her breast.

"No way," she whispered. But it was believable. Birthmarks were often remnants of past life traumas.

And the vision hadn't been a dream or nightmare. She had been wide-awake while holding the crystal dagger over Dane. The vision had come to her at that particular moment for a purpose. Could that mean she had used the dagger in a past life to defend herself against...

You never make it to your thirtieth birthday.

Was *Dane* the witch hunter?

"No," she whispered. "He doesn't believe in witches."

If he was going to hunt witches, she suspected belief was a strong requirement for getting the job. On the other hand, the man did debunk the paranormal. Which, again, didn't leave room for belief. Right?

Of course, Eryss knew if people didn't want to see the truth, they could convince themselves otherwise using science, superstition or any illogical thought process. Humans possessed a herd mentality and tended to go along with the majority. To follow those who demonstrated authority.

But the vision had been clear. Perhaps since her thirtieth birthday was so near, she was tapping into the universal energies that held her past secrets? The more she thought about it, the more clearly she realized that the crystal blade must be what she had used when she'd defended herself against the witch hunter in the past. Could it be? It had been given to her by Mrs. McAlister, who had been a Light witch. They had known one another in previous lives, usually in a teaching manner, they suspected. She could have gotten the blade from an earlier incarnation of Eryss.

Eryss had never been compelled to check her family tree. And she suspected if she went searching, she wouldn't find one written down. But reincarnation did not imply she was born into the same family every lifetime. That didn't make any sense. She was a different person each time. And yet, remarkably, she had always been female, and a witch. It happened like that sometimes. A person could be a teacher, a musician or even a socialite through the ages. Others ranged vastly from lifetime to lifetime in their occupations and personalities, either through choice or because they'd made the decision to experience a great variety of lifestyles.

What had the faceless man said to her in the vision? Something about a curse. And him not stopping until she burned.

The witch hunter had been *cursed* to kill her? That was an interesting detail. It was hard to believe—yet Midge had suggested the same.

Eryss shuddered to consider she may have been tracked through the centuries by a vengeance-seeking killer. Who had been cursed? And why stab her, then? Burning was the only way to kill a witch and to make her stay dead. (And yet, there was a rumor that dead witches burned at the stake in centuries past had been summoned in a Paris cemetery only a few years ago.) But usually fire and witches did not mix. Sure, you could kill one with a blade, and she would die. But that didn't ensure *final* death.

Was that why Eryss kept reincarnating? Because her soul had never received true and final death from fire? Midge had seen her stabbed many times over the centuries. But she hadn't mentioned anything about fire.

The thought of it made Eryss woozy. She grabbed a bottle of water out of the fridge behind the bar and sat before the laptop again. Running the vision over in her thoughts, she recalled what she had said to her killer.

Something like "Our souls will live forever with our love."

What could that mean? How could she possibly have been in love with a witch hunter? Was the man she'd stabbed in her vision *really* the witch hunter? Had she killed someone else? In defense or otherwise? Had she killed her lost love?

"Dane," she whispered. "This is so freaky!"

"What's freaky?"

Eryss spun around at Valor's voice. She hadn't heard her walk in. The brown-haired woman hoisted a bag of grains on each shoulder and strode over to the brew tanks, where she set them down against the wall, then brushed the dust off her hands with brisk slaps. Two five-gallon plastic buckets, the mill and an electric drill sat nearby, for her to hand mill the grains that Mireio would brew this afternoon.

Valor Hearst was a seventy-year-old witch who had performed an immortality spell on her twenty-fifth birthday so she'd stay young for a good century. She had never met a beer she couldn't reverse-engineer. She liked cars, motorcycles, biker boys and tattoos. Not necessarily in that order. The ultimate tomboy, she could also rock the glamour when she felt like it. But ordinarily she wore her purple-tinted hair straight and uncombed. Fashion was as easy as Sunday morning when she donned an old army jacket over a biker T-shirt and skintight jeans. The moonstone amulet on the leather cord around her neck never left her person.

"I had another portent this morning," Eryss offered. She could tell Valor anything. The witch knew how to keep secrets.

"Yeah, Mireio told me you'd been having nightmares."

And that witch couldn't keep a secret to save her life. Not that Eryss had told Mireio to keep it hush-hush. She trusted her sisters in the craft with the details of her life, as they all did. Geneva was the only one who had a tendency for secrecy.

"Did she tell you about my scientist?"

"Sexy, dark hair and eyes you could drown in?"

"That would be the one. He stayed the night again, and this morning…well, he saw the crystal dagger I got from my mentor. I'd had it out to perform a house blessing and Dane picked it up from the floor. He debunks paranormal-related weapons and started to explain why crystal wasn't a good weapon and how crystals don't have energy."

Valor made a *pfft* sound.

"Right, but when I took it in hand I got a vision of me stabbing a man."

"Did he look like your scientist?"

"I didn't actually see faces in my visions, but I wouldn't expect a past incarnation to look like me or the other person."

"True. Though ghosts do like to hang on to their previous incarnations. I sometimes think it's a courtesy to us living ones."

Valor had an uncanny ability to see ghosts. And there were a lot of them lingering in the city of Anoka. Poor girl.

"Though, now I think of it," Eryss continued, "we

were dressed in different clothes. Maybe medieval? The fabrics were rich and I'm pretty sure I was in a long dress. And the man had stabbed me. I could feel the blade in my chest. He said he wouldn't stop until I burned."

"Yikes. That is not cool." Valor slid onto a bar stool and propped an elbow on the counter. "I hope you killed him in your dream, after he said that."

"I think I did. It wasn't a dream, though. Dane and I were both awake. It was a vision. And I said something about love keeping us alive forever."

"Mercy, someone put a wacky curse on the two of you."

"He did say something about a curse in the vision. But seriously? Not me and Dane."

"Why would you think otherwise?"

"Well, he's not a witch hunter. It's a witch hunter who kills me, Valor. Midge read that in the soul gaze."

"He *is* a scientist. Don't they pooh-pooh witches and everything woo-woo? You did say he debunks stuff."

"Yes, but—no. He's not. Seriously? The guy would know if he's a witch hunter. I'm sure it was me holding the crystal dagger that sparked the vision. He just happened to be in the wrong place at the wrong time."

"What did he think of your vision?"

"I didn't tell him. How could I? I did tell him I'm a witch and he laughed about it."

"Yeah, doesn't sound like a hunter to me."

"His career is all about proving people like us don't exist."

"Better those kinds than the ones who are obsessed with proving we are real and get creepy real fast." She shrugged. "Anyway, I got the blueberry cream ale on tap for this weekend. You coming in to work, or will you be nestled all snug as a you-know-what with your man?"

"I hoped to be snug as a bug. But Harold is due back on Friday, so who knows."

"Mr. Stuart, the antiques dealer across the street? What does he have to do with your amorous liaisons? Am I missing an important detail in a strange new love triangle?" Valor waggled her brows.

"No, silly. Dane is in town to pick up a dagger from Harold. Oh my goddess."

"He's here to pick up a dagger?" Valor eyed Eryss with the most obvious "I told you so" glare ever.

Eryss shook her head. "It's for his job. Not a witch hunter thing."

Yet even she had difficulty not acknowledging there was too much coincidence going on here. And nothing in the universe was coincidence. Everything happened for a reason.

"You had better be very careful around that man," Valor warned. "And get that dagger from Harold before the so-called—" she made air quotes "—*debunker* gets his hands on it. For your own safety, Eryss. Be smart."

"I am. I just don't think Dane is anything but a kind man who knows how to kiss me silly."

Valor rolled her eyes. "I hear he's sex on a stick. I always think that would be so painful when someone says that." She shuddered. "Give me sex on a bike or in the backseat of a '65 Impala any day over a stick."

"I'll take it anywhere Dane wants to give it to me. Even in a snowbank, if that's on the table."

"You always have loved winter. You have any lavender growing over at your place? I want to imbue it in the last batch of October honey. I think it would taste fabulous."

Valor kept bees on the roof of her apartment building.

"Sounds delicious. Yes, I do have lavender. I'll bring some in this weekend."

Valor fist-bumped her. "Cheers."

* * *

After a morning of blowing snow from the driveway, Dane brewed a cup of hot chocolate (because coffee was blatantly absent from Eryss's kitchen). The snow removal had been surprisingly satisfying, and he'd blown a wide path all the way out to the main road and around the mailbox so the mailman could drive up close with his car. He was wishing for more snow tonight so he could go out again tomorrow morning.

Weird, the things that appealed to a man's sense of duty and personal satisfaction.

Now he settled into the couch in the conservatory with laptop in hand, and set the hot chocolate on the grass. So strange that the floor was fresh, springy blades of it. He couldn't begin to explain that, only that there must be a heating element threaded beneath this room. Otherwise the ground should be frozen solid, even with the conservatory on top of it. By rights, he should get on his knees and tear up a piece of the sod to discover what lay beneath. He could debunk her magical landscape. But Dane was confident what he believed was true. And maybe a part of him wanted to relax and take this vacation as it should be. No scientific queries regarding green grass in Minnesota in January.

He took a few moments to enjoy the surrounding greenery and the humid warmth. He could hear birds squawking and insects chittering...

"If only," he muttered, at the surprising leap of his imagination. But the room did evoke visions of a Victorian hothouse replete with colorful birds and perhaps even a monkey-climbing apparatus. Ha! There it was, his childhood imagination leaping out unawares. Best to tuck that away before anyone noticed.

On to more serious endeavors. He had the Haywood project that required proofing before he sent the final report on to the Agency. With that report, the Agency would reassure the small Nevada town that the Golgotha Cross, which had been excavated from the salt flats, couldn't possibly have been the reason behind the mysterious deaths over the past six months. It was most likely lead in the water. Water tests had shown dangerously high lead levels.

The Agency did suggest advanced testing and further research to their clients, which was what he liked most about the people he worked for. They didn't simply say "this is stupid; it couldn't possibly be real." They gave their clients avenues to explore what could really be behind something they believed was caused by the paranormal. And no, Dane didn't do it to tear apart people's dreams, as he'd once been accused by the housewife who was quite sure she was being visited nightly by a sexy hunk of a vampire. For the record, she'd been ODing on oxycodone and reading too many romance novels. For the unofficial record? It *had* been a vampire with a sweet tooth for the maple-sugared bacon the woman often snacked on.

Dane was about to open the file when he remembered the symbol in the kitchen. He'd noticed another this morning while showering. It had hung in the corner of the bathroom and was made from twigs and dried grass. An amethyst crystal had been woven into it.

A feeling of dread tickled his neck. Had Eryss been born into believing that she was a cauldron-stirring witch? What kind of parents would do that to their child? It was just wrong. And what magic, exactly, did she believe she possessed?

True-born witches were raised as witches, and he

wasn't sure if they were taught magic or simply possessed it innately. Were there witchcraft schools? He'd never dealt with witches, so he didn't have the research required to call her real or not.

The knife thing had been creepy. For those few seconds that she'd held the crystal blade suspended above his chest, Dane had thought something had shut down in Eryss. Or maybe too much had been going on in her brain. Had she had a vision of sorts? Similar to those she claimed to dream about? Something about a lost love. Hmm...would she have stabbed him if he hadn't said something to her?

He rubbed his chest now. The crystal blade had been sharp, and while he would expect it to crack and break upon impact, a good firm thrust could send it through skin, muscle and organs before breaking.

What was he thinking? Eryss was not the type who could ever wield a blade in violence against another. But there was something about her. Something...off.

He tugged his fingers through his hair and shook his head. He was getting off course. It shouldn't matter to him what went on in her brain. But it did. Because...he liked her.

Dane tilted his head back and eyed the glass dome overhead. The steel joins formed a decorative design that made a sort of star with eight points. A sigil? It couldn't be a magical symbol; it was just the way the structure had been put together. Though there was something hanging from the center, about a foot to the left of the rope that supported the emerald chandelier. Herbs? Well, those could be there simply for fragrance, not because of some witchy spell.

On the other hand, the room was fragrant with live plants and flowers. Herbs would prove unnecessary. Must be a piece of a plant that grew so high it had gotten tangled in the structure. Dane was okay with that explanation.

He sipped the cold hot chocolate.

"Dane?" The scent of tomato sauce and greasy cheese preceded Eryss into the room. He got up and took the pizza box from her, and she shrugged off her coat and tossed it to the grassy floor near the glass door.

"Pizza? This does not figure into the lifestyle of health and wellness for the Eryss Norling I know."

"Give me a break. I was busy at the brewery and forgot to eat. You must be hungry, too. It's the veggie style with a thin crust but lots of mushrooms."

"I can do mushrooms."

"I'll grab us some plates. What do you want to drink?"

"More of your delicious mint lemonade."

She winked and strolled out.

"Not a witch," Dane said as he opened the pizza box and the aroma hit him right in the feels. "But certainly a sorceress of my stomach."

Chapter 10

The pizza was a hit and Eryss was surprised they finished the entire thing. Dane had a hearty appetite. He was probably a meat eater, which was why she'd bulked up on the mushrooms for him. She wasn't used to cooking for men. But she wouldn't mind if he was around more often to challenge her meager cooking skills. How many days did they have left together?

She didn't want to count. It would ruin the blissful mood. And if she thought too deeply, she'd begin to wonder if the man could ever learn to love the brutal Minnesota winters. She'd certainly done what she could to induct him into the lifestyle of the cold and frigid.

Now they cuddled on the couch with the chenille blanket across their laps. Dane scrolled through his files on the laptop to show her the project he was working on. A month earlier, he had obtained a box rumored to possess a demon that could inhabit a person's soul if let loose. It had been found in the basement of a little old man living in Pittsburgh who had been convinced the box was whispering to him.

"It held just some bits of ash and stale air." He clicked on a photo of the small wooden box. "Ruined a perfectly good piece of redwood, as far as I'm concerned. Have you been to the Redwood National State Park in upper California?"

Eryss shook her head and offered a shrug. She hadn't traveled much farther than North Dakota and Wisconsin. If she must uproot herself, she was certainly in line for a change of scenery.

"Ah, hell. I'm boring you." Dane closed the laptop and set it on the grass. "I could talk about my work all day, and if you don't speak up I'll eventually explain the whole process in minutest detail. Why do you let me do this?"

"Because I like to listen to you. Doesn't matter what you say. Your voice is so rich and melty. It drips over me like dark chocolate."

"Wow. I don't know what to say to that."

"Maybe you should pretend I'm covered with chocolate right now?" She waggled a brow and he waggled one back. "I like what's happening between us, Dane. But it also bums me out."

"I knew it. It's the science talk."

"No, it's the fact that you'll be leaving in a few days. I'm not sure if I should be happy and enjoy this as a fling, or freak out because parts of me are wanting it to be so much more."

"I see."

"I mean, there's nothing wrong with a fling. But generally flings only occur with people I don't find myself connecting with too deeply. There's something about you."

"You believe we've loved in a past life," he stated drily.

"Maybe." She clasped his hand. "Look at me, into my eyes."

He met her challenge with a fixed gaze, those beautiful browns so dark and filled with mysteries she might never learn, but wanted to discover, slowly. Oh, so slowly. She did feel their connection. Their souls knew one another. It wasn't a sensation or even a sound or taste. Eryss simply knew it in her very bones.

"Why do I dream about you?" she whispered.

"Eryss, I don't think—"

She pressed a finger to his lips. "I'm sorry. I shouldn't have said that. This is too much for you. Magic is real, Dane, and the power of belief and your faith in science is strong. But I don't expect you to hitch a ride on my bandwagon."

"I've never been one for bandwagons. They're so loud." He chuckled. "You're right. The reincarnation and soul stuff is too much for me. I'm only here for a few more days. Can we...just have some fun?"

Eryss nodded. "Yes. I will stop trying to race ahead of what's happening here. Promise."

"Good. Living in the now is always best."

She took that as a reference to her claim that they'd shared past lives, and decided she would not push him. That would only scare him away. She slid a hand into his. "I'm in the mood for some extracurricular snuggling—"

But before she could continue, an abrupt crack shook the glass conservatory roof. Dane jumped to his feet and Eryss slid to the edge of the couch. They both stared up at the huge branch that had landed on the roof and now slowly slid off. A remarkable thud sounded when it hit the three-foot-deep snowbank outside the glass walls.

"The wind is insane today. I knew I should have

trimmed that tree this summer," Eryss said. "Do you think it cracked the glass?"

"It may have." Dane walked beneath the pane, head tilted back. It was two stories high, so he found it virtually impossible to notice a fine crack in the clear glass from the ground. "Do you have a ladder? And maybe some glass caulk?"

"Not inside. I think it'll be okay until the wind dies down. I can go out and inspect the damage in the morning."

"You don't trust that I can do that for you? I did plow the drive."

His man pride vibes were getting agitated; Eryss sensed his sudden tension. *Oops.* "Sure, you can do it. Tomorrow morning? It's only supposed to get wilder and windier tonight. I had plans to snuggle up before the fire in my bedroom, and I'll make popcorn."

He returned to her on the couch, a smile growing on his face. "You have a way of seducing a man with food, you know that?"

"I like to keep my company happy. The pizza was a fail."

"No, it wasn't." He kissed her. "Nothing you do is a fail. I'd almost wonder if you've bewitched me, but then I don't believe in witches."

"No, you don't. Which makes me a little sad, but I'm not going to press the issue."

"Let it never be said that Dane Winthur does not give a witch a fair chance." He sat and held out an entreating palm. "Do something witchy for me."

"Oh, no. I won't fall for that prove-yourself bullshit. I am not a circus sideshow."

"I know that." He snuggled up to her and kissed her cheek. "Just throw this disbelieving scientist a bone. I want to believe in you."

"Really? Or would you rather debunk me?"

"I, well…hmm."

"Right. No performances today, folks. So sorry."

"No, I'm sorry." He kissed her lips. "Forgive me?"

The pouty look was pushing it a touch too far. Almost. Eryss's sense of pride had not been damaged, and he was cute when he pouted. "Forgiven. If!"

"If?"

She undid a few buttons on his shirt. "You start the fire in my bedroom?"

"I think I know what you're asking, but do you realize that request can be taken two ways?"

"Oh, I do. And I expect you to fulfill them both."

The fire crackled, and the sugar maple logs sweetened the air. A playlist featuring Evanescence quietly haunted the atmosphere. The popcorn sat untouched.

Dane, sitting on the edge of the bed, pulled off his shirt, while Eryss lit a few candles and then a stick of incense on a bronze burner plate. Her hair spilled about her bare shoulders and the short dress barely covered her ass as she bent to place the incense on the floor before the bed. The room became infused with—what scent was that?

"Frankincense," she offered. Then, with a smile teasing her mouth, she stepped over the smoke curling up in tendrils from the burner and spread her skirt to capture the sweet scent.

"Yes." His eyes followed the hypnotic smoke imbuing her nether regions with sweetness. "Do you know that maidens once did exactly as you are doing in preparation to welcome home their mighty warriors after a long battle?"

"I do know that." She squatted just a little and closed

her eyes. Glossy hair shifted and fell over one cheek. She was a goddess upon her throne.

Dane shifted on the bed, adjusting his erection, which aimed to burst from his pants. Eryss slowly opened her eyes, fixing her seductive gaze to his. He swallowed. Such power she possessed.

"And did you also know," he said on a wanting tone, "that queens prepared for their kings, following their valiant service in war, by doing the same?"

Eryss nodded, smiling, basking in his growing hunger for her. She stood and began to inch up her skirt, then took steps toward him. Dane slid his fingers along her thigh.

"I am neither a warrior nor a king," he said, feeling the confession as deeply as if he had lived in one of those ancient time periods. And wishing, so terribly, that he could offer her such valor.

She gripped his hair and said boldly, "I will make you both a warrior and a king."

He bowed, following the gentle guidance of her hand.

And he kissed her there at the apex of her thighs, warmly, hotly, as if it were her mouth. He tasted her with lashes of his tongue, and worshipped her for the queen she might have once been in another life. He would gladly kneel before her whenever she requested, past, present and future.

Her fingers tickled their way through his hair, then gripped his head, and he took that as a sign of her pleasure—along with the long moan that harmonized with the music as he added his fingers to accompany his tongue in a sexual orchestration. She swore softly, sweetly, and her legs quivered. Catching one of her hands on the bed behind him, she steadied herself.

"Yes, there," she growled in a throaty tone. "Faster."

And with just a few concentrated flicks and teases of his tongue, Dane brought his ice queen to a rousing orgasm that shook not only her body, but his soul, as well.

Chapter 11

Dane sat up on the edge of the bed and stretched. Eryss had padded off to the bathroom. Taking a chance, he pulled open the drawer on the bedside table. He picked up the crystal dagger and studied it in the clear morning night. The skylights above the bed cast bright illumination. Combined with the stark white walls and bedding, they made the room feel like a winter wonderland escape, but cozy and with the scent of an exotic Indian market.

He placed the blade against the meat of his palm and then turned it to the opposite side. Both edges were sharp. Should he push just a little, he would draw blood. Impressive for a crystal. It was most likely quartz, but could be something else. He was surprised it didn't chip. And if it were actually used as a weapon? It would almost surely break off if embedded in skin or, even deeper, into muscle.

Unless it was enchanted or possessed a magical charm.

The thought unsteadied him. He'd just spent the night making love to Eryss, completely losing himself in her skin, sighs and kisses. Adoration was nothing compared to his obsession with her soft, wanting moans. He had worshipped as if a king on his knees before his queen.

He tapped the blade against the side of his hand. If the woman was a witch she shouldn't need a physical weapon. He smirked and carefully set the blade in the open drawer.

"I'm thinking oatmeal for breakfast."

He turned abruptly, not having heard Eryss come back from the bathroom. She wandered to the window in a long T-shirt that looked dreadfully thin, but he liked how the light shone through the fabric and outlined her shape.

"With blueberries and honey?" he suggested.

"I have honey. Valor is an apiarist. Her bees make the best honey."

"Does she also sprinkle in a little witchcraft to sweeten her wares?"

Eryss came over to kiss him, then tapped him on the nose. "How do you know my friends are witches?"

"I don't. Uh, *are* they? I mean, you do all work at a brewery called The Decadent Dames. If you were to go with the town spirit I imagine you might have called it something like The Cauldron."

"Ha! Too obvious. And the only cauldrons we use are the brew tanks. Though I do have a small iron pot I use for elixirs and spells. I guess you could call that a cauldron. Yes, my friends and I are witches. And you still don't believe. But that doesn't bother me because you're just—"

"Passing through?" He stood, letting the sheet fall away from his hips. He stretched up his arms.

Eryss drew her fingers down his abs and to the curls

nestled about his semierect cock. "Yes. I don't have much more time to enjoy you."

He sensed the sadness in her voice, and had to admit he felt equally sad knowing that soon he'd have to leave her. But this had never been a trip to discover a great romantic interest. On the other hand, he had discovered just that. And now, what would he do about keeping this gorgeous queen of his heart?

"What do we have going here, Eryss?" He pulled her against his chest and she nestled her mons against his cock. Now it was at full mast. "Beyond the sudden need to throw you on the bed and sink myself deep inside you?"

She teased her tongue out the corner of her mouth and gave him a delicious smile. "I thought we'd decided last night to call this a fling?"

"Yes, but I also sensed your need to go beyond that. *Is* it anything more?"

"Do you want it to be?"

She held such hope in her voice, he hated to disappoint her. Eryss was a phenomenal woman—but a woman who thought she was a witch. That was a problem for him. He didn't have the heart to debunk her.

And she did live halfway across the United States from him. "I'm not much for the cold."

"I've been keeping you nestled safely in my bed for days. And you did enjoy plowing snow."

"True. But also…"

"It's the witch thing, right? Listen, Dane, I like you. And this." She ground her hips against his cock, and he hissed out a breath that conveyed desire. "And everything we've been doing together. And when you leave I will not be happy about it. But we both know you're not much for, uh…snow. So there you go."

"There we go. Only…"

Only what? Why was he having such a difficult time simply allowing this liaison to be what it wanted to be?

"Only it's really good," she said, and glided her fingers down his abs toward his penis. When she gripped his cock firmly, he could do nothing but groan in agreement.

Eryss pulled out the glass jar of rolled oats from a lower cupboard. Dane had wandered into the conservatory, where he'd left his laptop. When he shouted her name, she stood up abruptly.

"Eryss? This is…ah, hell."

That didn't sound at all good. Leaving the oatmeal on the counter, she dashed down the hallway and through the open conservatory doors. An icy chill shivered across her shoulders. The first thing she noticed was that the plants were coated with snow, and the leaves were wilted and drooping. Some were even broken under the weight of snow.

"Over here! But be careful. There's broken glass. The window the branch landed on last night broke and fell in. It must have cracked more than we could initially see."

Eryss stopped on the grass where the snow had fallen. She wasn't wearing shoes, but could feel the earth tremble. It sent a shiver up her legs and into her being. "I can't believe we didn't hear that fall."

Dane's brow lifted. "We were quite industrious last night. And you did have the music on."

"Right. Oh, my plants. They've all frozen."

"Do you have a tarp? I can put up a ladder and fasten it over the opening in the roof until you can get a repairman to come out."

"No, I'll take care of that."

The broken glass was no problem for an earth witch.

Glass, after all, was just sand. As for the plants, Eryss had to act quickly if she wanted to save them. Some would surely be lost. Earth magic was desperately needed.

Bending, she placed her fingers in the grass and pushed down until she felt the earth. It was cool, but not terribly so.

"Eryss? What are you doing?" Dane wandered over.

She shouldn't do this with him as a witness. But right now she cared about the plants much more than freaking out a disbelieving scientist. And maybe it would be the kick he needed to get on board with believing in their possible shared past lives.

"Stand by the door," she said firmly. "I'm going to fix this."

"How? Wait. You don't think—magic isn't real, Eryss. You can't…" He sighed and wandered past her.

She couldn't care that he was going to witness something she probably shouldn't let him see. On the other hand, he wouldn't be able to deny what she was any longer. Seeing did make a believer. Or it should, anyway.

Closing her eyes and bowing her head, she began an incantation. Focusing on the elemental energies in the room and finding the shattered glass bits, she warmed them. Using the earth's vibrations and drawing them up through her system, she invoked the elements.

Glass shards rose from the snow-covered grass, dancing toward one another. She heard Dane's hiss of astonishment, but didn't shift her focus. Summoning an earth elemental, she asked for it to come to her as sand.

A tiny creature no larger than an egg popped up from the snow and shook its head. It spotted the moving shards and soared toward them, fixing itself to one shiny piece. The glass segments fitted together, melting and crystallizing as the elemental scampered over the surface, seemingly providing the sandy glue to mend them into one pane of smooth, clear glass, until the entire window was back in shape. It hovered above the ground, turning slowly, glinting in the morning light.

Behind her, Dane swore.

With a lift of her hand, Eryss directed the pane upward until it fit into the steel beams, and because of the lack of caulking, she directed the elemental to fly up and work its magic by melting the glass to the structure. It would hold until she could get a proper repair done in the spring.

With a thanks and blessing to the elemental, she dismissed it back to the earth from which it had come.

Now, for the plants.

Kneeling, she pressed her fingers farther into the grass until they dug into the soil, which had already begun to chill. She summoned the heat from the earth and the snow began to melt. Leaves dripped with moisture and some bent and furled upward as if to meet the sun, while others had been frozen beyond hope and remained lifeless. Infusing the soil with her own vita and spreading it out into the root system, Eryss bled her life into the flora until the scents of jasmine and rosemary freshened and curled about her body.

"I was wrong," Dane said behind her.

The room came alive. A dragonfly flitted above Eryss's head. The grass stretched upward and effused a green scent. Vines climbed toward their trellis. The emerald glass chandelier shivered, tinkling softly.

Eryss stood, but the incredible energy she'd just expended dizzied her senses, and she collapsed on the couch.

"Eryss!" Dane rushed to her and pulled the chenille blanket over her. Her work had also dried the couch and blanket, so it was warm and snug and felt like a safe landing place infused with vital energies as he tucked the wrap around her.

She nestled the blanket up around her neck and snuggled in, sighing a few times to release any of the negative energies her body may have sustained while healing the room.

And speaking of negative energies…she could feel Dane's consternation. His unwillingness to step beyond his rigid beliefs. His downright astonishment. It buffeted her air with a hot and bruising vibration. It took all her energy not to say in a snarky tone, *Debunk that, scientist.*

"What did you just do?" he asked. "Are you okay?"

"That," she said in an exhausted whisper, "was witchcraft."

"I know."

She knew she had just blown his mind. Now, to see how he would handle the truth. Wait. What had he just said? "You *know*?"

He nodded. "But I don't know what to say about…this. Let's go into the kitchen and…"

"I need to rest a bit," she said. "That took a lot out of me."

"I, uh…hmm. Yes. I think I should let you rest. Maybe I should…go outside, check the side of the conservatory for more damage. Yes. I'll, uh…the plants." He touched a fern leaf curled near the couch arm. "You gave them life. I saw it. I didn't expect this. I thought you were merely…"

She caressed his cheek. Soft stubble darkened his jaw. Worry danced in his eyes. Or was that fear?

"You need to distance yourself," she said. "And have a good scientific think. I understand. Go on. I don't mind. I won't be going anywhere today. It'll take that long to get back my energy."

"Is there something I can do for you? Bring you food?"

"No, I'm good. Please. Leave, if you have to. Do what you need to do. I'm good with that. Promise."

He nodded. "I'm not trying to run away. I just…" He pressed a few fingers to his brow and winced. "We do need to talk. I just didn't think… I'll check outside and then…"

"You need to be okay with what you saw. Go to the brewery and hang out in a corner. Do your internet searches. Argue with the scientist who wants to prove I don't exist. Concoct rational means to explain what you've just witnessed. When you've exhausted all possible explanations, then come back to me. And we'll talk."

"Yes, I'll…"

She took his hand and smoothed it. Dane leaned in and kissed her forehead. He stood and ran his fingers back through his hair. Without another word, he left her.

Was he running away from her truth? She would expect nothing less. Though she hoped for so much more. Like understanding. Had he run away from her through the centuries? Was that why she dreamed of a lover she had lost? Because he could never handle her being a witch? Why was she still unable to hold him after all this time?

He'd said he knew. She didn't understand what that meant, if not that he'd known she was a witch.

What was going on with Dane?

Chapter 12

Eryss watched out the corner of her eye as Dane appeared outside, on the other side of the glass conservatory wall. He studied it, scanning the whole side, around the back and up toward where the ceiling piece had broken out. He rubbed his jaw, then shrugged. His hair was coated with snow, and his shoulders were also snowy.

He should come inside and she'd muster up the energy to make some hot chocolate. But when she thought his gaze met hers and she lifted a hand to wave at him, he merely glanced aside and walked away, toward the garage.

He didn't come in. She waited another ten minutes before she recognized the sound of his rental car backing out and driving away.

Had she chased him off by casting magic in his presence? Of course she had. But in the moment, it had been the important thing to do. To show herself to him. For good or for ill.

With hope, it would eventually bring some good.

* * *

Dane had not gone to the brewery as Eryss had suggested. There was too much weirdness at that place. And there could be witches.

Real witches.

Not that he was afraid of witches. Yet he did have a wise caution toward the species. He'd been in the presence of only one during his stint with the Agency. She had actually worked for the Agency, and she'd provided historical backup on one of his first assignments—historical meaning she had informed him of the history of witches' persecution in Salem, a place he'd been sent to look into a claim that a doll was bewitching men into raping women. It hadn't been a bewitched doll, just a crew of misguided devil worshippers who had used witchcraft as a scapegoat for their own cruel choices.

And now there was Eryss.

He should not have left her alone, looking so tired and depleted. But he'd needed to step back and resituate his brain to take in things from a different perspective before he could have a rational discussion with her.

The witch.

The Agency debunked the paranormal species for the very reason that no human should ever have knowledge that such species existed. It was too dangerous. Thus, they put a scientific spin on the reason they couldn't possibly exist, and pointed the finger at the ridiculous believers. It was an effective means of diverting attention.

And for some poor souls, it offered them sanity. Freedom from the truth.

Even knowing paranormal creatures existed, every time he encountered another one Dane struggled with that sanity issue. It was so…impossibly bizarre. To know that vampires and faeries walked the same soil he did?

That there were shapeshifters and winged creatures that used the shadows for protection. And that witches, and even bloodsucking vampires, lived among the humans, and did it so well the majority of the population never caught on.

Until something went wrong, like a vampire's victim left dead in an alleyway, or a magical pendulum calling up demons in the middle of a ladies' afternoon church party.

So Dane had returned to the hotel and rented another room. Now he paced before the laptop set on the bed. A crumpled McDonald's bag had missed the trash, and his roasted coffee was cold and stank up the room. He'd accessed files on hoaxes and plants surviving frostbite and even how glass was made. Nothing could explain what he had witnessed when Eryss had knelt and put her fingers into the ground and literally raised the mended glass into the windowpanes and then…

"And then," he said in an awestruck whisper, "the plants!"

She'd brought them back from their damaged, lifeless state. Right before his eyes. Now, Dane knew that some plants were hardy and even survived harsh winters, and a light snowfall couldn't take out some flowers and bulbs. But broken stems and leaves had snapped back to health. Leaves turned brown by the icy bite of winter had become green again, and flowers that had shed their petals had resumed their full glory.

Witchcraft?

"Indeed."

Dane sat on the chair and shook his head. He'd exhausted the possibilities. A person *could* possess such extraordinary powers if she had been born a witch. So now he had to accept the truth.

He rubbed his brow tensely. How did he feel about it being the truth? Because the idea of witchcraft opened up all sorts of strange and not-so-welcome avenues. Mysticism, the occult and devil worship, for a start. Was Eryss a member of a coven?

Of course, the other women who worked at the brewery must be her coven mates. And they brewed up concoctions and sold them to the unwary public. What kinds of spells did they cast on the beer? He had drunk the beer. Was *he* under a spell?

He had not come to Minnesota on a witch hunt, but rather—

"The witch must die," he muttered now, memory jettisoning him back to his eight-year-old self when he'd held the sword before his mother's horrified eyes.

"No!" He stood and pushed aside the curtains to look over the snow-frosted parking lot below. The rental Ford sat beside a bare-branched maple tree.

Why was he questioning his beliefs?

"Because you know why you came here in the first place."

Who was Edison Winthur? Was he such a dreamer that Dane's mother couldn't handle his whimsy, and she'd divorced him? Why, then, had she married him in the first place? Surely, Edison must have been as absent-minded and whimsical when they'd married as the day they'd divorced?

Witches? Was that why his father had owned a witch blade? Or had he not known what the dagger had actually been used for?

What had Edison believed in? Would he scoff at his son's profession? Perhaps the man would argue against Dane's role in debunking the paranormal with fantastical reasons such that these things did exist. Why had Dane been denied those arguments? He wanted the man here. In his life. He wanted…simply to have known the one half of who had made him.

The divorce had occurred because Edison and Lillian Winthur were complete opposites. Just like Dane and Eryss. But Dane didn't need a woman like himself, or one who believed everything he did. He only needed to *understand* that other person's beliefs in order to accept and embrace her.

If he was going to allow his brain to accept that Eryss was a witch, then he should not immediately jump to the blaming and finger-pointing that would label her an evil entity or wicked. That was history and fiction and so much scapegoating. Women had suffered through the centuries for the idiotic misgivings of the majority. And the patriarchy. Men were historically the worst abusers and accusers. Some wore entitlement as if it were a family crest.

Dane shook his head and squeezed his eyelids shut. He must remain unbiased and unemotional about what he'd witnessed in the conservatory. Staying rational was his job! He could do that.

But how to keep back his emotions when Eryss had done such a good job of luring him into her life? He felt for her. Because he adored her. There was something about Eryss Norling that felt so right to him. And it wasn't because they had great sex together. He felt comfortable around her. Relaxed. As if he'd known her for a long time.

If reincarnation were possible, could he have known her in a previous life? She had intimated that they had known one another, and then she'd paused to see if he would agree. Yes, he believed in the soul, but it was incarnated into only one body, to live one life on this earth.

Or…maybe not?

"You are thinking like a madman." He checked his watch. What to do while stuck here? Perhaps he could have another go at convincing Gladiola to open the safe for him?

"Biometrics," he muttered about the safe.

He had no choice but to wait. Here. In this miserable little hotel room.

Or at Eryss's big, beautiful home filled with warmth and love and…witchcraft.

He shoved his hands in his pockets, and his fingers curled around something warm. He pulled it out to find a small blue stone. It was striated with gold flashes.

"Covellite. How did this…?"

Eryss had to have put it in his pocket. She of the crystals and foretelling symbols. This stone could be bewitched…

He was about to toss it onto the table by the phone, but then shoved it back in his pocket and sat on the bed instead. He pulled the laptop close and typed in "covellite," and then "healing stones." What came up was interesting.

"The doorway to remembering your past?" he read aloud from the web page.

Chapter 13

Eryss tested the dough that had risen on the counter throughout the afternoon. It had tripled in volume. She turned the oven on, then remembered to sprinkle sesame seeds across the top of the dough for abundance.

Then she recited a charm to keep herself from being upset when Dane left the state, because she had been the one to scare him off. She should have waited for him to leave and then repaired the window and the plants. But at the time, she hadn't had a moment to waste, or she would have risked losing so many more plants.

Finishing the charm, she pulled her fingers down from the crown of her head, envisioning a comforting white light surrounding her all the way to her bare toes. She wiggled them and pressed her palms together, tossing in a "blessed be" for good measure.

With the bread in the oven, she strode about the conservatory and noted that the plants had been decimated; about 10 percent hadn't made it. She started collecting spent blooms for tinctures, and would repot a few in an attempt to revive the roots, but some were simply dead. She could dry the heather and perhaps even get some use out of the alyssum, but the coltsfoot was a complete loss.

So sad. She should have checked the window last night. It was remarkable that she and Dane had been so loud they hadn't heard the falling glass. Of course, the glass had landed on a mossy pad that may have muffled the shattering. She checked the bee hut and found them nestled inside, snug as, well, bugs. And the butterfly terrarium held three chrysalises that would open in a few weeks. The temperature of the room had returned to a cozy seventy degrees, thanks to her having expended so much of her vita.

Now grounded and calm, she repeated her wish for love that she'd spoken during the anacampserote.

"Let me recognize it when it comes. And allow me to let him leave when he must."

She didn't suspect Dane would fall in love with her so quickly, and certainly she didn't believe in the whole love-at-first-sight thing. And she wouldn't perform a spell to put a man under her sensual thrall. Such spellcraft must be handled with utmost reverence for the heart.

Placing a hand over her own heart, she drew up energy from the earth through her bare feet and fixed it into her being. With a heavy exhalation to release doubt and anxiety, she nodded and said, "So mote it be."

At that moment someone rapped on the back door. Eryss's heart sped up. "Dane."

She rushed to answer the door, but when she gripped the knob she paused. Her heart raced with excitement. Giddiness sparkled in her veins. On the other side of the door stood a man who made her days bright and her nights delectable. He was smart, kind and funny. And…

She dared not doubt her intuition regarding their loving through the ages. She would not.

She opened the door to a short, stout man who beamed at her from above his thick, bright red knitted scarf. He held up a clutch of newspapers. She allowed her neighbor, who lived half a mile down the road, to collect the weekly shoppers shoved into her mailbox, but he didn't have to ask her permission to take them.

"I'm not sure now what I came up to your door for," he said.

"I have a stack of packing paper from the brewery," she offered. She saved the brown paper to give him for his projects. "Let me get it for you."

"I'm sorry for the way I left this morning," Dane said as he followed Eryss inside the house and toward the conservatory.

It was already dark outside, even though it wasn't yet five in the evening. Dane hadn't yet grown accustomed to the sun setting so early. He required surf and sunshine to feel alive and vital.

Eryss trailed the scents of bread and rosemary before him. She wore a long, flowing skirt with tiny pink flowers on a brown background, and her pink sweater was equally soft and sensual. Her hair, messily pinned on top of her head, spilled tendrils about her ears and neck. He wanted to touch the strands, press them to his nose and forget himself.

But first things first.

"It was rude of me to leave this morning without first talking to you. Hell, making sure you were okay."

"You were in shock after witnessing witchcraft," she said over her shoulder. "Something you couldn't flat-out debunk with a few scientific explanations." She stepped into the green room lush with floral and woodsy scents. "I figured you needed some time to sort things out. Come to terms with whatever beliefs you have, and decide whether or not they were worth opening wider, perhaps even inviting in new beliefs. And don't worry. I am okay."

She plopped onto the couch and picked up a basket of flowers she must have been sorting before he arrived, for she began to pinch off the petals and place the centers in a little copper bowl.

"So?" She looked up to him with a sweet smile.

Dane sat next to her, and her skirt wisped up onto his lap. He toyed with the soft fabric then leaned forward, pressing his elbows onto his knees. "So. I, uh… I do believe you, Eryss. I haven't been completely honest about my work." She cast him a searching gaze. "Before I get into that, can I have a look around in here? I mean, to make sure all the glass got swept up and—because you walk around with bare feet and—"

"Go ahead and verify whatever you need to verify, Mr. Scientist. I'll sit here, preparing these hibiscus petals for tea."

"Do you, uh…bewitch the tea?"

"Sometimes."

Right. And yet he was not going to insist on the impossibility of that, after what he'd witnessed. But he did indeed want to verify a few things. He slid a hand in his pocket and curled his fingers about the covellite. He wouldn't mention that. Yet.

Dane wandered to where the glass pane had landed and shattered on the moss floor. Squatting and gazing about the tight, loamy earth, he couldn't spy any slivers or shards of glass. And overhead he didn't see any strings or wires, nothing that may have facilitated raising the glass pane back up into the conservatory ceiling. No smoke or mirrors, for that matter.

The plant closest to him was a sansevieria with thick stems that he'd seen completely broken because the glass had hit it. He stroked his fingers over the glossy, wide leaves, which were intact and looking healthier than ever. Had she had time to replace the broken plants with new ones since he'd left this morning? Surely there were plant stores in the area.

No. There would be no purpose in Eryss putting on such a show to prove to him she had magical powers. Because really, she knew he was a skeptic. Or rather, she thought he was.

He was not. He believed in all of it. But he'd kept that truth from her, which could be construed as a lie. So now he had to get to his truth.

"Does it all check out?" Eryss asked, setting the bowl of flower petals aside and rising. She stretched out her arms as she yawned. "I did lose quite a few plants to frostbite. But I was able to save some for drying and to create some tinctures. I said a blessing to Airmid, goddess of plants and healing, as well."

Dane glided his palm over a glossy frond. "Shouldn't that have been a curse for not watching over your plants?"

"I would never curse nature. The falling window was meant to happen. I am thankful for everything I own, know and experience. The trees, flowers and grass? I am merely sharing this earth with them and I would never want to curse their vita."

Dane nodded. "You are forgiving, and your kindness is genuine. And…like I said earlier this morning, I do believe you are a witch."

With a careful smile, she approached him, though she

held her arms crossed under her breasts. She wasn't quite so ready to welcome him with open arms.

"So what prompted this sudden belief?" she asked. "You, the diehard scientist who debunks my kind? Who makes a point of telling others that what they think is real is not?"

"You should sit again." He gestured to the couch. "And whatever you do, please hear me out. I've only ever kept details about my job and certain beliefs from you because I didn't feel it necessary to reveal as much. We are required to not spill the beans. That's why our organization exists and how we manage to make it work."

"I'm not understanding," she said with a nervous laugh, teasing the ends of her hair. "You've lied to me?"

"Not at all. I just didn't explain everything." He gestured to the couch once more and she sat, tentatively. "I debunk the paranormal using science. And ninety-nine-point-nine percent of the time, whatever job or mission I've been sent on is nothing more than false beliefs and misunderstandings. Someone trying to be something they are not. Or someone believing in something that isn't at all what they want it to be."

"What about the other point-one percent?"

"The paranormal weapons, entities and/or creatures I encounter are real," Dane said calmly. He stood before her, unsure about sitting next to her. A confession would be given very soon. "And I know it's real because I've witnessed what real is. Trust me, I came to this job as skeptical in fantastical and mythological creatures as the next scientist. But once you've seen, you do believe."

"So why debunk something and go to all this trouble to prove that it isn't real?"

He splayed a hand before him. "You should understand that it's not wise for your kind, or vampires or werewolves, to be exposed. The less the public knows, the better. So if there is a vampire attack that leaves behind a victim with a suspicious bite mark, then the Agency's job is to swoop in and take care of matters."

"Like spin doctors?"

"Exactly. The founder of our organization actually started out doing spin work for a vampire slaying group. I'm not really allowed to speak of it, so don't ask."

"Would that be the Order of the Stake?" she asked slyly.

Dane gave a vague shake of his head. The woman knew her stuff. There was little need to expound on it.

Arms crossed over her chest, Eryss asked, "So you've come to Anoka to debunk witches?"

"Not at all. I've been truthful with you. I've come after a dagger. Actually, it isn't even a job. It was a curious weapon I discovered while going through some old files. It intrigued me because the former owner was listed as Edison Winthur."

"That's your last name. A relative?"

"My father."

"Oh. I…hmm…this is…a lot of information to take in."

"I'm sorry, Eryss. I didn't mean to deceive you. But you must understand that I am trained, first and foremost, to err on the side of humans being misled by false beliefs, and to protect them. You said you were a witch? There are many who believe as much and are no more than humans playing with mirrors and crystals. Kitchen witches."

"I get that."

"You do?" He exhaled in relief.

"But you do understand that I was born this way? That the spells and craft I perform are real and not silly things I've learned on the internet or in a book?"

He nodded. "After what I witnessed this morning? Oh yes. You most definitely are a witch."

She nodded. Uncrossed her arms. She seemed to be thinking deeply, then asked, "So how does that make you feel? Do you have encounters with the paranormal all the time in your work?"

"Rarely. I can count on one hand how many non-humans I've come across. You are my first witch."

"There's Mireio and Valor, as well."

He held up a few more fingers. "So that makes three. Are you angry with me?"

She shrugged and let out a sigh. "I don't see a reason to be angry. You've come clean with me. I appreciate that. But now I wonder what this means for my safety."

"Meaning?"

"Are you going to report me to your agency?"

"No, not at all."

"Do you hunt witches?"

"No. Never. Not me, anyway. Like I've said, my job is weapons. Interacting with another species doesn't often occur. Though I once went after a nasty chimera growling from high atop a redwood tree. It wasn't what I expected it to be."

"And what did you expect of a witch?"

He shrugged and winced. "Evil. Maybe a cackle or even green skin."

"Seriously?"

He again winced. "I'm kidding." But he wasn't. Not entirely.

She stood and hugged him, wrapping her arms around his neck and stepping her bare toes onto his shoe tips. "I do have a pointy hat somewhere. It was a costume. Mireio is always insisting we be witches for Halloween because it's the one time of year we can be truthful with people."

"I admit I am at odds with all this. I never expected the woman I find occupying my thoughts would be—"

"I think you're focusing too much on the label. Come here." She grasped his hand and tugged him over to the couch. Once snuggled beside him, she tilted her head onto his shoulder and again held his hand. "I was born this way," she said. "My mother was a witch—who never used the craft. She was trying to fit in with the humans. But she died about ten years ago from skin cancer."

"Shouldn't she have been able to cure herself with some potion or charm?" he asked, and then immediately saw the error in that question. "I'm so sorry. That was cruel. I shouldn't have said that."

"It's all right. You wouldn't be a very good scientist if you didn't ask the hard questions and seek the truth. It's what you do with that truth that determines what kind of man you are."

"I'm trying to handle your truth carefully and respectfully. I am sorry about your mother. Were you alone after that?"

"Yes, because my father went off traveling and found someone new immediately after that. I've been living on my own since I was fourteen. Well, under Mrs. McAlister's watchful eye. I knew Valor from grade school, so we've always been besties. She helped me through a lot. She's an old soul like me."

"Souls," Dane said, and then quoted one of his favorite lines. "'You do not have a soul, you are a soul. You have a body.'"

"Attributed to C. S. Lewis, though it was never proven he actually wrote that."

"It's a lovely sentiment, though."

"It is. Even more so coming from you. Did I tell you that when we first met, my soul recognized yours?"

"Really?" More of her witchy weirdness. Dane clenched a fist, but then released it. He was just going to go with it, remember? Because he had no choice but to believe now. "How so?"

"It's an inner feeling. A deep knowing."

"Is that to do with the reincarnation thing? Do you really believe we were once lovers?"

"Anything is possible. We have lived lives before and we did know one another. But in what capacity, I can't be sure. I have dreams of a long-lost lover. But I never see his face. So many times I dream of reaching for his hand and our fingertips touch, and yet we can never quite clasp hands. I know we loved without question and with our souls completely."

"That sounds romantic. It can't be me."

"It could have been you."

"Do you often dream of lovers?"

"Yes. But only the one." She smiled and tapped his chest, but retracted her finger quickly. "But lately I've been having the nightmares, too."

"I witnessed that. I could feel the tension in you even as I lay there, still in a reverie."

"I didn't want you to notice."

"Yes, well uh…" He dug out the stone from his pocket. "Did you place this here? Is it under a spell?"

She nodded. "It's for remembering things. Like past lives. But no spell, just the stone's own energy."

"I see. So you wanted to see if I would remember us together in the past?"

"Always worth a try."

"I wish you would have just asked me instead of being sneaky about it. I prefer truth and forthrightness."

"This coming from the guy I thought could never believe I am a witch."

"Yes, well, what is it they say? Seeing is believing?"

"Believing allows you to see." She touched the covellite. "It's just a stone to you, anyway. Something pretty."

He swallowed and held it up before him. "Pretty, yes. Capable of making me have visions?"

"You had a vision? Dane, seriously, tell me."

"No, I did not. I rented a hotel room again. Didn't want go into the brewery after…you know. Anyway, I did a little research on witchcraft with hopes of debunking your window thing. To no success."

She stood and ran a hand through her hair. "So…the dream that woke me the other morning?"

"Yes. Will you tell me what it was about?"

"I dreamed I'd been stabbed. And in turn had stabbed my attacker. We'd killed one another."

"That's morbid. *I* was a catalyst to such a dream?"

"I'm not sure. I went to a soul seer and she was able to interpret the dream for me. That was the first time I've dreamed of being stabbed by a man. Blood was everywhere. I can never see his face, but I instinctually know it has happened many times. The soul seer was able to tell me that it's happened *every* time I've been reincarnated."

Dane looked directly at her. "That's scary. And strange. But you know, it could have been a recall from some detective murder show you watched late one night."

"Dane, I don't own a TV. And you don't have to believe anything I say, but I have to tell you this. So you know where I stand."

He spread out his hands, gesturing for her to go on.

"The soul seer said I have never made it to my thirtieth birthday. That this man I've dreamed about always manages to kill me before then. And in turn, I kill him."

"That's crazy. Your thirtieth is in just a few days! As is mine."

Eryss shook her head. "And in my dream, or nightmare—whatever you want to call it—the man who stabbed me said he wouldn't stop until I burn."

"Why would he say such a thing?"

"Because he's a witch hunter."

Dane opened his mouth to speak, but nothing rational came to mind. So that's why she'd asked if the Agency hunted witches. "But in your dreams he never does burn you?"

"No. Burning a witch brings her final death. I mean, you can kill us in other ways, but our souls survive and live on. You know that, yes?"

He splayed out a hand. "Basically. I haven't done a lot of research on your kind. Your souls live on?"

"Reincarnation, don't you know? Sometimes even spontaneous regeneration. You need fire to ensure a witch's death is permanent."

"Interesting. As I've said, you are my first. I'm not up on witch lore." He tossed her the stone, not wanting to have the thing in his hands any longer. Spell or not, it was weird. But since she was spilling everything to him, he might as well step in deep. Any opportunity to learn must be taken. "I guess you walk a wide circle around fire?"

"I do. Fire magic is not something I'd ever try, but there are witches who have mastered it. Anyway, to get back to my dreams, I then say to the man that my soul will live forever, thanks to our love."

"Love?"

She nodded. "Apart from the recent nightmare, I've had a recurring dream for years. About a long-lost love. My soul mate."

"Whom you have implied could be me."

"Yes. I recognize your soul, Dane. It came to me as a

feeling that first night at the ball when we danced. You don't have to accept that, but I do."

"But this soul mate man and the man who stabs you are not one and the same?"

"I don't believe so. I mean, I certainly hope not. That would imply…" She gestured toward him, but snapped her hand back to her chest. "I have lost a lover that has been with me in many lifetimes. Possibly you. And then there's this other man, who basically kills me in every lifetime. Maybe that's the reason I keep losing the lover? Because I'm dead? This is confusing. I know you're not a witch hunter."

Dane's muscles stiffened. He'd just been thinking, as he'd sat in his hotel room searching the internet for information on witches, that he'd become a sort of witch hunter. But that was contained to research. He was not a person who armed himself with weapons and malicious intent against another.

The witch must die. Why had he said such a thing when he was just a child?

"No, I'm not," he said. "Do you know who this witch hunter is?"

She shook her head. "Haven't a clue. You don't have the desire to hunt me, do you?" she asked with a nervous chuckle.

"Absolutely not! Eryss, I would never. Historically, it's all a lot of false accusations and a patriarchal exercise of power. Witches do not…" He fisted his hand and rubbed the knuckles. It was a little harder to profess such a belief now when his convictions were being tugged every which way. "Do you really believe—"

"No." She tugged his hand into hers and leaned over to kiss him. "I don't believe that about you. And I know you're not a witch hunter. On the other hand, debunking witches *is* another way of hunting them, yes?"

"Hunting, to me, implies debunking rather than condemning or even killing. The sort of hunting the Agency does is always ultimately focused on protecting."

"That's a good thing."

"Yes, but I haven't lived before, Eryss. I know that. And yet—I'm questioning that belief now."

"There might be a way to find out. I can do a sort of past life regression on you."

"No, thank you. That's pushing it. You wouldn't learn anything, anyway."

"I thought you were a scientist. Aren't you the one who will leave no stone unturned to learn the truth?"

"I *know* the truth."

"Do you?"

He sighed heavily. The truth was far more dangerous than he'd ever believed. "What does it require?"

"Trust. And whiskey and fire."

Dane lifted a brow. "I'm intrigued. Damn me, but I am."

She kissed him. "Then let's do this."

Chapter 14

Red smoke swirled about Dane's head, imbuing his senses with sulfur and sage. It tickled his nose. The swallow of whiskey no longer burned, yet the alcohol warmed his chest. Eryss's chanted words blurred into nonsense as his eyelids fluttered. He felt as though he were falling backward…

He caught himself against the iron streetlamp and hissed when a dusting of soot sprinkled his cheek. He wiped it away with the back of his hand and then realized he'd smudged it over the ruffled hem of his white sleeve. Fool. And he'd taken an inordinate amount of time preparing for this meeting tonight. Had even bathed and slicked pomade through his light, curly hair, and trimmed his beard.

He pulled down the velvet coat sleeve in hopes the smudge would not be noticeable. He needed to make a good impression, or he would go mad with the pent-up desire that had been brewing ever since he'd laid eyes on her. The woman from the art gallery who had stood transfixed before John Byam Liston Shaw's painting Now Is Pilgrim Fair Autumn's Charge. *It was such an evocative piece. Witchcraft entered his mind just looking at it, though it was deemed an allegory to the fall harvest.*

He'd walked up behind the woman, transfixed by her porcelain skin, her plump mouth barely open. The scent of roses filled the air about her. He'd wanted to sniff at her hair, draw her into his senses. So he had, and she'd turned around, and just when he'd expected her to renounce him as a scoundrel, she had smiled brightly and laughed.

Ah, the night smelled fresh and devoid of the usual distasteful scents. But he picked up roses. So close. He felt warm hands cover his eyes and the rose leaned in to whisper, "I'm here."

He turned and drew her into his arms and kissed her.

A snap nearby startled Dane out of the vision, and he felt like he'd been suddenly dropped back into his body. The rush of blood heating his veins made him lift his arms and stare at his hands. And then he noticed Eryss smiling at him, the bright illumination gleaming in through the windows falling over her as if she were an angel glowing. Was the moon full? No, it just looked like it, all orange and hanging low in the sky.

Did he smell…roses?

He sat upright and slid his feet to the floor. Grass. A cursory glance didn't produce any roses. Before his bare feet sat the mandala Eryss had created earlier with various crystals, from rose quartz and carnelian, to the covellite and violet-and-green labradorite. Tiny Herkimer diamonds were set around the circumference to "heighten the experience," as she had explained. At the center, a yellow candle released red smoke. The same smoke she'd used to induce him into the trance with but a whisper of her witchy words.

The room's humid warmth made him smile, and he was thankful to be back in the present. And yet, had he really just looked into a past life? Felt the warmth of that woman's kiss, and smelled her rose perfume? Impossible.

"So?" Eryss asked eagerly.

Dane rubbed his palms together. He looked harder at the surrounding plants and flowers. Nope, no roses.

"You saw something," she prompted. "It's been five minutes."

"Eryss, now listen. I know you don't have a television, but I do. And I have a penchant for watching historical dramas. I enjoy them. So I'm quite sure that what I saw was a memorized conglomeration of things I've seen in movies and television shows. In fact, there have been times I've had occasion to wonder what it would have been like to live in the late nineteenth century—the bohemian age. There's a scientific term for this wondering. Something like dream incorporation."

"Sure, whatever. So you flashed back to bohemian times? What did you see?"

He stood to pace toward the window. Surprised at how unsettled he was over it all, he inhaled and exhaled deeply. The beeswax candle wisped tendrils of sweet smoke, and entangled with the foliage; the perfume was heady. But it wasn't roses. Could a witch bewitch him to see things? Had he really been hypnotized or in some kind of trance? The images he'd seen had felt weirdly... familiar, no matter how he tried to account for it with reason.

Perhaps any rational explanation was simply beyond reason and he should accept that. It wasn't as though the experiences connected to his job were normal to begin with.

He glanced at Eryss. Such hope in her eyes. She was always so bright and hopeful. He adored that about her. No matter how many times he'd laughed at her truths, she'd simply smiled and kissed him.

"Fine," he said. "If what I experienced in the dream, or whatever it was, was true—and I won't commit to saying it was—then I was in the nineteenth century. Or I assume it was my idea of me. I didn't see a face, because, well, obviously I was embodied, and one cannot see one's own face in a dream, yes?" He didn't look to her for reassurance. Such a confession felt weak and as if he were acting against everything his scientific education had led him to believe. "I was wearing a velvet coat and waiting for someone."

"A woman?"

He raked his fingers through his hair and sighed. "Isn't there always a woman in the dramatic romances?"

"Dane!"

He flung up his hands in defeat. "It was a foolish exercise. I'm sorry. I think we're finished with this topic. I'm going to head into town for the night. Harold is due back on a flight this evening, so I expect he'll be in first thing in the morning."

"Yes, of course. You don't want to stay here tonight?"

"I, uh…"

"Don't worry about it." She bent to pick up a few of the crystals. "I have a lot to clean up here in the conservatory. You go. Give things a good think."

She always suggested he do that when she wanted to exert her beliefs on him. Reincarnation? Was he ready to believe in that? Obviously not, since all he desired right now was to put himself as far from Eryss as he could.

"I'll give you a call," he said.

And it tore at his heart to walk away from her, pull on his coat and gloves, and leave the house. He knew he had hurt her with his abrupt departure. Again. He'd hurt himself, too. But it had gone beyond what he was able to deal with. He accepted she was a witch. The truth had been shown to him.

The reincarnation thing? Not on his life.

His one life.

Perhaps it was best if he stayed away from Eryss Norling until after he'd gotten what he'd come to town for. To really know what it had meant when he'd held the dagger as a child. Was it the same dagger he now sought?

If magic was involved, his world was going to grow only more unstable, and his beliefs would be cracked wide open.

Oh man, what had the witch done to him?

Eryss had been watching the antiques shop across the street for half an hour. Harold always tended to go in to work around eight in the morning, and today should be his first day back, if Dane had understood correctly that he was on a flight back last night. Of course, he could take the day off, but Eryss hoped the old man would want to go in, knowing that Dane had been waiting for him for a week.

She must get to Harold first. Why? Because she sensed there was something about the dagger Dane sought. And if it had been handed down through generations?

"He could be the witch hunter," she murmured, elbows resting on the bar and her cheek to her palm, so she had a good view across the street. "Is that possible? Without knowing?"

It seemed as impossible to her as witches must have once seemed to Dane. But she had a feeling, and feelings must never be ignored.

She only wished that Dane would have a feeling about trusting his instincts regarding reincarnation. He had obviously seen a past life, and that had freaked him out. Stepping back and giving him breathing room had seemed the best option. But she'd missed him terribly last night. Her bed had never felt so empty.

And what was that about?

Well, she knew what it was about. She'd fallen for the guy.

Eryss straightened abruptly at the sight of the tall, slender gentleman, scarf across his face to reveal only his eyes, headed toward the antiques store, one arm loaded with a brown paper bag full of stuff sticking out the open top.

"Harold!" She dashed out the door and across the street in only a skirt and sweater, no outerwear. "Hey, Harold!"

He entered the shop, then turned to glare at her as she came in right behind him. He had never made it a secret that he didn't like her type. He assumed she was a witch, though Eryss couldn't ever recall giving him good reason to believe such. Gladiola must have said something to him. "Miss Norling."

"How was your trip?" she asked.

"It was fine, just fine. I do enjoy the Hawaiian tropics. But terrible circumstances for our visit."

"Oh, yes, of course. How's your wife?"

"Lovely. She's taking the day off, but I suspect Gladiola has already beat me in today, as she usually does.

Uh, you're here rather early. You know we don't open for two hours?"

"Right, and I hate to barge in on you like this. I'm sure you have a lot of catching up to do. But I've become friends with Dane Winthur, the man who I presume your sister told you has been waiting for your return?"

"Yes." He set the bag on the counter and pulled away the scarf to reveal a thick white beard. It was the only hair he had, because he was bald up top. "I have an item for Mr. Winthur."

"I know. As I understand, it may be a family heirloom. I thought I'd pick it up for him. Surprise him with it."

"Hmm…" Harold eyed her suspiciously. While he was always courteous toward her, there had been the incident two Halloweens earlier when he'd come right out and accused her of being a witch. With great gusto. "No, sorry. I can only hand it to Mr. Winthur. It's a valuable item, you understand."

"Oh. I can pay you for it. Dane will pay me back. I really wanted to surprise him. He's been muddling about Anoka for a week, trying to get used to our winter. He needs a pick-me-up."

"I'll be here when he gets here. I texted him. He should arrive soon."

Shoot. Eryss sucked in the corner of her lip. She wanted to get her hands on the thing before Dane did. So…a touch of magic would be necessary.

Crossing her forefingers, she leaned forward and whispered—

"That'll be enough from you then, Miss Norling." Gladiola Stuart marched right up to the counter and startled Eryss out of the spell. "You run along. You heard Harold. He's waiting to hand the valuable item over to its rightful owner. Good morning."

The woman knew she was a witch, and would not brook any shenanigans. So Eryss nodded and turned to grasp the door handle. "Cinder falls," she muttered as she left. A curse for misfortune concerning finances, especially in retail. It wasn't strong and would dissipate in a week.

Feeling not a bit of guilt, Eryss crossed the street.

Harold Stuart followed the witch's retreat across the street and into the brewery. Those women brewed spells into their beers. He'd once purchased a growler and had taken it home to test the ingredients. He knew how to reverse-engineer spells.

But he couldn't kill a witch. He hadn't the stomach for it. Murder wasn't his thing. And besides, he'd promised his wife he wouldn't kill again after that incident twenty years ago involving the demon. What a mess.

Anyway, those witches across the street would finally meet their end. The witch hunter was in town.

"Our savior has arrived in the Winthur man," he said as he turned to head to the office.

"Mr. Winthur? He's no witch hunter."

"He is." Harold punched in the digital code for his office door. "He just doesn't know it yet."

Chapter 15

Dane was ready to leave town. And yet, he was not.

If he and Eryss worked out their differences, what kind of relationship could they possibly have long distance? He wasn't about to move to Minnesota. And she had a business to run here. She wouldn't move for him. After knowing one another only a week? That would be illogical.

So he had to mark this off as an affair he would never forget, and move on. But maybe the occasional visit and some sexting? He could get behind that. On the other hand, Eryss deserved a man's full attention, not a few heart and kiss emojis on a cell phone.

Eryss's dreams of him being her long-lost love and of being stabbed by a witch hunter had seemed like nonsense to him. Yet he did believe in witches, and perhaps they could portend the future.

But he wasn't the man she thought he was, though he

couldn't deny his inexplicable pull toward her. But her long-lost lover? Nope. No way.

That didn't mean, however, that he wouldn't pursue the chance of being her current lover for as long as possible.

He sighed and pulled on the tweed vest that reminded him of his father. As a boy, Dane had been obsessed with that single photograph of Edison, who had worn a tweed vest over a crisp white shirt that had sported rolled-up sleeves. When Dane had asked his mom about him, she'd tugged the photo from him and stuffed it away. Why had she hated Edison so? And after only three years of marriage? She had to have learned something about him that went against all she believed in.

Dane touched his cell phone. If he called her with questions, she'd divert him away from the truth, and he had played that game too often. It was time to get his own answers.

He would pick up the dagger, and then maybe a few extra days in this icebox of a tundra would be well worth it to his heart.

Dane strolled into the antiques shop, got a whiff of freshly baked chocolate chip cookies and veered toward the counter, where Gladiola sat smiling up at him.

"Good afternoon, Miss Stuart."

"Same to you, Mr. Winthur. How are you enjoying our weather?" She pushed the laden plate toward him.

Dane picked up a still-warm cookie. *Bless the woman.* "I'm acclimating. Four degrees below zero? Bring it on!"

"It's going to be twenty below tonight," she said eagerly. Then she lowered her gaze suspiciously to the leather loafers he wore over thin socks. "You ready for that?"

He almost choked on the cookie in his mouth. He grinned and forced a nod, because he couldn't speak—and felt it best he not do so, anyway.

"My brother got home last night. He's been waiting for you. You can go into the back room." She pointed down a long, narrow aisle lined with assorted antiques and artifacts. "Walk all the way back and give a knock on the door to the right. Take another cookie with you, too."

He palmed a cookie and nodded more thanks. Twenty below? He might have to fill his pockets with cookies to keep his body temperature regulated. Ha! Now there was an enterprising idea. A cookie-fueled body warmer?

Passing a wooden sled outfitted with rusty metal runners, he cringed to imagine sledding in this weather, or the proverbial wet-tongue-to-icy-metal scenario.

At the back of the shop he turned to the right and stopped before a brushed-steel door with a digital entry keypad. Oddly James Bond–like. A thief would have a hard time breaching that one. Did the old man and his family make such a bundle selling dusty old crap from bygone eras that they needed the highest security?

He knocked, but before he could get the second rap in, the door opened and the man inside welcomed him across the threshold. Feeling a bit like a vampire—and in the Halloween Capital of the World, why not?—Dane stepped into the cramped office, about twenty feet long by eight feet wide. It was as cluttered as the store, but had a narrow aisle from door to desk. Harold offered a firm grip and vigorous handshake. The man was about six feet tall, thin as a rapier, and wore a green-and-blue vest over his white shirt. Smart dresser.

"A pleasure to meet you, Mr. Winthur. When your office told me the coincidence in your relationship to Edison Winthur, I must admit I wasn't too startled."

"And why is that?"

"Well! The history behind this dagger. Do you know it?"

"Only that it is rumored to have once belonged to a witch hunter. But I can assure you, while I never knew my father, I am quite certain he was not a witch hunter."

And Dane would again assume the role of nonbeliever. He had no reason to take this man into his confidence. This was just another deunking job, as far as he was concerned.

"No, I don't believe he was. The dagger tends to find its way into the right hands, though. Have a seat!" Harold pointed out a chair that Dane had not noticed, tucked as it was among ephemera. "I'll get it out of the safe."

Choosing to stand, Dane watched as the man pushed aside a stack of accountant's boxes to reveal the cinder block wall, and set into that, a digital panel. Harold leaned forward, opening his eyes wide. A green light beam swept the scan and something clicked. The safe door popped open, and Harold withdrew a long, darkly stained box from within.

"Biometric," Dane commented. "You get your hands on a lot of valuable antiques in this little shop?"

"Oh, you'd be surprised the things that touch my palms, young man. But I must say this is the most intriguing. And beneficial."

"Beneficial? How is a sword beneficial?"

"It's not a sword in the official medieval sense. It's more a dagger. A baselard, I believe. It was a common weapon in the thirteenth century." Harold handed the box to Dane. "It's rosewood, the case. Very pretty, yes?"

"It is." It had a good weight to it, and was carved

elaborately with ivy, arabesques and berries over the entire surface, save the smooth bottom.

"Haven't opened it," Harold said. "And you should not, either. Not here, at least."

"Why not? Are you sure there's a dagger in here?" He sat now, studying the cover by running his thumbs along the seamed edge until he found the front of the box.

"Oh, it's in there. I acquired it some twenty-eight years ago and handled it then. But don't open it! Just... can't you feel it?"

Dane looked up into the old man's steel-gray eyes. He was waiting for something. And that was almost as disturbing as the sudden vibrations that seemed to hum from the box itself. Dane pulled his palms away from the wood.

"That's it! You're the one. I was wrong about Edison, but you—you! I knew it!" Harold clapped his hands together. "You're him. You just don't know it yet."

"Him?" Now unsure if he wanted to open the box, Dane tugged it against his lap. Something weird was up. Then again, had anything *not weird* occurred since he'd set foot in this town?

"Mr. Stuart, can you tell me how you came to have this dagger? And how do you know my father once owned it? I'm sure you are aware of what I do, but what is more intriguing to me than a dagger that may have once been used to slay witches is that my father touched it. I never knew him."

"I know that, boy. And there is a lot of history in that dagger. I traveled to Thailand with Edison Winthur on a spelunking expedition, which is how I came to own this beauty. Edison happened across the blade while we were in Bangkok, about thirty years ago. He bought it. Played around with it a bit, but lost interest quickly enough. Though he said something once like 'it picked me out, wanted me to buy it.' I thought it kind of kooky at the time, but I've since learned—or rather, remembered—that the universe will put a man where he needs to be, when he needs to be there. Because that dagger?" He placed a hand over his heart. "I have known it."

Great, another hippie woo-woo believer in past lives. Dane smoothed his palm over the wooden case. He desperately wanted to open it. The eight-year-old child in him wanted to rip off the cover and— But he was even more curious about any information Mr. Stuart could impart about his father.

"I did some research on the dagger and came up with the witch hunter information you have," Harold continued. "It meant nothing to Edison. In fact, as fantastical as that man's mind was, it insulted him that I would suggest the dagger could be his. He left the city before me," Harold said, "but left the dagger behind. I've had it all these years. Sort of a remembrance of your father. But as well, I always had hopes of finding its true owner."

True owner? Yeesh. Dane didn't want to ask.

"What can you tell me about my father? Why was he fantastical?"

"Oh, he was always talking about writing stories about faeries and elves. That kind of funny stuff. We met in a spelunking club, of sorts. Edison loved exploring caves and geodes. Liked to take in the energy of the crystals. Said it fueled his stories."

Dane almost choked on his own breath. He curled his fingers over the box lid, bracing for the wild story that would no doubt follow.

"We got high a lot." Harold chuckled. "We were young." He offered a shrug as explanation. "Your father was a remarkable man. He told me he wanted to have children someday. And he did. You were born the year after we met."

Dane nodded. "I have a difficult time believing he was so...fantastical. I understand he used to teach geology at Caltech. I started there."

"But the Agency came looking for you."

"How do you know that? I was the one who contacted you. You couldn't have possibly—"

"I know some things." The old man winked at him. "I've done research over the years. And no, your father had no idea about the truth behind that dagger. The damascening on the blade tells a story. Legend says it adjusts and reforms into a new design with every kill."

Dane cringed at that word. He gripped the cover.

"No, don't open it here. There's so much energy connected to that old thing, I'm not sure my heart can take it." Harold patted his chest pocket. "Had to take my nitro pills on the flight home. Whew! That trip wore me out. I'm not a young man anymore. Just...take it back to wherever you're staying. Open it up. Breathe it in. Handle it. You'll know. And when you do, give me a call. Because that, my son, is your dagger."

Dane shook his head. "It's not. It wasn't even my father's. It was just a trinket that caught his eye on a shopping trip."

And he had traveled all this way for that: a trinket. *Disheartened* was describing his mood right now.

"Dane Winthur." Harold leaned forward and tapped a stiff finger on the top of the box. "I made that dagger for you."

"What?" Dane stood, unnerved at the man's intensity. "This dagger is centuries old. As you've stated, thirteenth century. I'll have to bring it back to the lab to test—"

Harold stepped up to Dane. "I made it in a former life."

"Ah. Well. Not you, too?"

"Too?" The old man thought about it, his eyes seeking out the door. "Right. The witch. She needs dealing with."

Dane's mouth dropped open at the man's blatant suggestion that perhaps he might "deal with" the witch across the street. But he didn't say anything. Yet the shock he felt was combined with curiosity and desperation.

Harold knew about witches. Eryss. And past lives. And he had made this dagger? Every fiber in Dane's being wanted to laugh and put a spin on the ridiculous suggestion, but he was no fool.

Not anymore.

As he tucked the box under an arm, he got the intense sensation that he was standing out in the snow, dagger in his hand and blood dripping from the shiny blade. He could smell the metallic taint of the ruby snow, and a shiver at the back of his neck stiffened his muscles.

He shook his head. The vision blurred back to Harold's face.

"It's talking to you, isn't it?" Harold asked eagerly. "You were lost for a moment there. I saw it."

"I don't…" No, he wasn't going to dignify the man's conjectures with an affirmative reply. Not when he had such little sense of what the hell was going on. "How much do I owe you?"

"Nothing. It is *your* blade. You'll realize that soon enough!"

And Dane found himself swiftly walking away from the crazy old man, box clutched to his chest. As he neared the front counter Gladiola held out the cookie plate. He reflexively grabbed one, mumbled a thank-you and headed out into the bracing cold. As he stood before the antiques shop door, staring across the street at the brewery, the cookie crumbled and scattered on the sidewalk dusted with white salt.

"I am not a witch hunter," he muttered.

Chapter 16

Eryss watched Dane exit the antiques shop and veer directly for the parking lot down the block. He didn't glance in the direction of the brewery. Instead he clutched a long box to his chest, which looked just the right shape to contain an ancient dagger.

Did he look…determined? Almost driven to avoid looking across the street in the event he might spot her?

She blinked, sending the teardrop down her cheek in a hot, stinging trail. "Stop it," she admonished her dramatic heart. But it was too late. She'd fallen for the guy. Hard.

Valor strode in with a box of T-shirts in hand. She dropped it on the floor and tugged her ponytail back over a shoulder. "Was that your man I just saw rushing toward the parking lot?"

"He's not *my* man. Never was," she said with a choking swallow. *Yes, he was. Had been. Through so many lives.*

Oh, Dane. Who are you? "He's headed to the hotel to take a look at his new sword. Or blade or whatever it is."

"He didn't stop in to show you?"

"Apparently not."

Valor looked out across the street, where Gladiola was currently hanging Valentine's Day decorations in the window. "Huh. What's up with the old lady?"

"I don't know." Eryss joined Valor in looking out the window. Gladiola noticed them, crossed herself, then skittered back from the window. "Whoa."

"That was unusual," Valor said.

"Ya think?"

"I know Gladiola knows we're witches, but I've never known her to go all *cast out thee witches*, with protective gestures. Strange."

"Curious. And worth some research. You got time to look up Harold Stuart on the internet?"

"Nope. I've got a date. And you're the internet chick, remember?"

"Right. Have a good time."

As Valor left in a breeze of sage and motor oil, Eryss opened the laptop and skirted around the end of the bar to sit on a high stool. She typed in Harold's name and the city, but the only hits were the Stuart's Stuff antiques store. Hmm…what was up across the street?

Dane closed the hotel room door behind him and set the box on the edge of the bed. He almost opened the latch, but pulled out his phone instead and selected the camera app. Then he opened his laptop to the browser. He would take pictures as he methodically went along. An unboxing of sorts. It would have been standard procedure had he been back at the lab with any other newly acquired weapon or artifact. And all Agency field workers were required to record as much as possible.

This was exciting. And nerve-racking. Harold's weirdness had gotten to him. The old man couldn't know a thing about what this dagger meant to him or his father or anyone. He was just a fanatic capitalizing on the paranormal vibe for which the city was famous.

Opening the fridge door, Dane pulled out an overpriced bottle of water. Two swallows later, he tossed the empty bottle in the trash can.

"Okay." He patted his chest, then nodded. "I'm ready."

His father had bought this dagger on a whim thirty years ago. What would have happened if Edison had not died and perhaps had been around to hand this blade to Dane himself?

According to Harold, Edison had been uninterested in the weapon's lore. And yet Harold had confirmed his father's whimsical nature. It seemed such a man should have been fascinated by the dagger. How could Harold possibly have known to keep it after his father had abandoned it? To save it for the real owner, whom he suspected was Dane? At the time, Dane hadn't even been born.

Sitting on the bed, he stroked the edge of the wood box. He wondered if residue of his father's essence remained imbued within the rosewood. When he was little, he'd had a pillow his grandmother had made him from one of his father's shirts. Sometimes, as he lay there wondering what his father might have been like, he'd fallen asleep with tears spilling over his cheeks and into the fibers of the fabric. Would his father have tucked him in at night and kissed him on the forehead, as his mother had?

You don't have to believe in reincarnation for it to exist.

Had he ever crossed paths with a reincarnated form of Edison Winthur's soul? It was a fantastical notion. And it was something Dane wanted to believe in. If only to feel his father's presence now, as an adult, when he had the faculties to put that experience to memory and keep it forever.

And if witches, vampires and demons did exist, why not the renewed soul? Had he discounted something as myth when he so easily embraced those legends of which he'd been given proof? Vampires and werewolves? Yes, they existed, because he had seen them and witnessed their supernatural power.

Yet how to prove a soul's return to a new life after death?

Eryss believed she had been reincarnated many times. She simply knew it. In her soul.

Dane shook his head. The more he thought about it, it didn't get any easier to accept. He wanted to accept it for the simple reason that it would give him comfort regarding his father's soul. Or maybe not. Shouldn't his father's soul be at rest?

"Hell." All this talk about reincarnation had really messed with his beliefs. He didn't know what to believe anymore.

So he'd start with the tangible.

He glanced at the box. It didn't feel like the closure he'd been seeking. Come to think of it, he'd always had closure. What Dane really desired was an awakening, a *knowing*. What had his eight-year-old self been up to?

He should be sharing this moment with Eryss.

He straightened and crimped his brow. It didn't seem

right not to share such an interesting discovery with her. And yet, what Harold had said resounded within him. This was something so personal to Dane. He'd show her later tonight.

Still, he couldn't shake the feeling he was missing out on something—or rather, some*one*—by sitting alone in the hotel room with a box of hope and mystery beside him.

Then again, he did like making new discoveries on his own. It was always easiest to attribute findings to him alone when it came to filling out the forms for headquarters.

"Very well then."

He leaned over the box. The carvings were smooth and deep. Not Celtic. Maybe Scandinavian? His father's side was Dutch, as far as he knew. But this box could have been anything that Edison Winthur had picked up in a shop. Perhaps it was Swiss? Dane didn't suspect the box's design held importance.

"Let's see what was worth spending a week in the tundra for, shall we? I mean…me." He looked across the bed to where Eryss might have sat, feeling as much anticipation as he did. "Later," he promised his heart.

As he laid a palm over the box top, he smiled, because he knew he hadn't suffered the elements simply tucked away in this room, bemoaning the terrible timing of the antiques shop owner's dead family member. Instead, Dane had met Eryss Norling, and he was pretty sure his life would never again be the same.

Pushing back the unlatched lid revealed a tangle of crimped brown paper shreds often used to pack artifacts. The thin strips scattered as he nudged them aside and felt the hard, smooth edge of what must be the blade handle or hilt. Curling his fingers about it, Dane pulled it out and couldn't contain an appreciative whistle.

"Nice."

He'd laid hands on many a fascinating weapon in his service to the Agency. Some were wildly curved blades like something depicted in fantasy paintings; others glowed or were even so cold he could barely touch them. A few took a while to figure out. And the first time he'd ever held a titanium stake from the Order of the Stake, the tip had plunged out from the protective column so quickly it had poked his wrist and he'd dropped it in the garbage bin because he was so startled.

He laughed now to think of that. But this blade wasn't going to cut him on its own, and it probably wouldn't hum or glow, either. It looked…insignificant. Like your average ancient weapon. It was old. Cold iron? Early Renaissance? Thirteenth century, as Harold had said? Dane couldn't know without some research. It could even be older. The blade was about a foot long—longer than most daggers. It could almost be taken for a short sword. A baselard, most definitely.

The hilt was only an inch and a half wide, and was formed from two pieces of ivory bone riveted together. The shape formed an I, which was indicative of the baselard.

The blade tapered to a tip that wasn't pin-sharp, but it could do some damage if stabbed into something. It was damascened with a pattern that, upon comparison to the box, Dane realized was similar. More Swiss design? He picked up the phone and snapped a few shots from hilt to tip, then moved over to the window and tilted the blade to get the best light on the patterning.

Had he held this very dagger when he was eight? He couldn't remember what it had looked like then, and he didn't get a pang of recognition. But then again, he couldn't recall the toys he'd played with when he was little or the clothes he'd worn. And he'd held the weapon for such a short time back then.

The witch must die.

It was too incredible to disregard that dark but innocent statement made by one so young. One who could have had no knowledge what it meant.

Dane winced to imagine being stabbed in the heart with such an instrument. Then that thought suddenly flashed into vivid clarity...

He pressed his free hand to his chest, and for a moment, the feeling was real. He stood...not in a hotel room, but in the stark white expanse of a snowy field. Crimson spattered the snow. He gripped his chest. His breath fogged out, pulsing hot and burning, cutting into his muscles and bone.

Dane cried out, unsure what was happening. He tossed the phone onto the bed and was about to set the blade down when he twisted at the hips and saw another standing before him in the snowy landscape. Snow? Yes, the walls of the hotel room had dropped away and he stood outside. He shivered. Blood poured over his bottom lip. And the blade he held was no longer in his hand but sticking out from the chest of a...woman.

"No." He shook his head. Her scream crackled in his ears. He reached for her. He could not see her face...

And as quickly as it had manifested, the image dissipated. The warmth of the room hit his skin as if it were a sea wave rolled onto the surf. Dane inhaled and touched his lip. No blood. Slapping a palm over his chest, he realized there was no piercing pain. Nor did he shiver or see a glint of snow at his feet. And yet his fingers touched something wet.

"What the—?" He pulled them away from his shirt. They had blood on them.

After unbuttoning his shirt and pulling it off, he examined the skin just under his pectoral. He stood before the mirror and studied the weird presence of blood, but he couldn't find a cut. Yet the blood was real.

Did the blade have some sort of mystical power? It was entirely possible in his line of work. And if, indeed, a witch hunter had wielded it, it could very well be warded or even cursed. By holding it, he may have tapped into some long-shrouded energy.

Disregarding the blood, he turned the weapon lengthwise before him to inspect the blade, which was rusted and pocked from centuries of use. It was a double-edged blade, and it glinted in the stark winter sunlight.

Dane ran his thumb carefully along one edge, not pressing, but—

"Ouch!"

That had required no pressure at all to cut his skin. He pressed his bleeding thumb to his mouth and sucked at the stinging pain. It wasn't long or deep, but felt like a paper cut, the kind that seemed to burrow down to a man's very nervous system for the pulsing in the wound.

"I'm a fool," Dane muttered. "Can't even handle a weapon properly without hurting myself." Though when he smeared his thumb over his chest now, he winced at the lacking wound.

He set the weapon on top of the stuffing in the box and then pulled the laptop forward as he sat on the bed. He connected his phone to download the pictures, planning to search the agency database to correctly identify a year of origin for the blade.

Beside him, the bubble of blood on the blade seeped into the narrow blood groove and slowly made its way toward the hilt. Once it reached the bone, it infused the ancient material with Dane's very DNA. A memory his soul carried from lifetime to lifetime.

And the becoming began.

Chapter 17

Eryss sat on the floor in the basement below the brewery. At her shoulder level, a plywood shelf hosted a small altar the Decadent Dames used to bless the beers. Scents of sage and ashwood charcoal drifted into her nostrils. Valor had performed a blessing before leaving.

Next to her, a large plastic fermentation tank stood, freshly cleaned and ready for the next batch of beer. The brewery didn't have enough space on the main floor for all their equipment, thus the hole in the floor above, so that the beer Mireio brewed in the hot liquor tanks could be piped down to the fermenters. Kegs were stacked against the wall, and two walk-in freezers bookended the cozy basement room.

On the far wall, a steel door with four padlocks led to what Eryss had been delighted to learn was a secret passageway that ran underground to the businesses across the street. Such passages ran everywhere beneath Anoka, connecting buildings, but most had been filled with cinder blocks and closed up. She and Mireio had explored the tunnel once, only to learn the door on the other end had also been blocked up. It was a bummer.

Taking inventory of the T-shirts was necessary, and she'd let it go so long that Valor had let her know they had no size smalls in anything. So she ticked off another mark in the column for the pink T-shirts emblazoned with The Decadent Dames logo and set the stack aside. Before her loomed a six-foot-high shelf with shirts in pink, white, black and gray. The task would keep her mind off other things.

Like Dane walking out of the antiques store without bothering to pop his head in to see if she was at work. Not that the man should. It had been early. The brewery didn't open until midafternoon. But he was aware she went in to work before opening time. She sighed and pulled down the stack of medium gray shirts and began her tally. Time got away from her as she counted a few more stacks. When someone put his hands over her eyes from behind her, she touched the icy-cold fingers and smiled. "I didn't hear you come down."

"I have stealth. Taking inventory?"

"Yes, I let it slip for a few months and now customers are freaking because the pink shirts are out of stock." She turned and sat against the wooden shelving, inviting him to join her on the floor.

After taking a moment to inspect the altar, Dane sat by her side, stretching out his legs before him. How the man survived snowblowing in leather loafers was beyond her. He leaned in and kissed her. The fine stubble that had formed on his jaw and cheeks gently brushed her skin, and she smiled against his mouth. And as his lips quickly heated against hers, she tasted the coffee he must have just downed and inhaled his oceany, yet icy, man scent. A Viking from centuries past? She could imagine him as such.

"Your nose is still cold," she commented, giving it an Eskimo nuzzle with her own. "This weather does not agree with you."

"I disagree. I favor the snow. Though I extend an open invitation for you to come visit Santa Cruz and surf the sweet summer waves with me."

"Sounds like heaven. I've never surfed. I can swim, though."

"That'll work. Is that what I think it is behind us?"

"Yes. Everything we serve is blessed."

"And bewitched?"

"Sometimes." She wouldn't offer more. There were other, more interesting things to talk about. "So where's the dagger?"

"At the hotel."

"You're not going to show it to me?"

"I didn't know you were interested." She gaped at him. "I thought it was me and my sparkling wit that intrigued you." He brushed the hair from her cheek. "So it was just the dagger all along?"

She caught his mocking tease and set the T-shirts aside. "You know it. I'm a big fan of daggers used to kill witches. So, is it authentic? Does it check out?"

"I don't know. I'll have to research it back at the lab."

"The lab where you collect and analyze dangerous weapons used by paranormals? And possibly plot ways to kill them?"

"Eryss, we don't plot. And we leave the slaying to the Order of the Stake. We do, however, spin the truth to assure everyone that the creatures some people want to believe are real are nothing more than fantasy. Can you imagine the panic if a real vampire was discovered living in a New York penthouse? Or werewolves in the wilds of Minnesota?"

"There *are* werewolves in the wilds of Minnesota, as well as walking around town."

"*I* know that and you know that, but let's not start a panic, okay?"

She bumped his fist with hers. "Deal. I don't want that any more than the next witch or wolf does. Though I know Harold and his sister know we are witches."

"Yes, I—uh…how so?"

"It's just a feeling. The way he looks at us, and some of the things he's said. He knows. And we know Gladiola knows. But she's been pretty cool about it, until earlier today, when we saw her make a hex sign against us. Did Harold say anything about me? Does he know the dagger is supposed to have belonged to a witch hunter? And what about your father?"

"Whoa. Slow down." Dane kissed her again. His lips were still a little cool, so Eryss made sure she didn't stop until he felt as warm as her heart did. When he pulled away slowly, he bowed his head to hers and said, "I needed that."

"You're distracting us from the topic at hand."

He kissed her again. "Just detouring us a bit."

He cupped the back of her head and delivered a hard kiss that was bruisingly delicious and so worth the intensity. It was a claiming kiss, a kiss that wanted to own and mark her. It was a king's kiss to his queen. And she had never felt more worthy. Together they could be so—

He sat up abruptly, pulling Eryss from the idea of their future. "So, the facts," he said. "Harold did not mention you specifically. He is aware of the witch hunter legend. And what did you want to know about my father?"

"That's what I thought you were here for. To learn more about him. Why do you think *he* owned the dagger?"

"Our information says he did, and Mr. Stuart confirmed it. Harold was actually his friend. They met in a spelunking club, of all things. On an expedition to Thailand, my father bought the dagger."

"So did you learn what you wanted to about him?"

Dane swiped a palm over his face and winced. "Harold didn't tell me much about him personally. Supposedly my father picked up the dagger at a street vendor out of fascination, not because he had slain witches or thought it possessed any magical capabilities. He was not a witch hunter, if that's what you're thinking."

She hadn't been thinking that. Maybe. Okay, a little part of her had been thinking it.

"So how did Harold know you would ultimately come to get it?"

"That's the part I'm still not clear on. As I've told you, I found the file about the dagger while cleaning, and noted my father's name on it. That Harold knew my father is just a grand coincidence."

"Nope. Don't believe that." Eryss moved up onto her toes, squatting between Dane's legs. She kissed him quickly, then clasped both his hands. "Nothing in this universe happens without a reason. Not me having portentous dreams about a long-lost lover or nightmares about being stabbed. And you coming to possess a dagger formerly owned by a witch hunter when you are, at this moment, involved with a witch?" She blew out a breath. "I gotta scry on this one. Or have Midge look into it."

"Seriously? You think peering into a crystal ball is going to give you answers?"

"It can't hurt." She kissed his knuckle, and noticed the

cut on his finger. "Did the dagger do this?" She traced the cut and felt a weird energy spit out at her. And not a friendly one. So unfriendly, in fact, that she retracted. "Did you feel that?"

"I...feel what? It's just a cut, Eryss. Even I, someone accustomed to handling weapons, on occasion make a goof." He pressed a hand over his chest, rubbing the region under his pectoral. "I was so startled after standing there in the snow with blood spattered around me."

"What? Dane?" She knelt closer to him and bracketed his face with her palms. "Blood all around you? That had to have come from more than a small cut. What happened with the dagger?"

"It's nothing. It was just..." He heaved out a sigh and lifted his hands. "When I took the dagger out of the box and held it a few moments, I suddenly had...a vision."

She quirked a brow but didn't say anything. She wanted to hear this.

"I was bleeding from my chest and... I *felt* it. It was the weirdest thing. I've never experienced anything like it before. I *knew* I was standing in the hotel room, and yet I saw snow all around me, as if I were standing outside. And blood spattered the snow. A lot of blood. And the woman standing before me had a dagger in her chest. The dagger I had just been holding."

Eryss swallowed and stood up. She paced toward the empty kegs stacked against the far wall. She didn't know what to say. Didn't he understand what he'd experienced?

"I know what you're thinking." He jumped up to a standing position, as well. "I shouldn't have told you about it. It's nothing, Eryss. Just a wild imagination."

She put up a palm to block him, unwilling to listen to his ridiculous excuses. No longer would she allow him the easy way out. He knew the truth. And no amount of convincing on her part would be successful, until he accepted the possibility. By the goddess, the man believed in the various paranormal species—why couldn't he wrap his head around reincarnation?

She met his gaze. He shrugged and offered an innocent but unaccepting wince. Seriously?

"Right. I'm not going to convince a scientist who believes in bloodsucking immortals that he's lived before." She gestured toward the shelves of T-shirts. "I should get back to work."

"Eryss, please, you don't understand."

She grabbed a stack of white shirts and shook her head. "Nope, I don't. But I'm not going to argue with you. I have work to do. Maybe I can stop by your hotel room later with something to eat? I should be done in a few hours."

He nodded. "That'll give me time to research the baselard. Now that I have what I've come for, I, uh… I'm not headed back to Santa Cruz immediately. Thought I'd extend my vacation a bit."

For her? She wanted to hug him and kiss him and thank him for that thoughtful gesture, but Eryss couldn't force herself to touch him. Not until he stepped into reality and accepted what she already knew.

Dane Winthur had lived previous lives. And had been her lover in those lives.

"I'll leave you then. But, Eryss…" He took her hand and pulled her closer, even as she coached herself not to appear as if she was pulling away. "You know I would never do a thing to hurt you, yes?"

She didn't know that. And he didn't know that, either. He didn't even know his own truth.

She nodded and kissed him quickly. "See you in a few."

* * *

Eryss finished the inventory and checked with Mireio to see if she needed help tonight. There were three on staff, so Eryss was good to go. They'd opened two hours earlier, and regulars sat before the bar nursing the blueberry cream ale, while in the other room that overlooked the street, a rowdy group played a game of Jenga at one of the long oak tables.

She intended to head over to Dane's hotel, because she had to see that sword. Baselard. Whatever. And they had to talk. She had to know that he knew. But it was very probable he did not know.

Why would he seduce her and make love to her if he really was a witch hunter? That didn't make sense. So when he'd told her he didn't have ill intentions toward her, he meant it.

So far.

But what had his taking the witch hunter's blade in hand done to him? He'd had a vision. A bloody vision of death that had paralleled her own visions. And even if Dane didn't believe in portents, she certainly did.

So she swung by DaVanni's and picked up some hoagie sandwiches, then headed over to the American Inn. Dane's room was close to the pool, and the smell of chlorine and humidity wafted down the hallway. She knocked and heard someone swear on the other side of the door. She heard the lock click, and the door swiftly opened.

"Uh, Eryss? Hi?"

She held up the food bag. "I said I'd stop by?"

"Right. Uh...right." He stepped back and she saw he held the dagger. When he saw her notice, he shrugged. "I was just swinging it. You know, field testing it. For research purposes, of course."

"Of course." She closed the door behind her and shed

her coat and gloves, not caring to hang them up. She was too interested in what he held. "Can I take a look at it?"

"Can we eat first? I'm starving. Didn't realize that I'd skipped lunch until right now. What did you bring? I can't place the smell."

"The smell is processed meat and plastic cheese."

"I'm in. I've got some water in the fridge."

Dane had placed the dagger in a wooden box decorated with elaborate carvings. Eryss tried not to be distracted by it sitting on the middle of the bed, but the sandwich was lackluster, and she could almost feel the blade's energy hum through the air. Something felt different in the room. And while it could be her hesitant feelings toward Dane, she tried to remain neutral.

Finally, she set down the half-finished deli sandwich and wiped her hands. "We need to talk."

Dane nodded as he chewed. "That's why I'm still here."

"Good. So let's talk about what I can feel flowing from that damned box as if some kind of radioactive energy is inside."

"Seriously? You can feel energy coming from it?" He wiped his mouth and set the sandwich aside. "I know what you're thinking, Eryss. But I happen to know myself quite well. I've never had a murderous bone in my body. I have no desire to harm a witch."

She sighed and gave him a pleading look.

"What do you want me to say? Eryss, I'm on your team. The whole purpose of the Agency is to *protect* the paranormals."

She had to agree with that. And yet she still felt strange sitting here with him. Or rather, in the vicinity of the dagger. It wasn't beneficent. In fact, it might very well be evil.

"That is not my dagger," he reiterated. "I am not some former witch hunter reincarnated into a new life who has come to slay or burn you. Trust me on that one."

"Then why the vision about you stabbing a woman and she in turn stabbing you? It was exactly like *mine*, Dane."

"It was a fluke. You told me about your visions, and I subconsciously grasped on to those same images."

Chuffing out a frustrated breath, she barely stopped herself from pounding the table with a fist. "For what reason?"

"How the hell should I know? I'm not a psychologist. That's my mother. Listen, I don't think you understand how much I like you, Eryss. I mean, I'm here, *in Minnesota*, when I could be on a flight back to California. I want to be here *because of you*. You…mean something to me. And I'm not sure how to walk away from you."

Eryss swallowed back a protest. His confession struck her heart in the most unexpected way. Because she agreed with him. He meant something to her. And she didn't know what she'd do if he walked away from her. Not because she was madly in love with him, but because of the potential for so much more between them. And she wanted to explore that.

She got up and sat on his lap, wrapping her arms across his shoulders and tilting her head against his. "Just hold me," she said. "We'll figure this out."

Melting against his warm, masculine form, she slid her hand inside his vest. Nuzzling her nose to his cheek, she inhaled leather and ocean surf and oregano and to-mato sauce.

Dane slid his hand along her thigh and tugged her closer. "Feels good holding you. Like when I find myself gliding through the center of a barrel wave, surrounded by water, but none of it touches me. In that moment? I feel as if I'm where I was destined to be."

His confession reminded her that he didn't belong here in Minnesota with her. He could never be happy away from the surf and sea he called home. Could a long-distance relationship work? The idea interested her not at all. And yet she had been feeling a little too rooted lately. And she did have a goal of opening another brewery on either the West or East Coast.

No, that was thinking too far into the future. They needed to deal with right now before they could advance to what might be.

"Why don't you take a look at the dagger," he suggested. "I'd like your opinion on it."

"Okay." She stood, and when she did, he picked up his sandwich to finish it. Never deny a man his food.

Carefully, Eryss approached the box. The cover was not on it, and the dagger sat on a bed of crinkled brown paper shreds.

"It's a baselard," Dane said. "You know about that?"

"No, I'm not much for weapons. Do you know how old it is?"

"The thirteenth century is when baselards were first made."

She would never touch it without knowing its origins, and those were mysteriously intriguing. Holding her hands palms down over the blade, she closed her eyes and focused on the energy she could sense streaming from the weapon. It was vibrant and active, and…dark.

A sudden jolt pushed her off balance and she stumbled backward, landing in the armchair before the window.

"Eryss!" Dane rushed to her. "What happened? Did you touch it?"

"No," she said with decided defeat. "It repulsed me. It's warded."

"Really?" He twisted to look toward the bed. "I did feel some kind of funky vibrations when I held it. But you know me and vibrations." He picked up the dagger by the hilt, examining the damascened blade. It glinted in a beam of pale winter sunlight.

And Eryss pushed back in the chair, feeling a nervous shudder tighten her veins. She wasn't wearing any protective tourmaline or a spell, so with a whisper, she pulled on a white light and felt it hug her briefly from toe to crown.

"What was that?" Dane asked, looking up from the blade. "Did you just cast some magic?"

"I pulled up a protective shield."

He dropped the dagger onto the bed. "But I told you I would never harm you, Eryss. You have to believe me."

"I do believe the man who doesn't know himself. But once you do know? I'm a little worried—oh, crap!"

She pointed to the dagger, which was levitating over the bed behind Dane's shoulder. He spun and grabbed the hilt, but he had to slap another hand onto the blade, as if it were trying to move without his volition. "Get out!" he shouted.

Eryss wasn't a stupid witch. She fled the room, plucking up her coat and gloves from the floor as she did so. "Call me," she said from the hallway, "when you get that thing properly warded!"

Chapter 18

Dane clasped the dagger to his chest, eyes closed, listening intently to Eryss's footsteps fading down the outer hallway. The blade felt on fire, as if pulled from the forge, yet it didn't burn his skin. It couldn't. It was just another vision or strange magic that was making him want to run after her and—

"No," he said in a hoarse gasp. *A witch hunter?* "I can't be. This is insane."

He thrust the baselard away from him, and it landed on the corner of the bed. Cruel winter sunlight glanced off the blade, which flashed as if it were the sun itself. Dane hurriedly picked up the weapon and slammed it into the box, replacing the cover.

"It's not true," he said aloud. "It's probably enchanted. Things like that happen all the time with the weapons I take into the lab. They can make normal men do strange and mysterious things."

Yeah. That was it. Of course it had to be enchanted, perhaps to track witches. How else could the witch hunter have found them? Had the dagger recognized Eryss as a witch? Was that the reason it had levitated, almost as if in wait for someone to take it in hand and—

"No," he insisted, squelching those irrational thoughts. "Stay cool about this. Think like the scientist you are. Don't let your heart start edging in and messing everything up."

Had he just admitted that to himself? Because his heart *had* started to interfere, and he wasn't sure how that would change things. It shouldn't matter. He could have a relationship with a woman and remain logical and do his job at the same time.

But everything was different with Eryss. Even after having known her such a short time. Now he was thinking that his heart had intruded on his work when…

"Maybe it's the other way around?" He shoved a hand through his hair and studied the dagger he'd hastily shoved into the box. It was the catalyst to the mistrust he and Eryss had developed lately. It had to be.

So he'd keep his hands off the thing, and as soon as he returned to California, he'd make sure it was dewarded or disenchanted. The Agency employed people who could do things like that.

Dane paced before the bed. He had to go to Eryss. Make sure she was all right. The levitating dagger would have freaked out anyone. But first he had to ensure it wouldn't cause any more issues between them. What to do?

Suddenly he remembered there was a UPS store just a few blocks from the hotel. Harold Stuart might have been reluctant to ship the blade, but Dane wasn't. If packaged properly, it would be fine. He'd send the dagger on its way now, and catch up to it when he got home.

Trying to focus on the soup simmering in the copper pot before her was impossible. Eryss felt sure she'd dumped in far too much oregano, and she now tried to spoon the floating green herbs out for fear that all her chopping of carrots, celery and zucchini would be wasted.

Setting down the spoon, she raced upstairs to the closet and looked over her crystal collection. The rainbow fluorite was perfect for mental acuity. She snatched it and whispered an intention to imbue the stone with power, then tucked it in her skirt pocket. Calmly, she walked back down to the kitchen and decided the soup would be perfect.

As would everything else in her life. The brewery was running smoothly. The glass in the conservatory was holding well and would continue to do so until she could call in a repairman in the spring. Her health was excellent. And her love life...

With the wooden spoon, she poked at a chunk of mushy tomato. What about her love life and its incredibly dangerous attachment to someone who was very possibly a witch hunter? A witch hunter who didn't even know he was one.

And yet, his dagger knew.

The knock on the door chattered against the wood. Eryss could practically hear the rattling of a freezing scientist from California's bones in that knock. She rushed to open it and pulled Dane inside, going in for a kiss right away. His lips were cold, and she could feel his cold leather gloves snake around her waist through her long sweater. It gave her a good shiver and she snuggled in tighter against him, deepening the kiss until she forgot everything except how nice it was to stand in Dane's arms and lose herself.

He shed his coat and dropped it behind him without breaking the kiss. His hands, now gloveless, curved over her hips and cupped her derriere, pulling her up until she stood on her tiptoes. When he performed a dexterous lift and carried her over to the table, again without breaking the kiss, she cheered inwardly. He set her on the butcher-block surface, which did finally break their contact.

Eryss leaned forward to tickle his upper lip with her tongue, and she giggled.

"Someone happy to see me?"

"You have to wonder?" she asked.

"After what happened in my hotel room, I wasn't sure I should show my face again."

Now she pulled her skirt up to her knees and wrapped her legs about his hips, pulling him in close. "I'm not afraid of what you don't understand. And that's all there is to it. Are you hungry? I've made minestrone."

"It smells delicious. I love oregano."

Half an hour later Eryss patted herself on the back for not freaking out over the extra oregano. And the spice was an aphrodisiac, so everything had worked out perfectly. As Dane handed her the last bowl—he'd offered to wash the dishes again—she dried it and set it in the cupboard. This weird domesticity felt comfortable. Like she'd done it before.

And she knew that she had.

"So is this a lifetime pursuit, your job?" Eryss asked as she set the last glass on the counter and started to wipe up around the sink.

"Protecting us humans from the knowledge that vampires and werewolves live among us?" Dane nodded, but then quickly followed with a shrug. "I'm not sure I've thought as far ahead as my whole lifetime. I like doing it right now. It's interesting. It feeds my need for using scientific protocol to confirm or deny truths. It allows me to travel across the United States as I'm sent out to retrieve weapons."

"What does a promotion look like? Vampire slayer?" Eryss cautioned herself from saying *witch hunter*, but she was certainly thinking it.

"There's the Order of the Stake for that. I'm not a hunter, Eryss. I am a protector."

"I get that." She folded the dish towel over the edge of the sink and turned to face him. "I suppose having grown up without your father, you were compelled to protect your mother?"

"Yes and no. Lillian Winthur is the epitome of an independent woman. She doesn't need anyone to protect her. In fact, I would send out a warning to the next man who attempts to approach her with the misplaced fantasy of playing the rescuing knight to her not-in-distress damsel."

"A real tough cookie?"

"Strong. Smart. And she knows what she wants. Like you." But his smile wasn't completely there. He was likely trying to figure out if his comparing her to his mother had offended her.

"My mother was much the same, but she adored my dad."

Dane leaned in and kissed Eryss gently on the lips. He bowed his forehead to hers. "Sometimes life steals the good ones too quickly."

"Did you contact Harold again?"

"Yes. If I can get him out for a steak and beer I'll be

able to pick his brain. He wants to see me again, as well. Harold has his ideas about the dagger."

"Such as?"

Dane waggled a finger at her. "I don't want to go there tonight. I came here to escape that *thing* between us and just enjoy you. Can we do that?"

It sounded too good to work, but she wanted that, too. She nodded.

"Let's make love out in the conservatory," he suggested, grasping her hand and leading the way. "I need a nature recharge after scraping ice crystals from the car windshield."

Eryss spun around in front of him and danced into the conservatory, delighted as her toes hit the grass. "You get the right outerwear and you'll begin to marvel over nature's beauty. But I won't hold it against you."

"For an earth witch, I'd suspect winter to be a cruel and heartless season for you. Why don't you live somewhere warm where you can put your toes in the sand or grass all year round?"

Eryss looked down at her feet, nestled in the lush grass, and gave him an innocent shrug.

"Right. All hail your witchy magic. I want to know more, but right now all I want to do is kiss those toes that are wiggling in the grass."

And he dropped to his knees and lifted one of her feet, planting a warm, lingering kiss on top. Eryss managed to sit on the edge of the couch while he kissed her foot. The lash of his tongue along her arch disturbed her in an achingly delicious way. She'd never thought a foot could be sexy. But having a man trace his tongue along its structure? Mercy.

As he kissed her ankle bone, his hand glided up under her skirt. He drew circles behind her knee and, with one goodbye kiss to her foot, moved up, pushing aside the fabric to deliver another of those devastating kisses to the inside of her knee. Eryss let her body fall back onto the couch, moaning as she did so.

"You know all my spots," she said on a sigh.

"Your erogenous zones?"

"Mmm..."

"I know you have one right here." His tongue tickled an X on the inside of her thigh. "And here." He lifted her leg and delivered a kiss to the back of her other knee. He sat before the couch, on the grass, her legs bracketing his head. He sprinkled kisses along her thighs until she giggled, and he had to grip her firmly to keep her from squirming away.

But she didn't want to get away from him. If anything, she wanted to dive inside him and grasp that tendril of remembrance he couldn't seem to connect to, and draw it up and into reality.

And then she had an idea.

"Let's go upstairs," she said, pulling her leg free from his wicked torture, standing up and starting toward the doors.

"But I thought—?"

"Trust me!" she called.

Entering the bedroom behind her, Dane pulled off his shirt and unzipped his pants, watching Eryss light pink and black candles around the bed. Then she lit the incense in a copper pan—a ritual he didn't question now. It was just her manner, and the way she lived. He actually liked the mood it gave the room.

Sitting on the bed, he nodded toward the iPod and Eryss shook her head. "No music tonight. I want to try something. If you're willing?"

Coming from any other woman, that would probably imply a new sex position. Coming from a witch, Dane knew he had best be wary. But he trusted her, and wanted further entrance into her wild and mysterious world.

As she began to pour pink salt around the bed, he pulled up his feet. "A spell circle?" he guessed. "Is tonight the night you bewitch me then?"

She finished the circle, then set the empty salt jar aside. Pulling off her dress and sweater, she approached the incense to stand not over it, but beside it. Pink smoke curled across her pale skin.

"Are you willing to step into the past with me?"

"You mean like a past life regression? I thought you couldn't do that yourself?"

"I can't. But a little sex magic might enhance the charm and get us both there."

"Seriously?" He wasn't sure if he should be excited or nervous.

She stepped over the salt line and climbed onto the bed, kissing him and running her palm up his chest. "Together, as we indulge in one another, we might be able to share memories and experiences from the past. If we truly were lovers, it might come through for us. It won't hurt. In fact, all we have to do is make love."

He stroked the hair from her cheek and lingered, brushing his fingers over her skin. In the course of a week he'd gone from a scientist who knew better than to get involved with the paranormal entities that he knew existed—wisely standing aside and witnessing—to a lovesick fool who spread his arms wide and welcomed in the weirdness with rapidly waning caution.

"Speak your spell," he said, leaning in to kiss her. "Enchant me, witch. Bring me into your world."

"Repeat after me," she said, as she turned to sit before

him. She took his hands and brought them before her, and he followed by cupping her breasts and kissing the back of her shoulder. "Yes, stay in the mood. All love shared will only enhance the spell. *Infero.*"

He knew that meant enter. *"Infero,"* he repeated.

The incense smoke increased and wafted over the bed, coiling about their embrace in a violet curl. An inhalation infused Dane's senses with sage, salt and oranges. Eryss rapidly recited a few more words, in a low tone so he couldn't follow and repeat them, but he understood that he didn't have to. Then she stretched out her hands, tracing a design in the air that the smoke seemed to fill in, until it looked a little like the *om* symbol he was familiar with.

Dane wanted her all over him, on him, kissing him. He slid his hand between her legs and she gasped at his gentle intrusion. She spread her knees and leaned back against him. He tenderly touched her swollen clit and traced his fingers down the sides of her labia. She clutched at his thighs, gasping. Her breasts rose as she panted rapidly.

And the sensation of the sheets beneath him changed in a subtle way. Rougher, perhaps a different weave, like primitive linen...the woman on top of him cooed and her body shook so her long red hair spilled over his face, and he inhaled cool summer scents of grass and earth. He couldn't see her face. The change didn't disturb him so much as welcome him to continue, to explore, to kiss her freckled shoulder.

And when she lowered herself onto his erection, he hissed in pleasure.

"My love," she said, in a voice he hadn't heard before, but instinctually recognized.

"Alexandra," he said. "You have me for all the days and nights to come."

She laughed lightly as her rhythm increased. "You are a fantastical man, Ivor. Mmm, but I cannot imagine a day without you at my side. Or inside me."

And she leaned over him, hugging him as he thrust deeply within her, feeding the coming release, racing to the climax. Wanting to fill her, to put life there in her womb and begin the family they so desperately craved.

"To family," he said, as the climax overwhelmed him and his body shuddered beneath hers. He shouted out and clutched her forearms as he rode the intense pleasure. Incense coiled into his senses. He opened his eyes. "Eryss…"

"Dane," she whispered, and placed his hand over her breast. "Ivor. We are one…"

Her husband lay beneath her, shuddering in exquisite release, but she did not stop her motion, riding him faster, driving his hard shaft in and out and rubbing it hard against her pleasure peak. She would find that great release, as well. His body flexed in the candlelight, and the pine wreath hanging over the small window tainted their musky union with a piercing sharpness. He pinched her nipple, and that moment she sought erupted within her. As she cried out and spread her arms wide to allow the universe to join in the divine moment of ecstasy, she looked at her lover.

So many centuries lived in his irises. Multitude embraces met with kisses and hugs and unbridled sex. Dark stubble on his jaw matched the midnight curls that tickled the pillowcase. And with a glint of moonlight, she inhaled the smoky taint of cherrywood tobacco.

"Jean-Philippe," she said with a giggle, because he made that wrinkle-nosed smirk. "You are not finished?"

"Making love to you?" He tugged her down and rolled her to her back. Plush gold chiffon pillows tumbled over her face, but he pushed them away and kissed her quickly. "I'm only getting started!"

And he glided his tongue down her throat and between her breasts. He did not kiss her there, which made her wiggle in a pleading request, but he waggled a finger as he moved lower and then kissed her again and again and again at the peak of her blond curls. He knew she loved it when he suckled her there, but the man was such a tease, there were times she almost couldn't bear it.

As his tongue touched the apex of her inner folds, she gasped and tilted back her head. The sky was black, save for a glitter of stars, and the tiny apartment in Paris was suddenly clouded with red smoke that smelled of sage.

Violet waved her hand through the smoke, but then realized what was happening. She had not spoken a spell—but someone had. And she was not frightened, for deep in her soul she knew this was only a glimpse from another lifetime. And her attention focused inward as every lash of Jean-Philippe's tongue seemed to tighten her muscles more and dare her to surrender to orgasm.

Inhaling a breath of incense, she went deep and... Eryss glided her hand through Dane's thick hair as he kissed her and tasted her.

"Violet," Dane whispered, and when he looked at her his eyes smiled as widely as hers. "Eryss."

"Dane," she answered, bringing her lover up to nuzzle alongside her.

She hadn't orgasmed, and sensed the spell was weakening. And while she didn't want to return to her current body, she relented just as Dane filled her with his hot, thrusting cock. And the molten presence of him, in the now, looking like the man she'd met days earlier, anchored her and at the same time released her to fly.

They came together, bodies shaking and breaths roughly gasping over skin.

Dane rolled over in the bed and pulled Eryss up against his stomach and thighs. He smelled like life, sweet, sweaty and soft. He nuzzled her hair and whispered, "Here's to soul mates."

Eryss leaned over the side of the bed and broke the salt circle with a slash of her fingers through the pink crystals. The room seemed to briefly sigh, the bed shuddered subtly on the floorboards, then all fell silent save for Dane's soft breaths. He'd fallen asleep and she intended to let him rest. They'd had quite an experience.

Snuggling next to his delicious warmth beneath the sheets and comforter, she stared up at the skylight. There was no moonlight tonight because of the clouds, but she'd seen plenty while making love to Dane. And Jean-Philippe. And Ivor.

Ivor had been her original husband, sometime around the thirteenth century. It had been an amazing marriage. They'd loved so deeply. She had felt the emotions as if she'd been there. And in a way, she had been, traveling through time thanks to the enchantment of the spell.

Dane could not deny now that they'd loved one another through the centuries.

Chapter 19

Over breakfast of blueberries and clotted cream sprinkled with hemp seeds, Dane played footsies with Eryss while she tried to check her emails on the iPad.

"Just give me two minutes," she insisted, but with a smile on her face. "I want to make sure everything is running smoothly at the brewery."

"Fine." He was ready to go on his knees and take those cute bare toes into his mouth, but he controlled the urge. He would allow Eryss her two minutes. Besides, he could wait to discuss what had happened last night. It had been weird, wonderful and amazing.

And he believed every moment of it because he had been there. Past and present, combined.

His own phone pinged, and he reluctantly picked it up and read the news notification. "There was an accident involving a UPS truck. The highway was littered with the boxes."

"Bummer," Eryss said, her attention on her phone. "At least it wasn't bees or live animals."

"Eryss." He set the phone aside.

"What? Why so serious?"

"I sent the dagger back to the lab via UPS."

"Oh. Really? Why couldn't Harold have mailed the thing to you in the first place?"

"I don't know. The old man was weird about the thing. Doesn't matter. I packaged it well. I've shipped many an ancient weapon before. But what if it was in the crash?"

"Do you know how many trucks that company has? There must be hundreds in the Twin Cities alone. Are you worried?"

He sighed heavily. "Should I be?"

She met his gaze. It wasn't as though the dagger hadn't already achieved an immense task by finding its way to him. If it was attached to a witch hunter, then surely, over the centuries, it had a means to find its owner.

"No need to worry," she replied cheerily. "I have to run in to work." She set down the phone. "But it's not an emergency. So. We haven't discussed last night."

"I've been waiting for you to bring it up."

She popped a blueberry into her mouth. "How do you feel about what happened?"

"You're assuming I saw things? Or experienced things?"

"Didn't you?"

He let her off the hook with a nod. "I did. You were in my arms the whole time, and yet we were different people."

"Yet the same souls," she said, laying a hand over his.

He clasped her hand and squeezed. "Yes, the same through the centuries. I believe it, Eryss. We have been lovers before. And I don't know how I came to find you again this time around, but I'm glad for it. Do you think we knew this in our other lives?"

"I'm not sure. But did you see us as Ivor and Alexandra?"

"Yes, I felt so much love in that moment. Do you think that was us...originally?"

"I believe so. We were married. We were... I'm pretty sure we were trying to have a family."

"I know! I felt that. And you had red hair and freckles."

"I did? I didn't see myself, only you. You were blond and built like a Viking warrior. Maybe you were one. I'm not sure. Didn't see a lot of our surroundings. I felt as though it was medieval, though."

"We lived in a cabin of sorts. Near a village, maybe? It was winter."

She nodded enthusiastically.

"This is so wondrous, Eryss. I want to know more now. To do research. To familiarize myself with the times. You've always known you've been reincarnated. Haven't you ever felt compelled to know more?"

"No. It's always just a feeling I've had and known. We live many lives for a reason. The past is the past. We leave it behind us."

"Yes, but learning about that past might teach us about the present."

"Wow, you've really jumped off the science cliff, haven't you?"

"Don't tell my colleagues. Of course, those in the Agency would probably just shrug. I wonder if I should report this to Tor. I'm not sure. It doesn't feel necessary. It's not as if this is a job."

"But you had intended to hand over the dagger, yes? What will you do about if it's actually lost?"

"I've got to track that package. I don't want it to fall into the wrong hands. I never thought about it that way, but this personal quest for the dagger may have become a real job. But as for the dagger's relationship to me..." He clasped her hand. "I didn't see anything last night that wasn't loving and kind. There was no stabbing one another, for example."

"Neither did I. And that's a relief. I confess I had my worries you could be the witch hunter. I mean, the blade does act weird around you. But surely we would have seen evidence of violence last night." She kissed him quickly and grabbed his empty bowl. "We're good!"

As she sailed over to the sink, Dane checked his phone, which had just signaled he had another message.

It was not good.

Eryss picked up on his sudden tension. "What is it?"

"I just got a text from UPS telling me my package was on the truck that was in an accident. While some packages were recovered, mine was not. They apologize, and will be sending an email with insurance forms attached."

He set down the phone and caught his forehead in his palm.

"That could be a good thing," she said to him. "Everything does happen for a reason. So maybe the dagger was never meant for you, and the real owner now holds it."

"Sure, but then that means there's a witch hunter out there armed with an enchanted dagger, determined to track down witches."

"Right. Not cool. But instead of a witch hunter it could just be someone who passed the scene of the accident and grabbed a package. Either way, we need to find that weapon."

"*We* do? I do," Dane corrected her. "It's mine. I know that. And I won't deny it anymore."

"So are you saying you think the dagger was meant to find you?"

He nodded tentatively, agreeing against his will. "I suppose. I haven't given it enough thought and—"

"And charted it out in graphs and pie charts?"

"You tease, but…yes. But that still means nothing in the greater picture. Eryss, you mean a lot to me." He clasped her hand over the blueberries and cream. "I've never met anyone who has made me want to move to Minnesota."

"That's saying a lot."

"It is. And I mean it. You make zero degrees seem balmy."

"My kisses are rather hot." She winked.

"And your skin." He leaned over to kiss her cheek. "And your body, and the way you move it. Now I'm horny."

"I'm feeling it. Sex before dishes?"

"Do you see me arguing? Lead the way, oh witch of my heart."

After sex, Eryss drove Dane to the hotel and dropped him off. Mireio had a slight emergency with a leaking fermentation tank and needed help mopping. While Dane had offered to help as well, Eryss had insisted she could handle it. They'd decided he would stop by in a bit, and they would do lunch.

He told the receptionist at the front desk to keep his bill open. He wasn't sure how much longer he'd stay. He kept telling himself just a few more days. He did have work to get back to.

Of course, most of his work could be done anywhere. He needed to go into the lab only when he had a weapon to research. And he hadn't received any new field assignments, so he'd stay on this vacation as long as he could. He didn't even miss the waves. How was that for acclimating to new elements?

Was he falling in love with Eryss? Could he imagine himself in a relationship with a witch? It was a lot to take in. But the idea of love appealed to him. And while he instinctually wanted to approach from an observant, cautious angle, with graphs and charts in hand, a part of him was nudging for the full dive. *Just let it happen. Go with the waves, man.*

After pushing the key card into the lock, Dane shoved open the door and strolled to the window. He tugged off his coat, gloves and hat along the way—

And then noticed that something was on the bed that hadn't been there yesterday when he'd left. It had a note with the hotel logo attached to the familiar-shaped box. He'd had a delivery while he'd been out.

Dane's heart fell in his chest. He dropped the winter gear to the floor at his feet.

The tattered UPS box containing the witch hunter's dagger sat on the bed.

Chapter 20

With everything that Dane had learned since meeting Eryss and taking the baselard in hand, he could not be surprised now to see the box sitting on the hotel room bed. It frightened him, because it seemed to have a mind—a very mission—of its own. It also frightened him because that mission seemed to be inexplicably tied to him.

And the worst part of that fear? He wanted to open the box and grip the dagger—*because it was his*.

"I've wielded it through the ages," he muttered as he touched the cardboard packing box. "Could I have been a witch hunter in a past life?" Which could only mean... "I killed Eryss." Or Alexandra. Or...whoever she was.

Catching his breath, he sat heavily on the end of the bed.

"But if I killed her, that means..."

That she had killed him. According to her visions, that was how it had always gone down. Both of them stabbing one another. Because she'd had to defend herself against him? That was the only imaginable way to explain it. Surely she had not gone after him with intent to murder.

"What have I done?"

And yet it was difficult to grasp on to a feeling of guilt. Because those murders had occurred in an entirely different lifetime. And he must have had his reasons. Of course, he'd been hunting a witch.

"But in every lifetime? I'm not hunting one now."

Technically.

Dane brushed his fingers over his jaw, his mind racing with wild scenarios and ideas. In his past lives, if he had been born to hunt witches, then that would facilitate his life choice of killing a witch. But could he have been born normal, just an ordinary man, and then *turned into* a witch hunter? For what reasons? Had a witch done him or his family harm? Had he been cursed as a witch hunter? Had he been less of a scientist and more of a true believer in his former lives? Not like those innocents his organization sought to hide the truth from, but a true knower of all things paranormal and otherworldly?

In every lifetime? Always a witch hunter? That could only mean he was destined to become one now.

He shook his head. He was a rational man who didn't have a murderous bone in his body. The thought, the very *idea,* of doing harm to another did not fit right with his soul. He'd never thrown a punch unless in self-defense. He considered himself kind and considerate. He had never owned a gun. He armed himself only when necessary for a job, and had trained to fight defensively and against the supernatural. That was common sense due to the nature of the job.

While his knowledge on witches was minimal, he was aware that fire brought their true death. "Why has a dagger sought out a witch hunter if only fire brings true death?" he wondered. "Why *this* dagger?"

The box the UPS store had packed it in was damaged, but it wasn't bent or torn too terribly. They'd packed it in an inner box, as well, surrounded by packing peanuts, which spilled out as Dane tore open the first box. If the box had fallen out of the truck during the accident, it must have bounced off the road, as it didn't appear to have been crushed by another vehicle. But had it been stolen? How had the thief known to bring it here?

There hadn't been a thief, Dane decided. Because some greater supernatural force had delivered this dagger to the one person to whom it belonged. And whether or not he was the person who would ultimately wield the dagger, or the person who would prevent another from doing so, he had to accept that it was now his responsibility.

He must take the dagger in hand.

The inner cardboard box opened to reveal the rosewood box, which had been carefully swathed with a thick layer of bubble wrap. Dane peeled it away, and when finally the box sat on his lap, he drew in a breath. Because he could *feel* the dagger. Calling to him. Vibrating from within. It beckoned directly to him, he somehow knew. It hummed in his bones and made his heart beat faster.

And when he opened the box lid, the dagger slowly rose before him until it hovered, hilt down, blade pointing heavenward—the perfect position for a hand to grasp the bone hilt.

And Dane did.

Blade in hand, he stood in the center of the hotel room. And then he was not…

His vision changed, fading out and then focusing sharply on his surroundings and the scents of blood and snow. Chill air hit his face and forearms, dusting the wolf's fur he wore across his body.

Ivor followed the crimson droplets in the snow. His calfskin boots crunched on the fresh-fallen snow. He tugged off his gloves as the droplets formed into a pool of blood. The toes of his boots stopped at the dark curls on his father's head. The man's chest blossomed with blood.

He gasped, choked back a snort.

And standing over his father, Alexandra clutched a bloody knife. Crimson colors spattered her white dress. A smear of blood streaked her cheek and her red hair.

Ivor swallowed a scream. His heart lurched to the fore. He squeezed his fingers about the dagger he held. The woman he loved—his wife—had murdered his father. Rage deep within him pushed him to leap over his father's body and plunge the knife into his wife's heart.

Alexandra did not cry out. She only looked down at her hand, which was pressed against Ivor's chest, wrapped about the knife hilt she held. The blade had entered his chest and sliced his heart in two.

Alexandra gasped.

Ivor spit up blood and shook his head. "Why did you do it?"

"I love you," she managed to reply. "He was going to sacrifice you."

"No. He would never!"

"I will always love you," she whispered, and pressed her mouth to his forehead, "through the ages. Our souls will remain steadfast and true to one another. I will find you again. I'm so sorry, Ivor."

And she slid a palm over her belly, taking his hand to place it there, where he felt a gentle swell. He looked up into her eyes, which were glittering with tears. But before he could speak another word, his heart stopped and he fell into her arms.

The couple collapsed, spilling thick, hot blood into the white snow until their bodies were surrounded by a flood of their own life.

A blink tugged Dane from the vision. He smeared a palm down his chest, expecting to feel the hot blood because he could still smell its metallic perfume.

"She killed my father," he murmured.

Clenching the hilt, he straightened his shoulders and drew in a breath. "The witch must die."

Chapter 21

Eryss grabbed the flattened cardboard box Valor handed her. The city didn't have recycling, so she always took as much of the cardboard home with her as she could and stuffed it into her bin. It was late. The sun had set hours earlier, but a few bars were still open. The Decadent Dames closed at eleven because they liked to have lives that didn't involve working until the early morning hours.

Eryss's car was parked beside Valor's Jeep, the black paint job of which was barely visible due to the white road salt that covered it nearly to the tops of the doors.

"We so need a forty-degree day so I can wash this monster," Valor said when she noted Eryss checking it out. "Uh…Eryss?"

Eryss closed the hatchback and nudged up her thick scarf to block a chill from her neck. "What?" she asked, as Valor gaped at something behind her.

"I thought you said you and that scientist guy were getting along?"

"We are, very well—" Eryss swung around when Valor grabbed her, to face a determined man crossing the street less than fifty yards away. But the distance was decreasing quickly. And what she saw in his hand made Eryss recite a protection spell and put up a white light.

Valor's shield of protection, combined with Eryss's, held the force in a pale violet glow about the two women as if it were an extended aura.

Without slowing his relentless pace, Dane stepped onto the parking lot concrete. In his hand he held the dagger. And it glowed a subtle green as he spun it once and then raised it high, readying it to swing toward them.

"This is nuts," Valor muttered. "Can you repulse him?"

"Of course!" Yet Eryss was so thrown by seeing Dane coming at her with a weapon, it took her a few seconds to realize she stood forced to defend herself. And when finally she did, the blade swept toward her and she thrust up a palm and cried, *"Deflecto!"*

The dagger cut easily through the protection spell, but suddenly clinked and jerked back in Dane's hand, as if it had hit a metal wall.

"Dane, what the hell?" Eryss called as she backed toward the Jeep with Valor at her side. "I'm not a threat to you!"

The man gripped the hilt with both hands and lowered it before him, blade pointing upward. It was such a deadly pose. He could strike in a heartbeat, swinging any direction that would prove most dangerous to her.

"You killed my father."

"What? No! He died when you were young, Dane."

"The witch must die!"

And in the faint glow put out by the green blade, Eryss noticed Dane's eyes did not reflect the color of his deep brown irises, but glowed white. As if he was possessed or under a spell.

"It's the sword," she said. "When he holds it, some kind of wicked enchantment binds him."

"Then we've got to get it out of his hands," Valor said. "Let me try."

Clapping her hands together over her head, Valor sent a burst of her air magic through the chilly night. It hit the blade with a crackle of violet sparks. Dane hissed and released one hand from the hilt, shaking it as if burned.

Eryss used that moment of surprise to send up a swirl of snow from the sidewalk, a tight coil that curled about the hilt, around Dane's hand and up the blade. He cried out and dropped the dagger. It hit the icy concrete and skittered toward Eryss and Valor. Valor bent to collect the weapon, but as she picked it up she let out a yelp, then dropped it.

Unconcerned with the dagger, Eryss slowly approached Dane. His hand still crackled with the violet sparks of magic Valor had sent at him.

"What the hell?" he shouted. When he looked up at Eryss's approach, he sneered, but then his mouth dropped open in a gape. "Eryss?"

"Yes, Dane, it's Eryss. Do you think I'm someone else?"

"You—she...what am I—" He straightened and slapped his palms to his jaws, then swept them down in disbelief. "What did I just do?"

"It's okay, Dane. The enchantment ended when you dropped the sword. Are you okay?"

He was visibly shaking, but when he met her gaze his eyes were now a deep chocolate brown instead of that white glowing color.

"Me?" He pressed his hands to her cheeks, cupping

her face gently. "What about you? I'm so sorry. I don't know—you said it was an enchantment? It's possible. The baselard has been speaking to me since I first put my hands to it. It was waiting for me in my hotel room. And then I had another vision of Ivor and Alexandra. Oh, hell. We need to talk."

"Good call," said Valor from behind them. "But first we have to figure out what to do with this." She toed the dagger. "I can't touch it. Nor do I want to. And I don't think it would be a good idea to let the witch hunter pick it up again."

"He's not—" Eryss began, at the same time Dane said, "I'm not a witch hunter."

Valor's left eyebrow quirked. "You could have fooled me. If this is what love does to people, then count me out."

"Love?" Dane asked.

And while he was considering it, Eryss felt compelled to hug Dane, more to reassure him that all would be well than herself. She was still frightened. In the moments he'd held that dagger, he'd wanted to destroy her. He was the last man she'd ever thought to fear.

"Valor is right," Dane said. "I can't pick up that thing."

"Neither can either of us," Valor said. "It's definitely a witch blade. And believe it or not, you *were* on the hunt just now. Why don't the two of you leave and I'll take care of this. I'll give Trouble a call. That is, if you think everything's okay between the two of you, Eryss."

"It will be."

Dane pushed away gently from Eryss's hug. "No, I can't let you take the dagger. It's mine. It belongs in storage with the Agency."

"We can get it wherever it needs to be without your assistance." Valor toed the blade again, and it spun halfway around on the ice. "Seriously, dude. You going to risk touching it again?"

"No, but…"

His perplexity over what to do was obvious. Perhaps even now the dagger was calling to him, tempting him to pick it up.

Eryss tugged Dane's arm. "Valor will take care of it. She won't do anything except put it in a safe place until you inform us what should be done with it. It's okay for the night, yes?"

His body refused to relax, to turn and walk alongside her, away from the weapon.

"You said we needed to talk," she pressed.

"Who is Trouble?" he asked Valor.

"Werewolf friend of mine. He should be able to pick it up, no problem. I'll give him a call. You cool with that?"

"Not really." Dane glanced to Eryss. She nodded at him, offering an encouraging smile. "Fine," he said. "Call me as soon as it's been secured," he insisted. "And don't try to put any fancy mojo or spells on it. It's already enchanted. I'll need to see if I can turn up anything more on the dagger and its history."

"You know its history. We both do." Eryss slid her hand into his grasp. "We'll figure this out. Together."

He nodded and followed her toward the car. They drove out of the parking lot, Eryss giving a little wave to Valor, who was talking on her cell phone.

The werewolf had been close, heading to a bar in a neighboring town, when Valor called him. He pulled up in a camo-painted Ford F150, music blasting. Valor liked Trouble. But he was called Trouble for a reason, and she would never consider him anything more than a good time. She'd had the opportunity to hook up with him last year, and while she almost had, she preferred to draw a solid line between friendship and lovers.

He hopped out of the truck. Valor was only a little disappointed he wasn't wearing a black leather kilt, which was his normal attire, but black jeans instead. "You got a problem, sweetie?"

"I'm not your sweetie. And yes." She toed the dagger. "I need you to pick this up for me."

He propped his hands at his hips and looked over the dagger on the ground. Gave her a funny smile. "Seriously? Too heavy for you?"

"It's a blade used to kill witches."

"Ah. Well then. What do I get out of the deal?"

She smiled. "I just kegged some stout."

"That's a good start. You want to fill a few growlers and head over to my place for some Netflix and chill?"

She bumped his fist with hers. Beer and movies with a sexy werewolf? She could dig it. But as for the chill part? "Let's do pizza instead."

"I'm appalled by the way I acted toward you," Dane said as Eryss navigated them toward her home through a gentle snowfall. He was still shaking from the events in the parking lot, so he shoved his hands into his coat pockets. "I'm so sorry, Eryss. You must have been frightened out of your wits."

She cast him a quick glance that served as a sharp cut to his assumption. Eryss, frightened? Doubtful. She had countered his attack with swift and powerful witchcraft. The baselard had been no match to her and her friend's magic.

And that didn't unnerve him so much as freak him out. What was happening? He was *not* the witch hunter.

And yet, *was* he? The dagger had led him to Eryss tonight, and he'd been out of his mind with anger toward her about the death of his father.

A father who had died many centuries earlier.

"It's bizarre," he muttered, for the small car felt too quiet now. She wasn't in the mood to converse. And he understood that. But he couldn't fight the nervous energy jittering up and down his limbs. "Who is this Trouble person your friend is calling?"

"Werewolf," Eryss said curtly. She signaled and turned into her driveway.

Dane nodded. He'd seen a werewolf shift once. The creature defied all scientific rationale. Watching a man transform into the shape of a wolf-man in a matter of seconds? It had been the event that had cinched his beliefs and his desire to work with the Agency. Because no man should ever have to witness such and then be left with the unthinkable task of trying to figure it all out. It really was better for the common man not to know.

And it had refueled his childhood fascination for the unknown. A fascination that had been born the day he'd found the sword packed away in his father's trunk.

It was a strange coincidence that he'd lost his father in the thirteenth century and also in his present life. Of course, he knew Eryss would tell him there were no coincidences. And scientifically, the law of averages explained it, as well. How many lives had he lived? He had surely lost his father at a young age in a handful of those lives.

The car rolled into the garage and Eryss turned off the ignition. She got out quickly, closing the door behind her. Her anger lingered in the car. And Dane inhaled through his nose and nodded.

"I'll make things right with her. I have to."

* * *

Eryss had needed to get away from Dane for a minute or two. See if she could find her calm. He had to have noticed her tight grip on the steering wheel during the drive home.

And yet, if he'd been enchanted by the sword, she could not blame him for his actions. So finding a sense of calm was important, not only to her well-being, but to Dane's face. She'd never slapped a man before, but—oh, did it ever feel necessary now.

"Chill," she whispered as she paced the kitchen floor before the butcher-block table. He hadn't come inside yet. "He's as confused as I am. Surround me with white light," she said, drawing her fingers down from her crown to her toes. As an added measure, she grabbed the black tourmaline crystal from the windowsill and shoved it in her jeans pocket. It would serve as a protection from negative energies.

Valor hadn't called yet, but Eryss assumed Trouble might still be on his way to the parking lot. He lived about forty minutes away. He and Valor were friends. That werewolf was impulsive and loved a good fight, for any reason.

Men and their ridiculous need to prove they were the alpha.

The door opened and Dane stepped inside, kicking his shoes off on the rubber mat and shedding gloves, hat and coat as quickly. He searched her face, perhaps gauging her mood, so Eryss offered a weak smile. She was calm. She would not blame him for what the enchantment had made him do.

"Did Valor call?" he asked, remaining, wisely, by the door.

"I'd give her another half hour or so," Eryss said.

"Don't worry, the dagger will be safe with the two of them."

"I trust her because I trust you," he offered. "But I'm not sure how you can ever trust me again after what happened." He splayed his hands out before him. "I don't think I was in my right mind."

"You were not. And I can forgive you the enchantment. But the only way to overcome this is to never touch the dagger again. Do you think you can do that?"

"Now that I've learned it's enchanted, I have to bring it in to the Agency. We have methods of disenchanting it."

"Can't you call in a coworker to pick it up for you? Or try to mail it again? Dane, this is directly related to you and your safety." Eryss inhaled a sharp breath. "And mine. You said you had a vision of us? Did you mention something about your father?"

"You killed him." He walked forward and didn't approach her, but instead sat at a stool before the table, resting his elbows on the wood. "I saw us in a vision. We looked different, but of course I knew it was us. Ivor and Alexandra. And you stood over a man whom I knew was my father."

Eryss slid onto a stool opposite Dane and leaned her elbows on the table. "And?"

"You were holding a bloody knife. You'd stabbed my father in the heart. And because I was out of my head with anger, I rushed at you."

"Weren't Alexandra and Ivor married in that time period?"

"Yes." He clasped his hands before his mouth,. "My anger was so strong. My father—you killed him."

"I can't imagine how I could be so cruel."

"Nor I."

"But Dane, that was centuries ago. Are you saying

you've sought vengeance against me through the ages for…?" She couldn't even speak the heinous crime he'd accused her of committing.

He shrugged. "I think so. I'm not sure. I just know that I plunged a blade—the baselard—through your heart. And at the same time, you stabbed me. We died together, over my father's body."

Eryss sucked in a breath and stared at her fingers resting on the wood table. She couldn't bring herself to look at him. She had murdered his father? It sounded outrageous. And yet he was not a man to fabricate lies or stories. Just a day ago he couldn't conceive of having visions related to a past life. So now, what he told her had to be true.

And she had seen them together in that time period as Alexandra and Ivor. Yet only loving one another. Never angry, and certainly not trying to kill each other.

Then she remembered.

"In one of my visions, you said something about not stopping until you saw me burn."

Dane swallowed audibly. "I think I know that."

"Then why haven't you burned me yet? Why carry this out through the ages? Fire would be the thing to end all this."

"Eryss, listen to what you're saying." He reached across the table, then stood and rushed around to turn her to face him. "I mean it when I say I would never harm you."

"Yes, but maybe you've said much the same in the past. It's not you who is doing the harm, it's the dagger. It has power over you. It must have picked up the dark enchantment that first time we both perished, over your father's body. This is…so much to take in."

He hugged her, and when she wanted to pull away,

Eryss instead laid her head on his shoulder and clung to his warmth, wishing she could lose herself in his leather and spice scent. And also wished that she'd never incited the anacampserote spell to bring her past love to her.

But would he have come to her no matter what? If she'd always been murdered by Dane before her thirtieth birthday, that meant he would've arrived one way or another. Her birthday was only three days away.

"Do you think this happens between us in every reincarnation?" she asked. "Have we ever simply loved and lived and grown old together?"

"I don't know. But how could you have done it?"

She searched his gaze. "Done what?"

"Killed my father. I remember you said something about a sacrifice, but I don't recall what it meant."

It was as though a child had just asked her to explain an unthinkable crime. She felt innocence lost in fear. Was he somehow expressing his loss and sadness over the father he'd lost in this lifetime as well? The poor man. He was so lost.

"I don't know, Dane. I've never had a murderous inclination in my life."

"This life," he corrected.

"What are you saying? That I could have been a dark witch then? No. I know in my soul that I have always served the Light. I would never take a life without…"

She couldn't finish that statement, because obviously she *had* taken a life. And not just Dane's father, but Dane's, as well. Over and over.

"In self-defense," she whispered, then stood and walked to the sink to distance herself from her lover's touch. "Maybe I was protecting you from him?"

The bar stool scraped the floor as Dane sat again, not answering her question.

Eryss wished she could grasp a vision of the event, to really know what had happened. There had to be a way. She could return to the soul seer, she supposed.

Her cell phone rang and she saw it was Valor. Dane watched keenly as she answered. "Everything cool?"

"Yeah, I'm with Trouble. He's going to bring the dagger to his dad's place. You know Malakai Saint-Pierre is a swordsmith?"

"Right. But what are you thinking? Do you think he can disenchant it?"

"Not sure. But Trouble thinks he should take a look at it. Where's the witch hunter?"

"Here." Had she just admitted what she and Dane had both been dancing around? Of course he was the witch hunter. "We're talking."

"Be careful, Eryss. Just because the guy doesn't have a weapon on him doesn't mean he's not a danger to you. I know you like the guy, but—hell, maybe I should come stay the night with you."

"No, I'm good. I appreciate you taking care of the dagger, Valor. Give Trouble my thanks, too. Everything is cool here. Trust me." She smiled at Dane, who forced a grim smile onto his tight lips. "I'll call you in the morning. Thanks."

She set the phone on the counter and yawned. She wasn't so much tired as bone weary. Exhausted from the emotional roller coaster she'd had to ride lately. All she wanted was to sink into a nice hot bath and soak for an hour. She couldn't decide if she wanted Dane here or back at the hotel, at a safe distance.

"Trouble's dad is a swordsmith," she explained to Dane. "They've taken it there."

He stood and crossed his arms over his chest. "They had better not tamper with it."

"It's okay. Malakai and Trouble are werewolves. They know not to mess with magic and enchantments. But it might not hurt to have a craftsman take a look at it. See what he thinks. You okay with that?"

Dane heaved out a sigh. "Not really, but I haven't much choice, do I? Where do these werewolves live?"

"About a forty-five-minute drive from here. I'll take you there in the morning, uh, if we decide that's a safe thing to do."

Dane nodded. "Right. The whole enchantment thing." He rubbed his jaw. "This is what I don't get. I apparently have known through the ages that fire is what kills witches. So the fact that I never take it that far makes me wonder why. Have I not wanted to make your death final? Is there something that keeps holding me back?"

It was an interesting way to consider things. And maybe, just maybe… "I did say our love would survive the ages. Maybe love is what will end this?"

He tilted his head in question.

"Love must have started it. If we were married, we were obviously in love. So maybe love will end it."

"Like we have to get married again? I don't understand that. I mean, I'm not even…" He stopped, slapped a palm over his chest. "Well, you know."

She quickly nodded. "Oh, sure. This has just been a fling. I wouldn't expect either of us to fall in love so quickly."

But truthfully? She already had. Because soul mates and true love did mean something to Eryss. And she had called Dane to her. With the power of a love that had survived the centuries. But if he didn't feel it, a girl couldn't ask a man to love her. Not even if it meant saving her life.

"Do you want me to leave?" he asked.

Eryss wrapped her arms across her stomach, feeling

so alone standing halfway across the room from him, and desperately wanting a safe place to land. "Do you want to leave?" she returned.

"No," he said softly, yet with a surety that she felt in her bones. "I'd like to stay the night with you. But I understand I've done something horrible. I can sleep on the couch out in the conservatory. I just don't want to go back to the lonely hotel room."

"I'll get you a blanket and pillow," Eryss offered, and immediately went upstairs. She heard Dane open the door to the conservatory as she reached the top of the steps.

From a hall closet, she retrieved a soft blue chenille blanket and then tugged a clean pillowcase over a fluffy pillow. Clutching them both to her chest, she bowed her face into the blanket and sought that wise, rational part of herself that she knew was her soul.

She didn't ask. She simply waited for an answer. And the one she got displeased her.

Really? She *shouldn't* trust him?

Hmm…

Dane sat on the emerald sofa and stretched his legs, burying his toes in the grass. A guy could get used to living in a place like this. With a woman like Eryss.

If the guy were not controlled by some wicked, witch-hunting dagger.

She'd done the right thing by having her friend take the weapon away. Dane knew, without a doubt, that should he touch it again, it would once again control his thinking and he would go after Eryss with a vengeance. He didn't want that to happen. No matter what crimes she'd committed against him in his past.

Because it had been his past. Entirely different lifetimes. Entirely different people. Only the same souls.

He wasn't sure how to process that. This soul discovery stuff was new to him.

But what was done was done. There was no reason to carry a grudge through the centuries. Somehow the dagger had been enchanted with his anger and desire for revenge, and now it seemed to possess a life of its own.

He needed that thing destroyed. Or it would destroy him. And Eryss. The Agency did have a contingency plan for items too volatile to contain, and he would mark the witch blade as a candidate for that backup plan.

He tugged out his phone, did the math on the time difference from the States to Europe and, instead of calling, decided to text his boss for further instructions regarding the dagger.

The conservatory door opened and Eryss padded across the grass. She handed him a soft, snuggly blanket and tossed a thick pillow at the end of the couch. He wouldn't even ask to sleep with her. He had no right. And if she'd wanted that, she would have offered. He didn't deserve that intimacy with her.

Not until he could prove he did deserve it. And he wanted to, so he would prove it. Because…he didn't think a person could fall in love so quickly. But perhaps he had. How was a person to recognize love in the midst of such a conflicting storm of emotions?

"Thanks. This means a lot to me," he said. "You don't have to be so kind, Eryss."

"No, I don't have to be, but I want to. You should know that every bone in my body is screaming for me to push you away and wipe my hands of you. No woman would ever be stupid enough to allow a man to curl up on her couch for the night who, just an hour ago, came after her with a death wish."

"Then why are you allowing it to happen?"

She sucked in her lower lip. Dane hated to see that soft, rose mouth shaped in sadness. Another glint of a tear glimmered in her eye. He hated himself for that.

"Because you are mine," she said in a wobbly tone that betrayed her struggling emotions. "And I am yours. And what we've had up until now has been amazing. And maybe we just need to get over this one bump in the road in order to really learn how amazing the two of us can be together. I'd like to celebrate my birthday with you."

Feeling his own tears threatening, Dane clasped her hand and looked up at her. "I don't deserve you."

"Yes, you do. I'm no saint, nor do I belong on a pedestal. I'm a witch. And you're a witch hunter. We should hate one another. And maybe ancient, visceral parts of us do. But we're together for a purpose. We need to learn from one another. Souls don't cling to one another through the ages for no reason. We chose each other, over and over, and we'll keep doing that until a lesson is learned. And we're going to get things right this time."

"Even if it kills us?"

"If it kills us, we won't have gotten it right." She bowed her forehead to his and closed her eyes. Her hair swept his cheeks and Dane closed his own eyes, taking in her wintery sage scent. "Know me," she said. "As you have always known me."

He knew she was speaking of the first time they'd found one another, fallen in love and married. He'd witnessed that time, but he hadn't known all. Such as why she'd been compelled to kill his father. It was the key to solving this bizarre reenactment of their pasts.

After she stood and dropped his hand, she tucked the blanket around him, and Dane leaned back on the couch.

"Would you mind if I snuggled with you for a while? I'm so tired. And I know I need a shower, but—"

"Come here," he said. Lying down, he patted the couch before him and lifted the blanket.

She climbed under the soft chenille and snuggled her head against his shoulder. Dane glided a hand up her back and held her gently, without demanding anything, inhaling sage and the sweet summer grass.

And he wondered if love really could save them.

Chapter 22

Dane's hair was still wet. He'd taken a shower in Eryss's bathroom after he'd risen this morning to find himself alone on the couch. Now, freshly showered, he spied Eryss in the kitchen stirring something in a pot over the stove.

She greeted him with a smile and a kiss, and placed a bowl of oatmeal before him. "Fresh-squeezed lemon juice or water?"

"Both." Cinnamon, chia and blueberries were stirred into the breakfast oatmeal. "I think your shower pipe needs a twist with a wrench. It's starting to leak. If you have a toolbox I can take care of that for you."

"It's out in the garage. You can't miss it because it's pink."

"I'll do that before we leave. We're going to see the werewolf who has the dagger today, yes?"

She sat next to him and set juice and water before him. "I had intended to go to Malakai Saint-Pierre's home and see what was up."

"I'm going along. I know the dangers, and I promise I will keep at a distance. But don't shut me out of this, Eryss. This is not something we can defeat on our own."

"I agree. Will you allow me to put a protection spell on you? Something to keep the energy from the dagger away from you?"

"I think I can handle that."

"Then here's to working together." She held up her water glass and Dane met it with a clink of his own.

"Tell me what you want out of this relationship, Eryss. I'm curious."

"Are you thinking I want to get married, have kids and live happily ever after?"

He lifted a brow. "You said you performed a spell to bring your long-lost love to you. What other intentions would provoke you to do so?"

"Honestly? I've never thought beyond the *finding him* part."

He wasn't sure if she was lying to herself or just him, but Dane wanted to believe her. On the other hand, if she'd confessed to wanting a life together, he was pretty sure it wouldn't have upset him. And how crazy was that?

"Can we take it one day at a time?" she asked.

Dane lifted his glass again and she met it for another toast. "To one day at a time. And…to standing strong together. No matter what."

"No matter what."

Malakai Saint-Pierre lived out in the country, near Clover Lake, which was a good drive from where Eryss lived. She'd called ahead, and Kai and his son Trouble were both eager to talk with her. She mentioned she was bringing Dane, and Trouble had cautioned her to ensure he kept his distance.

"So, werewolves." Dane scrolled through his cell phone messages as Eryss drove north. "I've seen one shift but didn't stick around to shake its hand and chat with it. Tell me what I need to know."

"They're just like you and me when in their *were* or man shape. Regular guys. Though Trouble bears that name for a reason. When he and Valor go out drinking, that can turn into one heck of a hot mess. 'Course, it's good for a woman to get into such a mess at least once in her life."

"Is that so? How many hot messes have you partaken in?"

"There was a guy in high school. He may have been the one to teach me the virtues of beer drinking. Although he took it to excess. He liked beer, NASCAR and Jesus."

"Whoa. I bet the witch didn't play well with his theologies."

"Never told him my beliefs. Just marked it off as an adventure and moved on."

"Am I another adventure?"

"You are," she said with certainty. "But you're not the kind a woman can easily move on from. What about you? Have you ever had any wild and crazy relationships?"

"I've been lucky on the crazy front. No wild women to speak of. And I would call myself a regular guy. Very calm and rational."

"And deadly with a dagger."

"Apparently. But I thought you weren't going to hold that against me?"

"I'm not. Maybe we're both in our hot mess phase right now."

"You think? Well, if you're a hot mess, I'm in for the ride."

"You know all the right things to say. That's the place just ahead."

Eryss navigated down a narrow gravel driveway, which had been plowed to an icy slick space. Bare-branched maple trees stood among thick northern pines and straight birch trees with pale bark. The Saint-Pierres owned a vast amount of land that included forest. It must be a dream to have so much undisturbed nature right in one's backyard. Eryss could live anywhere so long as she had nature. She might even consider surfing, just for the experience. Opening a brewery in California was looking more and more like it deserved a mark in the "possibility" column of her life.

She parked before an architecturally stunning brick two-story, all angles and jutting roof and windows in shapes to accommodate the slants and lines of the building. Snow glittered on the rooftop, and the windows gleamed in the rare winter sunlight.

A tall man with broad shoulders and dark hair skipped around the corner of the house. He wore only jeans, boots and a T-shirt that showed off his bulging biceps and tight abs. Trouble Saint-Pierre. He waved and gestured for them to follow him.

"You ready for this?" Eryss asked Dane.

"You were going to put a protection spell on me?"

"Right. You want one against the werewolf, too?"

Dane bristled proudly and shook his head. "Nah, I can take him."

No one could *take* Trouble, but Eryss wasn't going to bust Dane's alpha pride, so the protection spell against enchantment was all she put over his aura.

Dane was feeling slightly less manly bundled in a winter coat, gloves and scarf, while standing next to the

werewolf with the abs on crack. If he'd gotten his name
for a reason, Dane knew he had to be cautious. Especially
since Trouble was, after all, a werewolf.

No, Dane was good. He was smart, and could take a
punch as well as deliver one. But he wasn't here to fight. It
was just that the wolf sent off weird I'm-ready-to-rumble
vibes.

"Dane, this is Trouble. Trouble, Dane." Eryss introduced them as they paused before a shed around back of
the house. They'd followed a snow-trampled path beside
a narrow stream to get here.

"The witch hunter," Trouble said as he slapped a hand
into Dane's gloved fingers and squeezed. Hard.

Squeezing back just as hard, Dane nodded. "I won't
take offense at such a label so long as you don't take offense at any assumptions I should make regarding your
name."

"Ha!" The man bounced on his feet and punched the
air playfully. "You want to go a few rounds and see just
how much trouble I can be?"

Dane put up placating palms. "We're cool, man."

"Yeah? I heard you went after Eryss with that freakin'
dagger last night. Not cool."

"I wasn't in complete use of my faculties."

Trouble squinted at Eryss, and Dane assumed he
wasn't quite sure what he meant. More brawn than
brains? Probably didn't matter much because one punch
from those fists would reduce any challenger to a whim-
per.

"Eryss tells me your father is a swordsmith?"

"Yeah, he's inside. This is his work shed." Trouble
looked to Eryss. "I think we agreed that he wasn't going
to get too close to the thing?"

"No problem," Dane said. "I'd like to come inside. It's cold out here. But I'll remain by the door. Promise."

Trouble met Eryss's gaze. She didn't try to insult Dane by acting as if she had a right to tell him what he could or could not do. Finally, Trouble opened the door and gestured them both inside.

The air was clear but smelled of smoke and iron, and it was humid. The warmth was a nice welcome after the frigid cold. Dane shed his gloves and unzipped his coat. Over by the forge, which wasn't lit, but was highlighted by fluorescent bulbs strung overhead, stood another man as tall as Trouble and equally as built.

Minnesota, the Nordic land of Vikings and lumberjacks, Dane mused. And werewolves. Of course, as he was learning, werewolves were naturally physically intimidating, no matter their form.

"Dad, this is Eryss and Dane," Trouble called, alerting the man who was bent over a wood table beside the forge. All dark power and unspoken growls, he looked up, but then smiled at them. "My dad," Trouble said to them, "Malakai Saint-Pierre. You've met, yes, Eryss?"

"We have," Kai offered as he strode over and took Eryss's hand. He kissed the back of it and winked at her. But his glance to Dane caused his nostrils to twitch, and he lifted his chin defiantly. "You the witch hunter?"

Dane was prepared to deny the accusation once again, but then thought better of it, and thrust out his hand to shake Kai's. He tried, but failed, not to wince as the beefy wolf slapped a palm against his and squeezed much harder than his son had.

"You look like a schoolteacher," Kai commented, taking in Dane's vest and shirt beneath the open coat. "Not a sword-wielding maniac."

"Maniac? I'm not—please, you're jumping to conclusions. And I've only just learned about the witch hunting thing. I am not a threat to Eryss. Trust me."

"The blade will determine that," Malakai said. "Come take a look." He strode back to the table.

When Dane stepped forward, he was stopped by a giant fist to his chest. While he'd only tapped him, Trouble's dark gaze cautioned him.

Dane put up his hands again. "Right. I'll just watch from the door, as agreed."

"Good boy," Trouble said.

The demeaning comment hadn't been necessary, and it raised Dane's ire. If he had the dagger in hand, none of them would dare to challenge or make fun of him. He watched keenly as Malakai held up the dagger beneath the light.

"This is cold iron," he said.

Cold iron was simply a fantastical term for iron. It was used to denote steel and/or weapons that may have detrimental effects on supernaturals. It was more of a historical term than anything.

On the other hand, Dane worked for the Agency. And he didn't have to spin his own knowledge on the stuff. Cold iron was different from any other iron in that it *did* possess a supernatural nature. Yet he'd have to do lab tests to determine that nature. Of course, a man who worked with metals—and who was also paranormal— would surely recognize cold iron.

"I'd date it to the early 1200s or even late 1100s," Malakai added.

"That is interesting," Eryss said. "We believe Dane owned it in or around the thirteenth century. So he must have obtained it or possibly inherited it."

Both Saint-Pierre men gave Eryss wonky looks. Trouble leaned his palms onto the table and studied her as if she'd just eaten a cockroach.

"We've both reincarnated through the ages," she explained matter-of-factly. "We were married in the thirteenth century. Then I killed Ivor's father, for reasons unknown to us both. Uh, Ivor was Dane. And then he stabbed me with that dagger while I stabbed him with mine. We've basically been doing much the same every time we come to a new life. We find each other, then kill one another before our thirtieth birthdays. Mine is in two days."

Trouble blew out a breath. His father eyed Dane through the dark shadows that separated them. The look was not one Dane would like to meet in a dark forest or even on a dimly lit city street. But he maintained his stance. It wasn't wise to show fear in the presence of werewolf.

"It won't happen again in this lifetime," Dane said firmly. "It can't."

"Shit." Malakai gripped the dagger hilt firmly and studied the blade. "Did you see that?"

"The dagger wobbled in your grip," Trouble said. "I thought you were just losing hold of it."

"I know how to handle a weapon, boy. It moved of its own volition." Again he glanced to Dane. "Did you say he was controlled by this last night?"

"I believe it's enchanted," Eryss answered. "Possibly since that first time we went after one another in the thirteenth century. For some reason the dagger seems to find him through the ages, and it makes him go after me."

"And you two are in love every time?" Trouble asked.

"I'm not sure. Perhaps sometimes we are enemies from the start. Other times I know we've been in love, in many lives. It's a soul thing."

"I know about soul things," Malakai commented with a broad smile. Eryss was aware he was happily married to a beautiful faery. "I also know this dagger is getting jittery. You should step out of here," he said to Dane. "Now."

"Well, I, uh—"

The elder werewolf swore and hissed. Dane saw the blade fly toward him. He had the instinct to duck, but at the last minute, instead of acting a coward, he thrust out his hand and caught the hilt in his hand. A swing of the blade cut the air.

And he felt something great rise within him—all the power he needed to defeat any witch or werewolf who should dare to challenge him.

Chapter 23

"The witch must die."

Eryss chirped out a sound when she heard Dane say that. He stood before the door, dagger held at the ready. His eyes were white. He was captured by the wicked enchantment that had been infused into the dagger so many centuries earlier.

A slash of steel cut the air as Malakai grabbed a sword from an iron hook on the shed wall and approached Dane. A firm hand at Eryss's back reminded her she was not alone.

"Let me get you out of here," Trouble said. "Leave this to them."

"Why isn't the enchantment protection working? He'll kill him."

"Who? Your witch hunter or my dad? My dad isn't going to take any man's life. And he sure as hell isn't going to sacrifice his own today. Come on. You're not safe in here. And your presence might even be what's riling that bastard up."

As the blades clashed together in a dull *tang*, Eryss allowed Trouble to pull her out through a back door and into the cool winter air. He tugged her toward the house. Much as she pined to stay and to know every move Dane made—and avoided—she relented. Trouble might be right. Her presence could aggravate the enchantment.

Dane matched the werewolf move for move. Backed around the forge and against a wall, he managed an overhead strike, bringing down the dagger and hitting the powerful beast on the shoulder with the hilt. Malakai growled and spun, returning with an attack, but Dane dodged him and dashed to the center of the shed.

"I can go at this all day, hunter," Malakai said. "I'm not going to take your life. And I know you have not the strength or fortitude to take mine. You ever kill a man? Or is it only helpless witches you go after?"

Charging with a battle cry that roughened the inside of his throat, Dane swung his blade close to the man's neck. The wolf merely smirked and gestured with his fingers for him to come at him again.

"It's only the witch I have a problem with," he said. "She killed my father. I will not rest until she burns."

Malakai clanked his sword against Dane's. Once. Twice. There was a slide of steel against iron, and the twosome spun away from one another, reassessing their positions.

"Yes, burning will kill a witch," Malakai offered, "but I think you're going about it the wrong way, buddy. No fire to your arsenal?"

"I must subdue her first."

"A blade to the heart will do more than subdue. You

don't want to harm Eryss." The wolf backed Dane up until his spine hit the wall. Sword blades kissed. The man's dark eyes narrowed at him. "I can feel the dark magic humming off the blade and coming from you, as well."

With a quick flick, the wolf managed to snatch the dagger from Dane's hand. The blade soared over their heads and landed in the cold forge in the center of the room. Dane stepped forward, right into the meaty fist that connected up under his ribs, pummeling his kidney. Hissing out his breath, Dane could not fight the wicked pain that doubled him over and brought him to his knees. He fell forward, landing on his palms.

The wolf gripped his hair and pulled up his head. "I'm going to melt that blade down and end this right now."

"No!"

A renewed burst of energy flipped Dane to his back on the dirt floor. He jammed a foot between the wolf's legs and toppled the mighty beast. Rising onto his knees, Dane pulled back his arm, making a fist.

The air surrounding her in the open-floor-plan cabin felt cool and spring-like, scented with lilacs and clover. Arms spread wide, Eryss stood with her eyes closed and fingertips outspread. She wasn't drawing in a protection about her, but rather, spreading out her energy in a healing burst that she hoped would penetrate the walls of this home and reach into the shed, where she couldn't imagine what Dane was doing.

Technically, she *could* imagine. She just didn't want to go there.

When she spied the frost on the windows high in the V of the cathedral-style structure that looked over the backyard, she called on an elemental to do the spying for her. The frost danced into a shape of a large snowflake and fluttered away from the window, toward the shed.

"What are you doing?"

She turned to Trouble, reining her energy and exhaling. "Nothing wicked, if that's what you're wondering. They've been in there a long time. I want to see what's happening."

"My dad won't hurt him."

"But Dane is enchanted. He's not in his right mind. He could hurt your dad."

Trouble scoffed and gestured to the kitchen. "You want something to drink?"

"No. I want to be out there."

"They've stopped poking their swords at one another."

"How do you know that?"

Trouble tapped an earlobe. "I can hear pretty damn good. Now they've taken up fists." He bounced on his feet like a prizefighter, throwing a punch before him.

Eryss ran her fingers through her hair. Her nerves went on attack. Was Dane a fighter? He was a scientist. Yet he did work for an agency that put him in encounters with paranormal beings. But that didn't mean he was a skilled fighter. Shit. Malakai would tear him apart.

She rushed for the door.

Trouble arrived there first, so she slammed into his chest. He held her by her upper arms. The wolf put out a sensual musk that would have had her purring at his feet were she not aware of his propensity to use that attraction for less than sincere motives.

"They're almost finished," he said. "Just let this happen. Maybe if he gets the shit kicked out of him, the hunter will retreat for good."

"But such violence is not what Dane wants. It's the enchantment—"

The shed door opened with a squeak, and out staggered a man, blood streaming down his cheek.

"Let me go!" Eryss shoved Trouble aside and rushed outside to Dane. He saw her coming and put up a hand to halt her. She respected his need for space and stopped, but twisted her hands together impatiently. "Are you okay?"

His cheeks were spattered with blood. His lower lip bled. He nodded slightly. *Back off* was the silent message he gave, and Eryss did so. He'd taken a wallop from Malakai, who now stood in the open doorway. The wolf was equally bloodied and bruised, which gave Eryss some small thrill. Her man had stood his own against a werewolf, one of the strongest of all creatures who walked this mortal realm.

"Sorry," Dane said quietly, then strode off down the path they'd followed when they'd first arrived.

Eryss took two steps to go after him until she saw Malakai shake his head. She turned to the werewolf in the doorway, who had one elbow propped high against the frame. He spat blood out onto the snow.

"He's a tough one," Malakai said. "But that dagger needs to go."

"I agree. Where is it?"

"In the forge. I'm going to fire it up and melt the thing down."

Why she hadn't thought of that surprised her now. "That sounds like the perfect solution to this problem. Thank you, Kai. And, uh, thanks for not hurting him too much."

"He'll be sore for days. As will I." He pressed a palm to his bruised ribs. "Take him home and do some witchy healing on him. The man doesn't want to hurt you. And he won't, as long as the dagger is destroyed. I'll give you a call when it's done." He stepped out of the shed and wandered toward the house.

Taking that as her dismissal, Eryss ran around the side of the house. She found Dane leaning against the car, with no coat or gloves on, and his shirt torn to reveal bloodied bruises on his skin. He didn't meet her gaze, but hissed when she touched his jaw.

"Sorry. I have some healing potions at home. Will you let me make this better?"

He nodded, and silently turned to get in the car.

Her hero had been taken down a few notches, and he was handling it the best he could. Yet he had proved his skill against one who should have been much stronger than him.

And how? Because the dagger had controlled him? Or because he had been fighting for her?

Chapter 24

Dane's cell phone rang as Eryss pulled the car into her garage. She looked to him, and he indicated he'd be in after he took the call. He waited to answer until she got out of the car. It was Tor.

"How's it going, Winthur? You get your hands on that dagger yet? I thought I'd have a report on it by now."

"Yes, well, it was never a job, if you recall."

"Right. But you had intended to send a report on your findings."

"Didn't you get my text?"

"No. What's up? Is it dangerous? Or just an antique?"

"It's…" He winced at the pain in his ribs. That kidney punch had literally taken his sight for a few seconds. He'd never felt anything so painful. "Out of my hands at the moment. I'm having trouble with it."

"You need backup? What's the issue?"

"It's enchanted."

"Got it. I can send in a disenchanter. Can probably get someone there in two days. Maybe faster if I can locate one in the area."

In two days Eryss would turn thirty. And if her visions were correct, she never made it to her thirtieth birthday. Ever.

"That might be necessary. A werewolf has it right now and he's…" Hell, he'd completely forgotten the wolf's intention to melt the dagger down. "I gotta go. I need to check on something. Do send the disenchanter. As quickly as possible."

He clicked off and twisted to get out of the car, growling at the pain that sputtered fire within him. The cold didn't even bother him, for every muscle burned. He forced himself to rush out of the garage and into Eryss's home. The kitchen greeted him with a warm aroma of sweet spices and lingering scents of savory foods.

"Eryss!"

"In the conservatory!"

"I need Saint-Pierre's number," he said as he entered the lush green room. Instinctually, he kicked off his shoes and almost groaned in delight as the grass caressed his soles. "I have to stop him. The werewolf is going to melt down the dagger."

"Yes." Eryss stood near a basket of what looked like crystals, herbs and candles. She gestured for him to sit on the couch, but Dane did not. "It's what's best, yes? With the dagger gone, then the enchantment will no longer have control over you."

"But it was mine. My father—the man who fathered me in this lifetime, a man I never got to know—once owned that dagger. Eryss, don't you understand?"

"I do understand. And it's not fair to you, but—" She sighed. "Fine. Call him. Do whatever you want. I thought you said you'd never harm me." She stomped out of the conservatory. "I'll get his number."

Dane sat on the couch and bent over, catching his face in his palms.

She was right. No matter how much he thought the dagger meant to him, it would never be right. It would always demand something of him he wasn't willing to fulfill. He was not a murderer. And he would prove that by ensuring that in this lifetime, both of them survived beyond their thirtieth birthday.

"You got your phone?" Eryss returned with an address book. "I'll give you the number."

"No." He could hear waning trust in her voice, and hated himself for his cruelties to her. "Let him destroy it. It's what's best."

She knelt on the grass before him, and Dane dared to dip his head and nuzzle his nose against her hair. The soft sweetness of her pulled tears from his eyes. "I've learned all I can about Edison Winthur. The dagger was not a connection between the two of us. But it was a weird way of connecting us. Maybe it was my father who brought us together in this lifetime?"

She reached up and stroked the back of his head. "That sounds lovely. Let's leave it at that then? It would be a great way to honor him."

"Thank you for always being so understanding."

She pressed a finger over his lips. "I suspect another apology coming on, and I won't hear it. We're good. Lie down," she said softly. "Let me take the pain from you."

"Why? Shouldn't I have to suffer this pain in recompense for the pain I've caused you? I can't believe what's become of me."

"It's going to end today," she reassured him.

Then she tilted up his face and kissed his eyelid. Even

that hurt, but he didn't say so. With all they had been through in so little time, she'd never stopped believing in him and wanting to comfort him.

"I don't deserve your kindness," he said.

"Stop being the martyr. Of course you do. I love you, Dane."

He lifted his head and met her gaze. It was calm and true. She'd spoken a truth from her heart, and it didn't surprise him. But he couldn't say it in return because he didn't know if he *did* love her. He should. But a man who loved a woman would never raise a weapon against her.

"Lie down," she said again. "Let me work some healing magic on you."

He relented and lay back. And she went about lighting candles and placing crystals on his chakras, and then chanting words he didn't know the meanings of, but yet could feel their power as the pain began to lift and his muscles relaxed, sinking him into a deep sleep.

Malakai stood over the flames flickering in the forge. It had been burning for two hours, and he was satisfied it had reached a temperature that could melt cold iron.

Trouble had wandered in with a bottle of water for him, and he drank it down in two swallows.

"You going to melt the witch hunter's blade?" Trouble asked.

"Only way to stop the enchantment. Hand it to me, will you?"

Trouble wandered about the shed, looking for the dagger.

"I set it over there." Kai turned to the wall where he'd propped the dagger before starting the flames. "Where'd it go? You pick it up?"

"I haven't touched that thing since I brought it to you.

You sure it's not mixed in with some of those?" His son pointed to a conglomeration of swords stacked in the corner that Kai had either given up on during the forging process or that he wanted to give a second go to.

He rushed over and sorted through the misfit swords, but none were the witch hunter's blade. How could he have misplaced the thing? He had left the shed only to go wash up after the fight and had taken a phone call from Rissa, his wife, and when he'd returned, the dagger had been lying where he'd last seen it, in the forge. He'd taken it out and propped it against the wall. And now…

"Curse the moon. It's gone."

Alexandra observed her new husband's father from afar. She'd been suspicious of him over the past months. She knew that Ivor practiced witchcraft, but only in healing and to bring him closer to the elements of nature that then helped him to hunt efficiently. It was a craft he'd learned from his father. Yet the father had about him a dark aura.

And now she shivered as her suspicions came to fruition. The father stood before an inverted star made of rowan branches, and wore only his calfskin breeches. His upper body was streaked with fresh raven's blood. He chanted to what Alexandra could only guess were demons.

And when he whispered the promise to bring his son to the altar as sacrifice, Alexandra turned and ran swiftly into the barren, snow-littered oat field toward home. She clasped a hand over the crystal dagger she always carried over her sternum and tucked in her stays. A gift from a village healer. Alexandra was not a witch, but she did believe in the power of healing.

As the cabin she and Ivor lived in loomed closer, she

*could hear the huffing breaths gaining on her from be-
hind. He'd followed her! And when her toe caught in her
skirts and she tumbled forward, Alexandra pulled out
the dagger. Her shoulder hit the snow and she rolled,
prepared to defend herself from the menacing evil that
pounced.*

Eryss cried out, "He was going to sacrifice you!"

Her voice startled Dane, who'd fallen into a snooze
on the couch. Eryss still held her hands over his stomach; she'd been sending her earth energy into him for
healing, hoping to connect with the ancient origin of his
soul. And she had.

She tugged her fingers away, waiting for him to rise
from the reverie. What she'd seen when she'd been in
that trance answered so many questions!

"Did I fall asleep?" Dane smoothed a palm over his
stomach. "I feel…still achy, but actually…" He sat up
and touched his jaw, then tested his shoulder where he
must have taken a fist from Malakai Saint-Pierre. "No
more pain. And I thought my lip would be swollen for
sure. Wow. Thanks."

He leaned in to kiss her, but Eryss put a finger over
his lips. He pouted. "Right. I suppose I don't deserve a
kiss from you."

"You do." She kissed him quickly. "But you need to
hear the real news. I went into a trance to heal you, and
our souls connected again."

"Did you see us in another life? I heard you call out.
What did you say?"

"I did trance out as Alexandra again. Our beginning
is the key to our present. I was by myself, wandering
through the woods, and I came upon your father. Actually, I think I was following him. And remember you said

you'd dreamed something about a sacrifice but didn't know what that meant?"

"Yes. Go on." She watched him tighten a fist on his lap.

"Your father was a dark witch, Dane."

Dane reared back from her, but since she knelt before his legs, he didn't get up and walk away—though she sensed he wanted to do just that.

"And believe it or not," she stated, "you were also a witch."

"Ridiculous."

"But true. But you weren't dark like your father. I know that you only used the craft for good. You were going to teach me your ways."

"Eryss—"

She pressed a finger to his lips. "Just listen. I saw your father performing an incantation. And he promised some malefic force he would make the ultimate sacrifice to gain power. I think your father was the first witch hunter."

Dane hissed. "I was a witch? How could I have not known? And my father came after me?"

"You weren't willing to believe I was a witch when we first met, even though you work with our kind."

"What else did you see?"

She knew he wasn't going to like what she said next, but it could mean finally coming to terms with this whole situation.

"Your father was going to murder you," she said.

Now Dane pushed up from the couch and strode through the grass with his hand at the back of his neck. He paced back toward her, flung out his hand in dismay, then shook his head and turned away. He was clearly struggling with yet another truth that could be accepted only by blind faith.

"That's wrong," he said. "You twist your own beliefs onto something you need to be true."

"Dane, you now understand you've lived many lives. Why is it so difficult to believe your father could have once been so evil? You said you heard him say he was going to sacrifice something."

"Yes but—I am not like my father!" he raged, pounding a fist against his chest. "And I never will be."

He marched out the doorway, and moments later Eryss heard the kitchen door shut, followed by the rental car's engine humming into motion.

"No, you're not like Edison Winthur," she said, alone in the conservatory. "But your original father? You could become something so much worse."

Dane charged into the antiques store and spied Harold Stuart strolling down the aisle back near his office. "We need to talk." He walked right up to the man, stopped and got an affirmative nod from him as Harold gestured toward his office door.

Once inside, Dane closed the door. "What do you know about Edison Winthur that you're not telling me? About the baselard? You know what it's capable of. Don't you?"

Harold crossed his arms high over his chest, then with a raise of his brows, dropped his arms and nodded. "I've been waiting for you a long time, boy. Your father was never willing to take on the task of witch hunter, so I knew it wasn't him but rather his son who would become my rightful heir."

"Your…rightful…?"

"Every creature society has fictionalized is real. I know that. You know that. That's why you do what you do, isn't it? Protect the paranormals from human discovery."

"How do you know about the Agency?"

Harold shrugged. "I make it a point to know a little about a lot when it comes to the paranormal. I have remained much the same, while you, you have changed. Drastically. For the better, of course. You might say I've been doing this for centuries."

"Centuries? What are you?"

"Human. Just like you are. But I've been around a few times. Just like you and that witch who works across the street."

Dane put up a palm to stop the man. Knowledge about the paranormal world aside, something didn't add up. "Did you *plan* to get me here? How did you know? I was the one who found the record on the baselard and contacted you. I don't understand."

"I've been waiting a long time for you to return to me, my soul son."

"Your soul son? What are you saying?"

"I was the man who fathered Ivor Svendson so many centuries ago. And your wife killed me."

Chapter 25

"But how did you—" Dane paced the short stretch from the office door to the chair. "This is too much coincidence. You can't be my—how do you know about Ivor? And now? I was recruited to the Agency…"

"I figured you'd come across the witch blade sooner or later. That thing has a way of finding you through the centuries. Or at least, after you decided to fight on the side of the good and not practice witchcraft."

"Not practice witchcraft? But Eryss…" Had accused Dane—or rather Ivor—of being a witch. And his father. Harold could not be that same soul if he believed witchcraft evil.

"I've got time to talk about all this," Harold said, "but I know you don't. Thirtieth birthday and all."

"How do you know about that?"

Harold shrugged, then splayed his hands before him in confession. "I've been keeping notes. Making sure my next incarnation finds her."

Dane gaped at him. "How many times has Eryss killed you?"

"Just the once. But that's all it took. The dark enchantment took hold of you and the dagger."

"Dark enchantment? But it didn't come from Eryss. She said—were you a witch? Were you going to sacrifice me, your son?"

Harold chuckled. "I've changed paths since then. I would never harm you, my soul son. Ever since I was stabbed by the bitch and the darkness seeped from my soul into the blade, I've been on a more righteous path."

"Righteous? You mean killing witches?"

"I don't murder. But as for you? Time to burn the witch, boy. Once and for all."

Incensed, Dane gripped the old man by the throat and pushed him against a wall where sales ads and historical ephemera were pinned. "You are *not* my father. Edison Winthur died twenty-seven years ago."

"I don't always reincarnate as your father. In fact, I rarely do. Only three times that I'm aware of. Edison was just another soul caught in our story. Haven't you had flashbacks? You know it's true. You need to trust what you've seen. I know the witch knows you're the one who has slain her through the centuries. That's due to me, boy. My only goal each lifetime is to get that dagger in your hands and you standing before the witch. But this time you've got to do it right. Use fire!"

Dane released the man and spun, running his fingers roughly through his hair as he frantically tried to digest everything. Harold knew it all. And he had actually been the catalyst to bringing him and Eryss together so Dane could murder her?

Harold was Ivor's father? The very man Alexandra had murdered, who had been the catalyst for Ivor killing her.

"From what I've seen in the flashbacks, I looked upon my father with pride. A man who was human, just like me."

"In your original incarnation, you were not born human. Your mother was witch."

"Then why marry her and have a child?"

"I began to practice the dark arts after our marriage. It intrigued me."

"Intrigued you? To sacrifice...? Eryss tells me—"

"The witch lies to keep you on her side. She fears her death and she'll say anything to prevent it. Where is the dagger? Why don't you simply do it?"

"I am not a murderer!"

"Blood and revenge fuel your soul, boy. You want that witch dead, and you know it."

"No! And the dagger is being melted down as we speak."

"What? You cannot destroy that dark magic! It is infused with my intent and desire to avenge the woman who took my life!"

"Yeah? So why don't *you* do it? You want her dead? You take her out."

"The enchantment lives in your blood. That's not my role."

An enchantment that had somehow emerged when he'd found the dagger at eight years old. What would he have done had his mother not wrenched that hideous thing away from him then? Perhaps he would have made a choice to walk the world as a witch hunter—and know it.

"I'm not going to make that choice to fill such a role now. I can only thank you for bringing me here, where I met the most wonderful woman I have ever known.

And now that the dagger is gone, we can get on with our lives. Stay away from Eryss and her friends, if you know what's good for you."

Dane opened the office door, but as he was leaving Harold said, "You can't destroy that blade. It'll find you. It always does."

"Did Eryss come in?"

Upon seeing the redheaded Mireio polishing one of the brew tanks with a white cloth, Dane strode to the end of the bar in the brewery. Agitated after his conversation with Harold, he probably shouldn't have walked straight over, but he needed to see Eryss. To hold her. Because only she could make the world right. Because he—did he love her?

Mireio popped around and tugged at her short skirt as she eyed him with a flutter of lashes and a smile. "Nope. I thought you two would be together today. She's been spending a lot of time with you."

"Yes, we've been together a lot."

"Her birthday is tomorrow." The woman's demeanor grew suddenly cold, and she narrowed her gaze at him. "I know what's supposed to happen."

Dane said, "I won't harm her.

Mireio lifted a brow.

"Promise," he reiterated. "But I left her this morning to visit with…" He gestured toward the window. The antiques store was directly across the way. A few people lingered in the middle of the street, but he paid them no mind.

Come back down to earth, he coached himself. *Don't let the crazy old man who thinks he was once your father rile you.* "I thought I'd see if she had come in."

"Just got a text saying she was stopping by. You want a beer?"

"No."

Mireio walked over to the taps and filled a small glass they used for flights with a dark beer.

Dane glanced out the window again, to where a half dozen people stood before the brewery, facing the street. His attention was diverted by the clank of the glass on the bar top. "No, I'm not thirsty."

"You should give it a try. It's a new blend. Dark and chocolaty."

"Maybe next visit."

"Oh, come on." She pushed the glass toward him.

Dane flinched. "What kind of spell did you put on that? And why would you even attempt such a thing with me?"

Mireio pressed her fingers to her chest, affronted. But she wasn't that good of an actress.

"I'm not stupid," he defended himself. "Why are you so eager for me to give it a try?"

"Sorry." She expelled a sigh. "You're right. I'm trying too hard. There's just a touch of a love spell on that one."

He gaped at her. "Seriously?"

"I want everything between you and Eryss to be good."

He reached to clasp her hand and said, "It is good. I promise."

"What about the witch blade with a mind of its own?"

"It's been melted in a forge. Nothing can come between me and Eryss now."

"That's so romantic." Mireio caught her chin in hand and cast a glance out the window. "Wait a second. Why is everyone...?" She rushed to the window.

Dane followed, now finding it odd that so many people

stood outside. Some milled in the middle of the street, holding up their cell phones as if to record something or take pictures.

Mireio swung around and gripped him by the shirt. "You said it was melted!"

He peered over the top of her bright red hair, and when one of the people outside moved to the right, he saw it. The dagger hung suspended in midair in the middle of the street. And one man reached to touch it.

"No!" Dane thrust Mireio aside and ran out the door. "Don't touch that! It's dangerous!"

The people cleared a path for him as he made his way to the dagger—and almost grabbed it. A second before his fingers could curl about the hilt, Dane realized what would happen if he did touch it. He'd become a white-eyed, maniacal witch hunter. And this crowd of humans did not need to witness that. Nor did they need to witness a magical sword levitating in the middle of a city street.

The very job he did for the Agency—protecting humans from the truth—would not be breached right now. He had to rescue this situation. But how, without touching the dagger?

"It's a trick, everyone!" He put up his palms in a placating gesture. "Advertising! For...the brewery's next beer!"

"Pretty convincing trick," someone said to his left. "Where are the strings?"

"It's..." He searched his arsenal of lies and scientific reasoning for a way out of this. "Magnets!"

"Dane!"

He glanced over the conglomeration of curious faces and saw Eryss walking down the sidewalk. Shit. Talk about bad timing. He shook his head at her, hoping she'd get the hint not to approach.

He could feel the dagger's energy coaxing him. Calling out to him to take the hilt in hand. To own the power it granted him.

To kill the witch.

Chapter 26

The crowd gathering in the middle of the street before the brewery startled Eryss. Yet this *was* Anoka. People did weird things all the time in the city. It was never odd to see a person having an extended phone conversation while planted in the middle of the street, causing cars to drive around them. Or even a ten-minute lip-lock outside the brewery doors? Commonplace. But what was going on now? Had a parade been scheduled that she hadn't heard about?

Harold Stuart stood in the doorway of his shop, a smug smirk tightening his face. He saw her and made the sign of the cross. Really?

But when, amid the crowd, Eryss noticed the crop of glossy black hair with a curl that dashed across his eyebrow, she quickened her footsteps. People were shouting "Grab it!" and Dane was obviously trying to settle them down by waving his hands and telling them to leave, that it was only a trick.

"A trick?" Eryss pushed past a few people.

Then she saw the dagger suspended midair before Dane. Someone reached out to grasp for the hilt, and he grabbed the man's wrist and admonished him not to destroy the trick. A trick? He must be trying to divert attention from the real magic. Oh, crap.

"I thought Malakai melted that in the forge?"

Dane must have heard her because he looked beyond a pair of heads topped with ski hats, and their gazes met. Desperation filled his dark brown eyes and he shook his head, pleading for her not to come closer. The dagger must be compelling him to take it in hand. And there was very little he could do about resisting. But he must be trying fervently to avoid the inevitable, for he didn't want the crowd to witness what would happen should it come to that.

"Get away!" Eryss yelled. "That is a dangerous weapon!"

But her entreaty seemed only to excite the crowd, and they pushed in closer. There must be two dozen people standing about, and others were coming from around the corner where a trilogy of bars held reign. It was afternoon, a time the city was often busy with shoppers, even on frigid days like this one. What a nightmare!

Eryss glanced to the brewery. Mireio stood outside the door. She held up her hand and waved. "Can you grab it?"

Eryss shook her head. She couldn't touch the thing. It would repulse her, surely, and then what a show the curious bystanders would see—and record on their cell phones. Shit. This was not good. But what sort of magic would work against the dagger's? Dark? Malefic? Nothing that she could summon. The dark arts were out of her realm of experience.

So instead, she'd have to work on the crowd before

Dane could no longer hold them back. Planting her feet and connecting to the earth, she quickly glanced toward Mireio and gave her a nod. Her friend understood, and returned the nod. Mireio raised her hands over her head, bringing her forefingers together.

Moving vita through her body and down through her feet and boots, Eryss pushed through the hard concrete slicked with ice crystals and sought the ground beneath. And once there, she harnessed the earth's energy and pulled it up, warming the air and curling it about the legs and bodies of those standing in shocked curiosity.

Mireio's magic summoned water, and suddenly Eryss heard sniffles and sobs. Everyone had begun to cry. *Good one, Mireio.*

With the emotional vibrations at their highest level, Eryss was able to whisper, "Forget what you've seen. Go home."

And the crowd dispersed and wandered away, some hand in hand, comforting one another, and others walking off as if nothing odd had occurred. They simply went back to shopping.

Only when just she and Dane stood in the middle of the street did she hear him hiss, "I can't resist much longer. Get away. Now."

She didn't need to be told twice. But it hurt her heart to leave him alone with such malevolent evil. "I'm sorry," she said to him. "I love you, Dane."

Eryss turned and ran for Mireio, grabbing her hand when she reached her and tugging her inside the brewery. And then she realized her mistake. Outside, Dane grabbed the dagger and tried to fling it away from him. But the hilt stuck to his grip as if glued there.

"He'll come after you," Mireio said.

"I just realized that. Let's go out the emergency exit."

The twosome headed toward the back of the brewery. "We've got to at the very least lead him out of town and away from witnesses."

And even as she unlocked the rear door and turned off the alarm, the front door opened to emit Dane. He looked about. Eryss tugged Mireio down the hallway of the Bank Building, in which the brewery was located. She paused at the door on the opposite side of the building, where she was parked across the street in the lot, and waited for Dane to make eye contact with her through the window at the back of the brewery. At the sight of his white eyes, she sucked in a breath.

"Let's go," she said in a wobbly tone. "I don't know how to stop this, Mireio! That dagger is indestructible."

The redhead sailed around the side of Eryss's car and got in. Both their doors slammed shut. "This has been happening for centuries," Mireio said. "If it's a curse, there *is* a way to break it. You know that."

"Right, but—" And in that moment, when she again made eye contact with the reluctant witch hunter, Eryss knew the answer. "Love."

"What?"

A warm gush filled her heart. Tears spilled down Eryss's cheeks. "I said it to Ivor in my flashback. Ivor is—was—Dane. Just as we'd killed one another, and enacted the curse, I said our love would save us. We just need to love one another."

"Yeah? Well, while you're feeling the love, would you please get us away from crazy sword-wielding witch hunter?"

"Right." Eryss pulled away from the curb just as Dane swung at them. The blade tip cut across the driver's door, making her wince—not at the damage to the vehicle, but because it felt like a cut to her very heart. "I do love him, Mireio. I really do."

"You haven't known him that long."

"I've known him forever," Eryss said with a wondrous certainty. She turned the car to drive around the block and away from the man, who raced after them. "He doesn't want to hurt me. I know that, too."

"That's all well and fine, but if your theory on love breaking the curse were true then he'd stop right now. So he must not love you."

And that was the clincher.

Of course, Dane hadn't fallen in love with her. His life had been crazy freaky wild since arriving in town a little more than a week ago. He'd stated very clearly he had a life in California, and much as he cared about her, he couldn't see continuing a relationship between them long distance.

Yet she could entirely get behind uprooting her own life and moving to live near him. Because that's what she needed to do. To give her roots new life in new soil. Her soul craved this love. It demanded she fight for it now.

Mireio turned around on the seat and looked out the back window. "He's fast!"

"It's the dagger. I'm going left." That would take her toward the freeway. She could lose him there. But she didn't want to lose him. It took all her strength to switch on the turn signal and curve onto the freeway.

"He's stopped," Mireio reported. "I love that you found your soul mate, Eryss." She turned around and slid down in the seat, then clasped Eryss's hand. "And I know what that means. It is phenomenal. Meant to be. Not to be ignored."

"I'm glad you understand."

"I do. But *why* did you have to pick the one guy on

this earth who wants you dead? And why *does* he want you dead?"

"I killed his father." Eryss navigated toward a turn-off from the freeway. She didn't need to get away from Dane anymore, so after taking the exit, she turned toward a coffee shop.

"You did? When?"

Eryss loved that she could make such a confession to her friends and their replies were never laced with disbelief, just curiosity.

"In the thirteenth century. Apparently Dane's father was a witch. So was Dane! That's how the curse started, over his father's dead body. There's dark magic involved."

"Hmm, then dark magic should get you out of this."

"Maybe. But neither of us practices dark." She parked before the coffee shop and turned off the ignition. Both women remained in the car. "Dane came to town because he thought the dagger could tell him something about his father—from this lifetime—whom he never knew. But it's weird that, instead, he learned about his *original* father."

"It was meant to be."

"I feel bad about the man's death in the thirteenth century, but I know I did it to save Dane."

"And he couldn't see beyond that betrayal."

"Exactly. He reacted, as would anyone when they'd just witnessed someone stab their father. Oh! How could I have been so irrational? I would never murder someone. Why didn't I try to talk to Dane—Ivor—about it?"

"Sweetie, you are not the same person now as you were then."

"Right! I wasn't even a witch then. Dane was the witch! How weird is that?"

"But your souls have always been the same. And your

soul has grown and learned things. Times were also very different then than they are now. Trust me on that one."

"If that's so, even if I could find a dark witch to help me, there's no way I would use dark magic to stop this. It doesn't feel right with my soul."

Mireio sighed. "Then you're going to have to somehow make the guy love you. And good luck with that when he's doing the enchanted white-eyes thing." She shuddered. "That creeps me out more than staring down a sword. Seriously."

"I'm going to call him." Eryss tugged out her cell phone.

"I'll run in and grab us some chai and give you some privacy."

As Mireio strolled toward the coffee shop, Eryss spread her white light over her and cloaked her location with a simple spell that would jam the GPS on her phone. Then she dialed Dane.

He answered immediately. "I'm so sorry, Eryss! I tried not to touch it, but my muscles moved of their own volition. And everyone was standing around. This is a disaster. I need to do spin on this."

"Dane, chill. Mireio and I performed a spell. Everyone who walked away will never remember what they saw. Trust me."

"Really? Thank you."

"As for coming after me with the dagger...again..."

"I can never apologize enough."

"No need. I understand. If I could have removed the dagger from your proximity I would have, but I can't touch the thing, and our Light magic doesn't work against it. We need a third party."

"The disenchanter," Dane said. "He's arriving this

evening. He works with the Agency. Since we can't destroy the dagger, we can at least take away its power."

"Where is it right now?"

"With me. I'm back at the hotel. I was able to let it go. And I checked the mirror. No white eyes. It just feels so *right* in my grip, it's hard to explain."

"It's the enchantment."

"I'm sure it is. Where are you? No—don't tell me. Don't return to the brewery today, please. I feel as if I'll know and go looking for you. And don't go home."

She had nowhere else to go but home, but she wouldn't tell him that.

"Dane, are you going to be okay?"

His sigh said so much. Eryss felt her heart shiver in response. She wanted to pull him close, hold him and kiss his eyelids and tell him that she loved him. And to know that he returned that love.

"Doesn't matter if I'm okay. It's you I'm worried about, Eryss."

"We both need to be okay. But I'm not okay if you're not. That's just the way it is. Like it or not—I love you."

Had she heard him sniff at a tear?

"I love you," she repeated. "This lifetime. The *you* you are right now. The scientist who loves to surf and protect paranormals from mortal naivety. And while I know I've loved you in the past, I think it's different every time. Because we are different people every time. And yet we've been very much the same through the ages. We find one another. And sometimes even love one another."

"I'm sorry I've hurt you, Eryss. And I'll come and tell you that and kiss you and make love to you the moment the disenchanter has worked on the dagger. I promise you that. I'll give you a call soon."

"Goodbye." It was difficult to hang up because she hadn't heard what she'd wanted to hear.

That he loved her, too.

Chapter 27

After lighting a beeswax candle on the kitchen table, Eryss blew gently over the flame and whispered, "To love." The flame snapped back at her, and she flinched away from it.

She wasn't going to take that as a portent. She was too tired. And it had been a trying day. Would she and Dane ever be able to face one another without the threat of death?

"The disenchanter is on his way," she reminded herself. "Hopefully he makes it here before my birthday." Which was…she checked the LED clock on the stove. "Four hours from now. I need a bath."

And with a yawn, she aimed for the stairs. Her cell phone rang as she took the bottom step. It was Valor. "Hey."

"You sound tired."

"I am. What's up?"

"Where's the witch hunter?"

She wished her friends would not call the man she

loved a witch hunter, but Eryss knew an argument wasn't going to change the truth. "He's at the hotel."

"With the dagger?"

"Yes."

"Good. The disenchanter is here."

"Oh, excellent. Will you drive him over to the hotel? I was just going to hop into a nice hot bath. Long day."

"Not a problem. We'll go straight there. You get some rest. I'll give you a call as soon as the dagger is taken care of."

"Thanks, Valor."

Setting the phone on the bathroom vanity, Eryss stripped her clothes off and tossed them in the hamper. The water always took a while to warm up on cold winter nights, so she let it run over the rose quartz crystals she'd placed in the tub, while she combed her hair and patted some cleansing oil on her face in preparation to wash it away.

She tapped her fingers against her chin, eyeing her reflection and feeling as though she'd forgotten about something. But with a yawn, she stepped into the tub and groaned with pleasure as the hot water surrounded her.

Downstairs in the kitchen, the candle flame flickered and a tuft of ash broke away and landed in the chenille threads of Eryss's scarf. The ember took to amber light, and a flame burst into life.

The disenchanter was probably eighteen years old if he was a day, Valor decided as he followed her down the hotel hallway toward the room number Eryss had given her. He reminded her of a lanky, LARPing game freak. And he still hadn't grown into his long arms and legs.

He'd identified himself as the guy who was going to save the day when he'd walked into the brewery asking after Dane Winthur.

Kids.

"This one." Valor stopped before the door and knocked. "Dane?" She eyed the disenchanter's thin summery jacket. "You from California, too?"

"Arizona. I expect to get paid double for coming to this frigid town."

"Do they do that? Pay you double for suffering a few degrees' drop in temperature?"

"A few degrees?" He shivered and then pressed an ear to the door to listen. "I don't think anyone is in there."

"He's gotta be. The dagger has gone missing from the Saint-Pierres'—oh shit!"

Valor stepped back in preparation to kick the door, but the disenchanter stood before it like an idiot.

"Move!" she commanded, and he jumped to the side. Valor charged the door, and one well-placed kick beside the key card pad shook the door lock loose. They wandered inside. There was a half-packed suitcase on the bed, but no Dane.

And worse yet...no dagger.

Valor tugged out her cell phone to call Eryss, but it rang through to voice mail. "She's still in the tub. We've got to go to her. Come on!"

Dane gave the plastic lighter a few flicks as he navigated the darkness toward Eryss's house. All his life, he'd carried a lighter on him. Or rather, he had started doing it as an eight-year-old. To be cool.

Or because he'd been compelled by a wicked enchantment that had brewed within him for decades. Fire.

Now he understood.

Dane pulled up before the house, and saw smoke siphoning from the kitchen window. Had someone beat him to the fire?

Dagger in hand, he stepped outside and stood looking over the Victorian structure, feeling no need to rush forward. Flames licked through two broken kitchen windows. And the roof at the front corner above the kitchen had begun to burn with wicked gold flames.

Clenching the dagger tightly, he nodded. "The witch is burning."

A sense of finally finishing a long-tormenting task filled his chest. And he studied the dagger now in the darkness as the flames brightened his peripheral view. The designs on the blade began to disappear, and soon the cold iron was smooth. And the bone hilt cracked, as if with age, within his grasp. And he felt something crack within him. So sharply that he slapped a palm over his chest.

Something exited his heart and chest, as if a blade were being pulled free from the muscle and skin. He groaned and winced and his knees buckled, but he did not collapse.

Shouting to the heavens, he spread his arms wide and cried in victory and anger, and from the betrayal that had been visited upon him by his first father.

And the pain receded and he was able to stand firmly. Why was he holding this weapon?

Stabbing the blade into the nearby snowbank that edged the witch's driveway, the witch hunter released the most powerful influence that had haunted him through the ages.

And in doing so, the wicked enchantment that had curled about his heart...let go.

Dane sucked in the cold air. What was going on? Where was—he stood before Eryss's house. And it was burning! What in hell?

"Eryss? No!"

He raced for the side door and gripped the metal knob. He wasn't wearing gloves, and his skin burned from the contact. He swore and released it. He had to get inside. She could be in there, hurt or passed out from smoke inhalation.

Had he actually just stood here and felt a cruel tendril of satisfaction at seeing her house in flames? It had been that damned dagger.

But now—now he was no longer under its spell. He'd pronounced the witch dead and the baselard had listened, releasing the enchantment that had haunted him throughout the centuries.

"She can't be dead. Please!"

He turned and eyed the garage. There must be something in there he could use to knock down the door. Then he grasped a moment of rational thought, tugged out his cell phone and called 911. He reported the fire even as he stomped through the snow around the side of the house to the glass-walled conservatory. The dispatcher reported they would have a team on site within six minutes.

Dane shoved the phone in his pocket. "Six minutes is too long. Where are you, Eryss?"

He tripped over the end of the big branch that had fallen days earlier and cracked the glass ceiling. Tumbling forward, he landed in the snow, then scrambled around to grip the thickest end of the branch. It was about eight feet long, so he stood, pressed his foot to the center and broke off a good length of it. Using it as a battering ram, he smashed one of the conservatory windows, turning his head away to avoid the flying glass. Gray smoke billowed forth. He smashed again and again until two panes had been taken out. Tossing the branch aside, he then entered Eryss's summer sanctuary.

Pulling up the winter scarf from his neck to cover his

nose and mouth, Dane blinked at the heavy smoke. If it was thick out here in the conservatory, it must be impassable in the rooms beyond. He spied the open door to the main house and dashed for it. When his foot nudged something on the grass, he dropped down and felt the prone body lying half inside.

His fingers slipped into Eryss's hair. She wasn't moving, and when he shook her she did not respond. He lifted her and carried her limp body, clad in a thin silky nightgown, out through the broken window. Then he trudged through the yard until the thick snow hampered his footsteps and he could no longer carry her due to coughing.

He fell to his knees, gently setting Eryss on the snow. Moonlight allowed him to see that her hair was wet. He shook her shoulders and head, trying to rouse her. Was mouth-to-mouth appropriate for smoke inhalation? Had she merely passed out?

He bent and pressed an ear to her chest, gasping with hope when he heard the thump of her beating heart.

"Come on, Eryss, not like this. I won't let the flames harm this witch. No!" He clasped her shoulders and hugged her up against his chest, bowing his head against hers. "Please, not like this. We are supposed to go together or not at all. That's the deal."

A deal he'd just concocted, but damn—where was the emergency team?

He set her back down gently and, pinching her nose, tilted back her head and breathed into her mouth. Once, twice.

"Eryss, please don't leave me. I'll stay here in Minnesota if you want me to. I'd do anything for you. We've got to do it right this time. Please?"

He bowed his head to her forehead, slipping his hand

along her cheek to her cool lips. Pressing a kiss there, he lingered over her mouth and whispered, "I love you."

And he meant it. It had been spoken without thought, undeterred by scientific rationale. It had come from his heart.

And as if words had magic, Eryss suddenly sucked in a breath. "Dane?"

"Oh, my love, you're alive." He kissed her nose. "Thank God."

"I...the candle. It was my fault."

"It's okay, lover. I'm here. And I love you."

The fire truck's siren sounded not far off. The headlights from a vehicle illuminated the driveway, and someone got out and ran toward them. "Eryss!"

"Valor, she's alive," Dane called. He pulled Eryss gently onto his lap and shrugged off his coat to pull it over her shivering form. "She's alive." He beamed up at the other witch, who stopped before them.

"Did you set her house on fire?" Valor asked.

"It was ablaze when I arrived. She said something about a candle. I got her out."

Valor eyed him suspiciously for three very long seconds, then nodded and pressed her hands together in a namaste bow. "Bless the goddess."

"I found the dagger in a snowbank," said some teenager from behind her.

"The disenchanter," Valor said dismissively. "Keep that thing away from the witch hunter, will you?"

"Oh. Right. I'll take it out onto the street. And I'll back the car out. The fire truck will want to get up close. You Winthur?"

Dane nodded.

"Everything okay?" the disenchanter asked.

"It is now." Dane pulled Eryss in closer, and she nuzzled

her head against his neck. Her cool fingers slipped inside his shirt, and he pressed a hand over them to warm her up.

Someone from the fire rescue crew called out, and Valor turned to go meet them.

"You said you loved me," Eryss said. Her eyes beamed up at him. "Did you mean that?"

"Without question."

"Love has saved us," she said, and dropped her head onto his shoulder.

"That it has." He kissed the crown of her head. "Happy birthday, lover."

Later that night...

The Decadent Dames brewery resounded with the acoustic rhythms of a local alternative band that always brought in a crowd. Glasses clanked and chatter filled the festive air as the band suddenly segued into a rousing version of "Happy Birthday."

Mireio and Valor carried the sheet cake decorated with pink roses and violet forget-me-nots to the main room, where Eryss sat on Dane's lap in one of the easy chairs backed with a skull motif.

Eryss kissed Dane, and amid the loud chorus of "Happy Birthday," she whispered in his ear, "Happy birthday to you, too, lover."

"You made it to thirty," he said. "We both will. Let's go for thirty-one together. What do you say?"

The room suddenly quieted, and Eryss noticed everyone had leaned toward them expectantly. Only when she saw Mireio nodding frantically toward the lit candles on the cake did she get the hint.

"Yes!" Eryss called gaily, and leaned forward to blow them out.

A week later...

Sitting on a massive boulder that edged the Pacific Ocean, Eryss tilted her head against Dane's shoulder. She wore a sweater and leggings and had even brought along mittens and a scarf, but the night was actually warm, somewhere in the sixties. The bonfire Dane had lit earlier warmed her cheeks.

The moon was full, and while normally she intuitively assessed her body and how it was feeling and could guess when her cycle would next show, she could only now confirm something she'd known since that morning after the fire had destroyed her home.

The home was a loss. It had been her fault, leaving the candle lit while she'd gone upstairs to take a bath. No witch hunter had been allowed to hold fire to her in a death threat. Had it been the curse, though, that had set off the flames in her kitchen? She would never know for sure. Fortunately, Dane's love had broken their curse. And now they intended to move forward. Together.

But she wasn't sure how to tell him about what she knew.

"So what do you think?" he asked, leaning in to kiss her cheek. "You like Santa Cruz?"

He'd shown her around the city the last four days, and even helped her scout out a possible location for a new brewery. Both had discussed plans to travel more, and to make the relationship work, no matter the travel involved. Eryss had made her home in Minnesota, but now she had no home. And staying with Dane, for a few weeks anyway, felt right. But she couldn't abandon her job back there. And he knew that.

"I love the city and the weather."

"My apartment may be small, but I'm not averse to

looking for something bigger. That is, if you'd consider moving in with me."

That was the first time he'd come right out and invited her to stay, beyond merely "just visiting." That sexy smile of his would never allow Eryss to refuse him a thing. Moving in with the man she had loved for centuries?

"Could we have two homes? One here and one in Anoka?"

"You plan to rebuild?"

She nodded. "All my friends are back in Minnesota, and while The Decadent Dames can operate without my physically being there, I would miss the seasons. Even winter."

Dane rubbed his chin, making a show of giving it some thought. "I have wanted to travel more for my job with the Agency. And having two home bases could be beneficial. Would you be cool with living with a man who does what I do?"

"Hunt witches?"

"Eryss."

"Sorry, had to get that one in. I know you would never hurt me, or any other witch, for that matter."

"The enchantment has been depleted from the baselard, and it now resides in a warded box in a very safe locale. We need never worry that that thing will take control of me again."

"And I certainly don't mind you protecting humans from the truth. But there's a new addition to our situation you need to know about before you make me a copy of your key."

"And what is that? Because whatever it is—we can handle it. Together." He kissed her mouth. "We've been doing it forever. And this time around? I know we're going to get it right. I love you, Eryss."

"I love you, too, Dane," she said in a whisper. And then, because she didn't know how else to tell him, she simply said in a rush, "I'm pregnant."

Both his dark eyebrows shot up. His eyes darted to hers and then the corner of his mouth lifted. And the smile grew in his eyes before it exploded into a real and genuine smile on his mouth. "Really? You're serious? But I thought you said...?"

"I had a birth control spell enacted. It's never failed me. Ever. But I recall Mireio mentioning the new moon on the morning after we'd first had sex."

"I don't get it."

"The new moon ushers in fertility and creation. I think it overrode my spell. Are you angry?"

"Angry? Hell no. I'm...honestly, I'm surprised."

"Just as surprised as I am."

"So we're going to have a baby?" The smile refused to budge from his face.

"Yes, we are."

"We." He squeezed her hand and kissed the back of it. "I like the sound of that. Will he or she be a witch?"

Eryss shrugged. "Maybe. Are you...? Is this—"

He kissed her then, and she knew that he was okay with it, and that no matter what life threw at them, they'd be good. Together.

Soul mates.

* * * * *

Author Note

I hope you've enjoyed Dane and Eryss's story. I write most of my paranormal romances set in my world of Beautiful Creatures. If you are interested in some of the other characters in this book, they may have their own stories.

Read about Malakai and Rissa in *MALAKAI*.

Read about Tor in *THE VAMPIRE HUNTER*.

Midge makes a cameo appearance in *HIS FORGOTTEN FOREVER*.

And watch for more from the Decadent Dames soon. Valor's story is available in Autumn 2017! And after that Mireio meets the man of her dreams in 2018.

For more information about all the characters in my world and a complete book list, stop by my website: michelehauf.com.